We Are 100

by

nathan timmel

For Lydia

Prologue

Boom

Evan stared into the mirror.

It had taken some time, but he actually looked like a janitor now.

As soon as that thought flashed through his head, he chuckled and glanced at the laminate on his chest: "Custodial Services." Everything was so politically correct these days, even "Janitor" was an outdated term.

But he didn't mind.

Whatever made people happy. If no one was getting hurt, then what harm was there in spicing up a title?

The smile faded as a new thought entered his mind. He never thought he'd be pushing a mop, especially not at his age, but no matter. It's not like the position, or the work, defined him.

This was all part of the plan: get in, go unnoticed, make your move. "Sleeper cell," so to speak.

At first, he had been nervous. Especially when applying for the job. What did it look like to have a full-blown university professor, one with tenure and only a few years away from retirement looking to unclog toilets and empty waste bins?

He worried they'd look into his past; he thought they'd uncover what he was up to immediately.

But they hadn't.

Human resources bought his story, because it was 90% true, and only 10% "enhancement."

Sure, "lie" might be a more appropriate word, but whatever. Maybe "enhancement" was the politically correct term for "lie."

When asked why he was downgrading so heavily, he responded, "Well, I lost my wife two years ago. I turned to booze, which lost me my job, and now I just want to do something physical. Something away from the prying eyes of others, people always wondering how I'm doing, how I'm dealing with everything..."

Evan drifted off for effect, then, after a pause, finished with a heartfelt, "I just want something low-key to keep me busy."

The brown-haired woman with kind eyes was sympathetic, and hired him.

There are outright lies, such as the part about him being a drunk and losing his job, and then there are lies of omission.

Did he really want to just do *nothing*? To stay quiet and keep busy? Oh, God no. He wanted revenge—to do something to get back at those responsible for the loss of his wife.

His wife.

He had been at her side when she passed. Assisted suicide. The medication keeping her alive became too expensive, and she wanted to go out on her terms. She wanted to leave before deteriorating to the point she'd be unable to express herself.

Now, two years and three weeks after standing over her casket, Evan Francart would "express himself" in a way Madonna hadn't envisioned when she wrote her song.

To that end, he checked the gun sitting in front of him. Evan didn't want to fire it, but knew he might have to in order to prove a point: *Hey, I'm serious.*

When he first held it, the handgun was heavier than he expected.

In the movies, people were always throwing guns around, treating them like batons... He figured they were at least somewhat light.

After his first week at a shooting range, he realized how silly those action movies were. Holding the gun sideways was dumb beyond words, and the way actors shoot randomly and hit their target every time? Nothing in real life is so easy as it appears on the silver screen.

Also, guns in movies never seemed to have any kick to them. That's what surprised Evan the most, even more than the noise. He'd been expecting the loud bang, but the first time he fired it the recoil blew his hands back and he almost hit himself in the head. After that, he held on tightly, with slightly bent elbows to absorb the kickback.

One year of meticulous training later, and Evan felt as comfortable hold-ing (and shooting) the gun as he did driving a car, or brushing his teeth. The action was now routine.

Anyway, the gun was backup. Evan hoped he wouldn't need to use it, but somewhere in the pit of his stomach knew he probably wasn't going to get off so easy.

Evan closed his locker and made his way over to the custodial carts. He'd never worked the day shift before.

Day services were kept on hand in case a bathroom needed to be re-stocked, or someone spilled something, but for the most part the day shift was kept out of sight. The real cleaning took place at night. Once the sun went down, the kings of the boardrooms went home and the peasants came out to remove all messes under cover of darkness.

Even in a high-end office like this, he was surprised by the disregard for cleanliness. Evan found gum dropped and smooshed into the carpet and piss stained bathroom floors; the male executives were toddlers, spraying wher-ever they pleased. The 1% were animals. Or, if not animals, maybe their wealth allowed them to act without care. They knew someone like Evan would tidy up after them.

When he'd started, Evan was an oddity, a lone white face among a sea of Latino workers. Immigration issues flared every election cycle, but the sad fact of the matter was that people who arrived without papers usually did the work no one else wanted. Or, in the least, the work white people didn't want.

(Those toilets don't unclog themselves now, do they?)

For a moment, Evan felt a tinge of sadness. He knew his actions would destroy a few jobs, and therefore put families in need of the paycheck back on their heels. But it was all for the greater good. He absolutely believed that.

He had to.

Evan made sure the cart was in order, then pushed it over to the service elevator. His wait was short.

Not much taking place on the loading dock, he figured.

Once inside, Evan hovered his finger over the button before pushing. 14th floor. This wasn't a New York skyscraper, but it was decent enough for the Midwest.

The 14th floor housed the boardroom of Glenback Pharmaceuticals. If he was right—and, checking his watch, he believed he was—the big dogs would be about five minutes into their meeting.

The elevator moved at a decent pace and deposited Evan straightaway. Civilians used the passenger elevators, and no one working had been in need of moving from floor-to-floor. Evan's lucky day, he supposed.

Pushing the cart into the main hallway, Evan closed his eyes and said a silent prayer. If anyone asked what he was doing up there, he would say there was a mess in the men's restroom. Sink overflowed. Pipe burst. Something.

But no one noticed him. People went about their business, typing away on keyboards, taking phone calls, and shuffling paperwork. In a way, wearing a janitor's uniform was like wearing Harry Potter's cloak of invisibility. If you weren't wearing a suit and tie, you were "less than," and therefore not worth looking at. Maybe that wasn't the case on some of the lower floors, Evan mused, but it definitely was up in the penthouse.

Evan generally pushed his cart down deserted hallways at night; having to navigate people in a hurry was challenging, but not horribly so. When he arrived at the boardroom door, Evan took a deep breath. He could still back out now, if he really wanted.

Instead, Evan turned the handle. Though he was quiet as he entered, all heads turned to greet him.

"Excuse me, we're in the middle of a meeting here," someone said, but Evan wasn't sure who. His concentration was elsewhere.

After parking his cart, when he turned to face the group of six men and three women, the gun was level in his hand.

"Evacuate the building," Evan stated, his voice monotone.

This was the moment he dreaded, the reaction. Would they comply? Would one of them act like a hero and jump him? Was one of them armed?

Evan's eyes slowly scanned the room, trying to absorb as much detail as necessary. The fact no one was moving was reassuring.

"You're Janice," Evan said to the woman sitting just off from the others. The fact she wasn't actually at the table was the giveaway. "Leave."

Janice looked to her boss, the CEO, Michael Dexter.

"He's not in charge," Evan explained. "I am. Go."

Janice stood, nervously.

"Evacuate the building. You have ten minutes."

Janice took one last look around the room, almost apologetically. Even though it was too soon to know exactly what was happening, she knew she was being spared. A mix of thankful and regret stirred in her, but if anything it was a 90/10 split toward thankful.

Evan watched Janice exit.

This was it. Two years since his wife had passed. One year of mourning, one year of planning. Oh, and three weeks of putting everything together. Can't forget those three weeks.

The silence was palpable, but Evan actually enjoyed it. The less he had to explain, the better. When it was finally broken, Evan sighed, but only slightly.

"Is Janice in on this?"

Evan recognized the man who had spoken as Sean Patrick Moore, the CFO. The question wasn't completely absurd; the release of one person near-immediately must have looked odd, but the timing seemed out of place. Didn't they want to know who he was, or what his demands were?

Evan chose his words carefully.

"No one is 'in on' this. I am acting alone today. Janice is a secretary, and therefore not directly involved in your criminal actions."

Evan figured that would get them curious, and awaited follow up inquiries. After a short pause, CEO Michael Dexter stepped up to the plate.

"Who are you, and what do you want?"

If Evan was disappointed by the unoriginal response, he didn't show it. Cliché was to be expected; the idea someone could be inventive in such a situation was a challenge most people cannot rise to.

"My name is Evan Francart," Evan explained flatly. "And I want to make a statement."

As he finished his sentence, the fire alarm went off.

Evan couldn't help but smile wryly as he thought, *Clever girl, that Janice. Fastest way to get people out of a building? Tell them it's on fire.*

Evan glanced out the window. Fourteen stories down, he could see people beginning to trickle out the front doors.

Michael interrupted his train of thought: "What kind of statement? If this is about money—"

Evan cut him off. "Everything is about money."

He paused.

"But if you're worried I'm here to take yours, that's not the case."

The flow of employees from the building increased to a nice, steady stream. This was good. Evan knew he would be remembered as a terrorist, and probably a murderer, but they were going to have to give him credit for protecting innocent lives.

Evan glanced at his watch. A few more minutes and the building should be clear.

"You know," he explained to his captives, "for a company that prides itself on shredding documents in order to keep secrets, you're pretty sloppy about letting just anyone take those documents to the shredder."

There was no response, but Evan didn't expect one. After letting everyone digest those words, he continued.

"That means that no matter how well you protect your secrets from the public, the press, and even your underlings, someone will always know what you're up to."

Evan stared hard at Michael.

"Look," Michael began, "I don't know what you think we're '*up to*,' but this meeting..."

Evan finished the sentence for him: "Is about acquiring a small company, taking command of their flagship drug, and raising the price so that you can receive bonuses while people who can no longer afford it, die."

Evan took one last look out the window. The number of employees exiting the building had slowed to almost nothing.

He decided to give stragglers one more minute.

"My wife was on Chlozopran."

If every member of the board had been nervous a moment ago, everything that was happening to them finally sunk in. To put it in street parlance, *shit just got real.*

"My wife was on Chlozopran, and after you bought the rights to it, you jacked up the price, and over the course of two years we had to drain our bank accounts and mortgage our house to keep her alive. I'm guessing you've figured out how it all ended by now."

"Look," Michael Dexter began. His voice sounded almost sympathetic. Almost. "I'm sorry about your wife. Really. What we do here is to *try* and save lives. If we raise the price on a drug, it's because of overhead. The money we make goes—"

"Into R & D?" Evan interrupted. "Is that what you're going with? You need more money to make better drugs? OK, if there's so much research going on, then why did you get a $15 million bonus last year? *Bonus.* On top of your already obscene salary. Why did Mr. Moore get five million? The bonuses in this room add up to almost $50 million. Your salaries are over one hundred million. Company profits last year came in at $200 million. Why can't that number be twenty million? It's still profit, right? If you're in the black, what's the difference between $20 million and $200 million? What's the difference between $2 million and $200 million if you're profitable?"

Evan paused again.

"The only difference, as I see it, is the amount of your salary, and bonus. You want more, so you charge more."

Evan waited for a response.

None came.

"You charge more, and people die," he concluded.

Evan reached under a flap on his cart. A button awaited his touch.

It had taken him three weeks to bring all the components to the building. Some parts stayed in his locker until he needed them; others were hidden in the nooks and crannies of the basement, places no soul ever wandered.

After last night's shift, he'd remained at work, diligently putting everything together in the custodial break room. No cameras in there; no one pays attention to the janitors. In the lobby? Sure, were cameras everywhere in the lobby. But the lepers, the untouchables who did the grunt work for the kings? No need to keep an eye on the disposable people who don't exist in your world.

Evan was surprised at how easy it was to assemble. A few wires, a trigger switch, and a firing mechanism. His benefactor had provided such clear instructions that even a child could have pieced it together.

Evan stared directly at Michael Dexter. Under the flap, his finger tapped the button lightly.

"And now you're planning on doing it again. You want to acquire Metsger Pharm, just so you can own the rights to Diaphoneme. Once you own it, you'll raise the price, and kill more people."

He looked around at the others.

"And you're voting to let it happen."

Evan thought of his wife one last time.

He didn't know whether or not there was an afterlife, or if he'd be seeing her in it, but he knew this was the end of his time on this particular mortal coil.

"Well," Evan sighed, nodding his head thoughtfully. "I hope all your second homes and tropical vacations were worth it."

Evan pushed the button he had been caressing.

The explosion was so large it set off seismographs at Iowa State, the university thirty-plus miles away in Ames.

Two days later, Karen Jordan, a kindly grandmother living a quarter mile from the Glenback Building in West Des Moines, would find Michael Dexter's finger on her kitchen floor. It was a present from her golden retriever, Molly, who found it while out "doing her business."

Chapter 1

Susan Chamberlain

Susan's phone rang at 3:42 PM.

She had been absentmindedly reading tweets, but not for work. She'd completed her daily tasks and was piddle-farting around at her desk. "Killing time before five," as she put it.

At thirty-eight, Susan was considered a veteran in the FBI; she'd entered the academy straight out of college. There was no confusion, no questioning what she wanted to do with her life. Susan had decided her path while in high school.

She'd seen *The Silence of the Lambs* when she was fifteen. Yeah, it was rated R, but that didn't matter to the clerk at Blockbuster.

The clerk was probably sixteen, and he thought she was cute. He blushed as she put the movie on the counter, and had an impure thought while stealing sideways glances at her ponytail and freckles. The clerk let Susan rent the movie hoping to impress her.

She had wanted to see the film in the theater, but at ten years old her parents weren't about to let that happen. Plus, living in a one-horse town meant it was also a one-screen theater. She couldn't just buy a ticket to a different movie and hop over to the one she wanted to see.

It's not that Susan even knew what the film was about; it was just that pervasive in 1991. First it was an enormous hit, then it won all the Oscars…

Susan remembered her older brother teasing her, telling her how he'd seen it *three whole times*.

Susan was patient.

She went on with her childhood and did all the things children are supposed to do when they're ten, but she never forgot the film existed. Whenever the family had 'Movie Night,' she suggested it. Her dad almost relented, once, but then Mom stepped in with the word "inappropriate" and that shut everything down.

So when she finally had the opportunity, Susan rented a copy herself.

Susan remembered loading the bulky, VHS tape into their player. Sure, DVDs existed, but the digital revolution was still young in 1996. Her family wouldn't make the technological leap until 2000, when the price of a player got low enough.

Watching the film, Susan realized why she hadn't been allowed to see it five years earlier. It was almost too frightening for her at fifteen.

What made everything so scary was the normalcy. Nothing was over-the-top or dramatized to the point of absurdity. Every character felt real; every moment felt as if it could happen.

Especially the kidnapping of the senator's daughter.

Susan had always been told to keep her guard up, not to talk to strangers and all the things parents tell their kids (especially daughters). But seeing someone kidnapped like that, even if fake… Well, it shook Susan to her core.

As frightened as she was, Susan was also inspired; Jodie Foster was tough as nails.

Sure, it was *just a movie*, and Jodie Foster was *just acting*, but that didn't matter. The movie provided Susan with focus; made her realize that she could make something of herself and get out of her shitkicker Wisconsin town. Even if that only meant moving to a different city in the same state.

Plus, even if Jodie Foster was *just acting*, she was a woman in a male dominated industry. Hollywood was the home of the casting couch, where you had to offer your body to get ahead.

The fact Jodie made it through without having to sacrifice her integrity impressed Susan more than her character, Clarice Starling.

(And Clarice had impressed Susan to no end.)

Always an "A" student, Susan used her GPA to obtain several scholarships; "We're always interested in bright, young women at our university," they all said.

After finding a college rife with courses in criminal behavior and psychology, law enforcement and legal issues, Susan packed up and rarely looked back. Which isn't to say "never," because she still went home for the holidays and she still loved her parents, but once she got to college, she finally felt accepted.

Every election cycle, politicians champion 'Small Town Values,' but having lived in a small town her whole life, Susan was concerned by 'small town mindsets.' Small towns sometimes translated to small thoughts, where different was *bad*, not 'just different.'

Small town thoughts on race, sexuality, and even society as a whole were, to Susan, limiting.

In college, there were so many ideas, so much acceptance, so many thoughts bouncing around people's heads (and actually coming out of their mouths) that it was almost overwhelming.

Almost, but not entirely. Mostly, it was exciting. Intellectually stimulating. So, once she got to college, Susan stayed. When the school year was up, she got an apartment and a job instead of returning home.

Being a cocktail waitress wasn't the best job in the world, but it wasn't the worst, either.

She served drinks at a slightly upscale restaurant, which meant the prices were high and the tips decent. Plus, it allowed her to keep her days free, which was important when school started back up—no interference with classes.

Every so often, Susan would reflect on her time in the restaurant industry. She mused that if people were conscripted for a year of serving the pub-lic—kind of like a draft, only without the military aspect—society as a whole would be a better place. Unless you've been in someone's shoes, you've no idea what their life is like. The more people that had to spend time doting on others would teach empathy, and kindness. Because once you got the taste of humility on your lips, you became a better person.

Not that every customer was rude; the majority were kind. But when you got someone in your section that was demanding? Who thought they were better than you because you were working a "menial" job? That was frustrating, to say the least.

Being a cocktail waitress did give Susan a "Six Degrees From a Famous Murderer" story.

Working in a slightly upscale restaurant meant that she worked with some lifers. There were servers who had been there for years. Decades, even.

Not because they weren't ambitious, but because they were good at serving. As chance would have it, they were a group of tightly knit members of the gay community.

The manager, and a half-dozen servers, were the most outgoing, friendly folk Susan had ever come in contact with. They were her first real contact with the gay community, because if there was a gay community in her small town, it was a "community" of one, Brian McMahon. Except he was in the closet, because in a small town in Wisconsin it was best to remain silent and suspected than be out and targeted.

Susan wasn't judgmental, and was more than happy to weave her way into friendships with her co-workers. It was through them she got her "Six Degrees" story: one of the waiters had been targeted by Jeffrey Dahmer.

The lifers were out drinking in 1990, well before Susan arrived. One member of the posse, Ron, had gotten hammered. Too hammered. Brett-Kavanaugh-in-college hammered.

Dahmer had started hitting on Ron, and Thomas—then a fellow server, now the manager of the restaurant—intervened.

Basically, he got Ron out of there; he took Ron away from Dahmer.

Not because he sensed danger in Dahmer, but because in Thomas' own words, "Ron was too drunk to be good in bed."

Thomas knew Ron would be a bad lay; he had no idea Dahmer was targeting Ron specifically *because* he was fall-down drunk.

That's what made the story believable.

It wasn't dressed up with hints of a Spidey-Sense warning, "This guy is evil! Save Ron!"

Nope, it was just a friend saying, "You're too drunk for sex. Let's get you home."

Thomas probably saved Ron's life that night, something they discovered just a few months later as Jeffrey Dahmer became a media sensation for his murders and cannibalism.

Susan was enthralled by the story; the fact she knew people that had been in direct contact with a famous murderer was thrilling.

Fun stories and great social settings aside, waitressing wasn't her career, it was a means to an end. When the end arrived, it was worth it. Nose to the grindstone, she'd graduated in four years with a 3.985 GPA and a degree in Criminal Justice. Susan was accepted without question by the FBI.

Becoming a NAT—New Agent in Training—was like being a freshman in college. NATs lived in dorms and underwent twenty weeks of training.

Susan was surprised by the amount of time spent in classrooms; she'd pictured a lot of firearm and hand-to-hand combat exercises. While the FBI did provide extensive information in both subjects, the majority of her time was spent learning about the cerebral side of being an agent: informant development, investigative techniques, ethics, surveillance, interviewing, interrogation, intelligence, and probably several other "i" techniques that made her head swim at the time.

Like with college, Susan put her blinders on and focused. Several exams and two physicals later, and she was an agent.

Susan was assigned to the Kansas City branch, which she liked. It was just far enough away from home to give her distance from the past, but close enough to return for visits without too much hassle. Plus, it kept her in the Midwest, which she was familiar with. These were her people.

When the option of transferring to another location was offered, she politely declined. Susan worked hard and made it to a place in her life where she felt good. Comfortable.

Kansas City felt like *home*.

Susan didn't feel the need to climb the corporate ladder; she loved being a field agent. Problem solving was her thing, not micro-managing other agents and filing paperwork on cases. Time had given her seniority, meaning that on most cases these days Susan was the SAC, Special Agent in Charge.

Being an experienced agent meant the occasional trainee showing up under her wing, but Susan liked being a mentor. She just couldn't see herself as a manager. Teaching through experience was one thing; living your life inside the office building was another, and the problem with seniority is that the longer you were in the field, the more you were in the office. Oxymoronic, yes, but it rang true.

Susan had to accept annual pay raises and diplomatically sidestep promotions to remain an agent's agent. Like a comic's comic, or musician's musician. Someone the insiders respected.

So, from her roots in Wisconsin to the decision to become a field agent, it all brought her to a crisp autumn day at 3:42 PM when the phone on her desk rang. The top floor of a pharmaceutical company had just exploded in Des Moines, Iowa.

It was less than a three-hour drive, but when bombs go boom, time is of the essence. The FBI would be flying a chartered jet to the scene ASAP.

Susan would be briefed on the tarmac.

Chapter 2

Michael Godwin

Michael didn't set out to be a member of law enforcement.

Growing up in a mostly Black section of Somerset, New Jersey, yet attending a mostly white school, made him a member of two worlds. He discovered that his family had just enough money to be considered out of touch with his neighbors, but wasn't wealthy enough to be considered middle class by his white classmates.

Which meant that Michael didn't technically fit in anywhere.

Not that he didn't have friends; he did. But Michael often felt like the cross-section of a Venn Diagram. At home, he had one set of friends; at school, he had another. Those two groups never crossed paths, and that left Michael... not exactly *excluded* by either group, but sometimes they would just do something without him, and assume he was hanging with his other set of homies. So to speak.

Added to that, being Black meant he grew up being told, "Never talk back to a police officer, or you'll get shot." Being around white kids meant he couldn't relate to them, because they had no fear of the police at all. Yet his Black friends assumed that since he was going to a better school than they were, it also meant he was trying to escape his blackness.

Michael couldn't win, so he stopped trying. He decided that people would either like him for who he was, or they wouldn't. Beyond that, he wasn't going to try and act a certain way around certain people just to be accepted.

Not surprisingly, that method worked. It worked so well, in fact, Michael adopted it as his attitude for life. "I'll be nice to everyone, but not everyone will like me, and there's nothing I can do about that. Moving on."

"Moving on," for the record, was Michael's motto. Even if he didn't always verbalize it. Basically, he wasn't one for dwelling. On the past, his mistakes, anything. When Michael screwed up, he vowed to learn from it and move on. When others screwed up, he forgave, and moved on. Life could only be understood in the rearview mirror, but you moved in one direction: forward. So that's the direction you should face.

High school tried to stereotype Michael—*hey, you're the Black kid! Are you going to try out for *insert-every-team-sport-except-swimming-here**—but he wasn't having any of it. Michael was an academic, a learner. In fact, the one stereotype he begrudgingly accepted was his seemingly natural ability to play the bass guitar.

(Fuck you very much South Park for nailing that one.)

He didn't match the Hollywood stereotype of a Black male. Generally, if Hollywood was making a story about a Black man, it was that of an athlete whose dad left when he was three years old, whose mom was a drunk, and who was raised by his grandmother. Oh, the odds that man overcame to become an athletic hero... Audiences shed tears, and the Academy handed out Oscars.

Michael came from a typical household: mom, dad, sister. A loving unit. That was the normal Black experience—having a mother and father that stayed together and loved one another, but not if you watched the news or movies. There, the Black community was forever in turmoil; missing dads, crack-dealing teens... Anything to reinforce the idea that Black folk weren't just *different*, they *weren't as good*.

Being of two worlds and having an outsider's and insider's perspective on each gave Michael his first interest in law enforcement. Why was the Black community so at odds with it? Why was the white community so non-plussed by it?

As much as he could accept the disconnect he felt in his twin-world life, he couldn't stop analyzing it. Which is why he ultimately decided to become a part of the world that divided his two worlds: law enforcement.

He'd psychoanalyzed his decision repeatedly; was he looking for acceptance in the world of white people? That didn't work out in the long run, just ask OJ. Sure, you'll be liked, but you'll also be kicked to the curb the instant you step out of line.

Was he trying to bridge his two worlds?

That seemed more likely.

The only way to truly create change is on the inside. Protesters can hold placards and shout slogans, but real work is done from within. In the least, Michael would get his answers. Was the world of law enforcement inherently racist? He'd find out, and if becoming an officer was a mistake, he'd do what he always did: move on.

As he studied his chosen field from afar, Michael realized he liked the idea of detective work. Sure, there was honor in being a flatfoot—being out on the streets, interacting with the public and getting his hands dirty—but just like with sports vs. academics, he liked working the muscles of his mind more than those on his body.

To become a cop, all you had to do was graduate high school and pass the entrance exam.

That was inviting but limiting. Michael could work his way up the chain of the police force—patrolman, detective, dare he say chief of police? But was there a way to broaden his horizons?

That's when Michael realized he was limiting himself. The police weren't the only problem-solvers out there; there was the CIA, the FBI, the Secret Service...

Michael researched all his options.

The Secret Service was discounted immediately. He wasn't interested in counterfeiting or financial crimes, meaning he'd have to shoot for personal protection. But Michael wondered: could he really throw himself in front of a bullet because it was his job? If he respected the person he was protecting, sure. But Michael was pretty sure agents didn't just get to pick their assignments. If he ended up with a foreign dignitary who was a complete douchebag...

No, definitely not his thing.

The CIA was tempting, but he wasn't sure espionage was up his alley. Then he took a long, hard look at the FBI.

The FBI seemed to offer the best of every world—protecting people, but not affixed to a single location. Cops have to live in (or close to) their precinct. As an agent, he could switch locations without upending his life or losing seniority.

With his mind made up, Michael took a few extra steps on his path to being an agent. High school gave way to community college. He knocked out some core courses there and saved a ton of money on tuition.

Sure, community college got a bad rap; the best joke he'd heard about it was, "Why go to film school and learn how to make a horror movie, when you can go to community college and experience one?"

Funny, and only somewhat inaccurate.

That said, when he finally graduated, his student debt was manageable. Plus, he had an employable degree, and a plan.

Every year he heard about student debt crushing people, yet at college all he saw were unfocused young adults taking out massive loans to get a degree in art history.

"Good luck with that," he'd think every time he talked to a patchouli-scented white girl.

Ever the advance planner, Michael lined up his courses to gain a degree in computer science.

He knew the degree was a hot commodity for the FBI, and like his life motto, if the FBI didn't work out? *Moving on…* A degree in computer science would provide him with plenty of other opportunities should he dislike law enforcement.

While a student, Michael ended up working in the field of home health to pay the bills.

A friend referred him to Lutheran Social Systems, a charitable organization whose efforts centered on getting high-functioning people with mental disabilities out of institutions and into group homes. These were people without severe medical conditions. They didn't need a *nurse* on hand 24/7, but they did need constant care and monitoring—caring people to cook meals, provide daily activities, and take them out of the home and into the public.

Michael arrived at work every Sunday morning at 8:00 AM, and left Tuesday mornings at 8:00 AM. He got paid for 40 of the 48 hours he was there, but considering he was technically earning money while sleeping for a portion of the overnight section of his shift, he was OK with "donating" eight hours of his life every week. Having Tuesday through Saturday free was worth the minor sacrifice, and just meant that when autumn rolled around, he didn't schedule any Monday classes. Plus, since most of the clients went to bed around 7:00 PM, the job gave him plenty of time to do homework, read, or even watch TV. All while getting paid.

It was decent work, and being around members of the special needs community taught him more than he ever knew about compassion. So much so, that part of him almost wished he felt home health was his life's calling.

But it wasn't.

Thus, at the age of 24, Michael Godwin became an employee of the United States of America.

Michael was assigned to the Kansas City branch. He worked a couple wire fraud cases—it was hard to believe people were still willing to empty their bank accounts for the future promise of a huge payout by a Nigerian prince, but they did—and then two weeks into his service someone blew up a building in Missouri's hat.

Michael was going to shadow a veteran agent and get his first field work experience.

To say he was excited would be an understatement.

Chapter 3

Introductions

Susan watched as a black Toyota Highlander made its way to her.

She smiled but didn't laugh. It amused her how certain cliches rang true: the FBI loved SUVs, and they loved them black.

If the trip were a one-off, it could be any SUV. But if several cars were driving in tandem, oh, they had to match. Same brand, same model.

Image was important, after all.

It was chilly, but not yet cold. That would probably change as the sun receded into the horizon, which it was doing rapidly.

Forty-five minutes had passed since the bomb went off, and like with any event, no two news outlets had the same story. In the rush for clicks, the media barfed up whatever they could, accuracy be damned.

From what she could surmise, a janitor (or someone dressed like a janitor) had gone to the top floor of Glenback Pharmaceuticals' headquarters and set off a bomb. That information came from a personal assistant allowed to leave the room before detonation. She was being interviewed by local police. By the time Susan arrived, the poor woman would have told her story ten times to ten different officers.

Tedious, yes, but you had to interview the same person multiple times to discover inconsistencies. Not that Susan believed the assistant was in on the crime, but you had to follow every possible angle.

As of now, Susan knew of no demands that had been made before the bomb went off, no hostages that were retained or spared, and no reason for the action.

It was odd.

Generally, if you've gone to all the trouble to take a high-value person captive—and the CEO of a multi-billion-dollar corporation qualified as "high-value"—you were doing it with very specific intent. You waited for the media to arrive, made demands, and whether or not you killed everyone at the end was immaterial.

The pattern was: you told people what you were doing, and why. This guy just blew the place up without saying anything.

Susan ran scenarios in her head. She tried to keep it light, because she knew one of the biggest failings of law enforcement was getting too attached to any one idea. If you believed the butler did it, then you were going to find a way to prove the butler did it. Meanwhile, the guilty party got away. Focusing on one aspect of anything took away your ability to examine options. Susan wanted to think, but not precondition herself into believing anything. It was a tricky field of landmines to navigate, and better agents than her had tricked themselves into ignoring facts for gut feelings.

The SUV making its way to her caused Susan's mind to shift from "examining all options" to the Toyota acceleration scare of 2009.

People had become convinced that the cars were death traps, that they would just start speeding up and nothing could be done until the car crashed. Toyota had to recall millions of cars, and lost billions of dollars in revenue. Every time you turned on the TV or went online, there it was: *Toyota Accelerates Out of Control.*

Turned out, people were just panicking, and pressing the gas pedal.

That's all it was.

Completely simple explanation for a problem that baffled so many people, mainly because confusion, not solution, had become the media narrative.

To that end, Susan wondered—given the lack of demands made—if this would turn out to be something small. The general public was fueled by the media, and thus always went large: "Al-Qaeda!" "Terrorism!" Headlines got clicks, and clicks meant money.

But what if this was just a jealous husband? Someone out to settle someone else's hash, and did so dramatically and without regard for who else went with?

Well, *almost* without regard.

He had emptied the building. That meant he had a specific target, and probably a specific message to give.

So where was it, the message? Would there be a note at his house, waiting to be found once his identity was known?

The Highlander coming to a stop ten feet from her put an end to Susan's musing.

Two men got out; one she recognized immediately. Gordon Sumner was the director of the Kansas City bureau. He was on his phone, which was unsurprising. Sumner spent so much time on the thing Susan once cracked he'd probably get a brain tumor from the cell signal. Sumner had smirked in response, but didn't buy a headset.

The other man was younger, and unknown to Susan.

As Sumner made his way over, the young man grabbed his overnight bag from the back of the vehicle. Susan determined it was her co-agent on this assignment.

Susan's own bag sat at her feet. It contained a toothbrush and toothpaste, then two sets of necessities and nothing more. Two pair of socks, underpants, jeans, and shirts. And, of course, her FBI-adorned blazer. She'd have to wear that on site, but she didn't have to fly in it.

If the assignment ran longer than two days, she'd hit a department store for spare clothes, but cases like that were rare. Most FBI work took place at a desk; you gathered information in the field, and then analyzed it back at the office.

Sumner arrived and nodded in greeting. They'd known one another for years and didn't exchange minor pleasantries as if bumping into one another at a Starbucks.

"Right," Sumner said into his phone, and then paused. "Right. I'm at the airport. Call you in five."

Sumner hung up.

No "goodbye" was offered; Sumner always spoke with an efficiency of words. He said what he needed to and moved on. When Susan first arrived at the agency, it was somewhat startling, especially in person. One second you were talking to him, the next he was walking away. He wasn't rude—Sumner always acknowledged the conversation was ending—but it wasn't formal, either.

"This is Michael Godwin," Sumner gestured as Michael walked up.

Susan reached out her hand at the same time Michael did. Susan offered "agent," as her greeting, but before Michael could respond Sumner jumped in.

"Susan Chamberlain," Sumner informed Michael, and then continued without pausing. "We've still no confirmation as to what kind of attack this was: foreign, domestic, lone wolf... As information is gathered on the ground, it'll be sent to you in the air. By the time you arrive, we should know whether or not we're taking over and making this a federal case, or if the locals can handle it."

"Locals can handle bombings?" Michael asked, somewhat confused.

"If it turns out to be a lone actor," Susan responded, "then yes. If there are ties to an organization, it's on us."

Michael nodded in understanding.

"Building security is compiling all camera footage they have for the past three days and transferring that to us," Sumner continued. "Analysts will go over that; you'll get interview assignments as we identify anyone going into or coming out of that location who shouldn't have been there. If this guy had a partner, we'll know it soon enough."

Sumner paused, and eyed his agents.

"Questions?" he asked.

Susan's face was locked in, serious; Michael's betrayed his excitement. Neither spoke.

"Good," Sumner said, satisfied with their non-response. "Go."

And with that, Sumner turned on a dime and tapped a button on his phone. He was engaged in conversation by the time he got back to the SUV.

Michael looked at Susan as she picked up her bag.

"You're the senior agent," Michael offered. "After you."

They were in the air and flying north ten minutes later.

Chapter 4

The Plane

Michael had never been on a private jet.

It was insanely gratifying. Even though he was working, it was still better to walk right on a plane and sit down than it was to stand in line after line and then be felt up by a member of the TSA, the "Take your Shoes off, Asshole" mall cops of the airport.

There was no on-flight service or movie, but my God, with so few seats and only he and Agent Chamberlain on board, he could stretch out his legs.

Michael exhaled in satisfaction. He could get used to this.

Michael turned his attention to Agent Chamberlain; she was thumbing through headlines on her phone but didn't appear to be unapproachable or busy.

"Do I call you Agent Chamberlain?" Michael offered. "Or Susan, Suzy..."

"In public, we call one another agent. In private, whatever you're comfortable with."

Susan's response was warm, and Michael relaxed. He'd hoped he wouldn't get stuck with a personality disorder, and it looked like he dodged that bullet.

"You don't have a Susan/Suzy preference?"

"I used to as a kid, but a friend beat that out of me using his own actions."

Michael arched an eyebrow, confused. Susan chuckled at the memory she was recalling.

"I had a friend named Jim in high school. Just one of the guys in the crowd I hung out with. Good guy. After high school several of us stayed in touch, and one day we all got a very formal email saying he would prefer if we all referred to him as 'James.' He'd gone to college and took a psychology class, or realized his penis was smaller than other penises... something silly happened, and he demanded to be called 'James.' Well, I responded with a light joke, and referred to him as Jim—something I'd done for years—and he got offended and lectured me. Made him come off like a..."

Susan paused, hunted for a word, and then chuckled again and landed on "douchebag."

Michael smiled.

"I don't mean to be harsh," Susan explained, "but that's the best way to put it."

"No, no..." Michael put his hands up to show he wasn't judging her. "I understand perfectly."

"Anyway," Susan finished, "I'd never really had a preference, but after that lecture, I decided I was confident enough with who I am to not be bothered by whatever name someone wants to call me."

She paused.

"As long as it's not 'douchebag.'"

Now Michael laughed.

"What about you, Agent Godwin?" Susan asked. "Michael, or Mike?"

"Well, aside from the whole 'having a friend named Jim' part, it's the same: whichever. I've never had a preference. And hearing you relate it to his penis, I'm glad."

Susan laughed: "That was my way of saying he was over-compensating for shortcomings elsewhere."

"Fair enough."

Susan checked her phone.

"No messages from the office yet," she explained. "Since we've got forty-five minutes in the air, no updates to discuss, and you're going to be working under me, I need to know who you are."

"Also fair enough."

"Good. First question: baseball or football?"

If Michael was taken aback, he didn't show it. Sure, it was an odd first question—most people opened their getting-to-know-you session with something about college, "What made you want to join the FBI?" or a question about their relationship status.

This was outside the norm, which is why Susan asked it. How a person responded to knuckleballs was important to her.

"That's a trick question..." Michael started. "You're trying to figure out if I like the strategy of baseball, or the aggression of football. The problem is, with the roughing the passer rules in football, it's becoming a non-contact sport, like baseball. Which means my answer is basketball. My turn?"

"Your turn."

Michael thought for a moment.

Susan's initial salvo had caught him slightly off guard, but in a good way. Working with a new agent was like a first date, only with potential life-or-death consequences while in the field. If something went down all you *really* needed to know was whether or not you could trust your partner to have your back.

But, since working side-by-side with someone meant discovering their personality, he could see where Susan's approach was coming from and decided to Judo her method back at her.

"Facebook, or Twitter?" Michael asked.

"Ouch," Susan winced theatrically. "Bad move... you're not supposed to follow up to an either/or question with another either/or question."

Michael feigned disappointment in himself. "I just exposed how unoriginal a thinker I am, didn't I?"

"It's OK," Susan laughed. "I will answer, and then give you a second chance. Facebook or Twitter..."

Susan trailed off in thought while Michael toyed with the idea of whistling the music from Jeopardy, but then realized that would be another sign of unoriginal thinking.

"I have decided that I am insulted," Susan said, her voice cheerful in order to show she was not, in fact, offended.

Michael arched an eyebrow.

"You didn't include Snapchat, because you think I'm too old for that," Susan continued, "but you also think I'm so old that I'm into Facebook. You're judging me, Michael."

"So, Twitter," Michael laughed.

"Twitter it is," Susan confirmed. "Ask another question."

Michael didn't hesitate; he'd used the time she contemplated her answer to come up with his next inquiry.

"Best concert you ever saw," Michael volleyed.

"OK Go, Worthington, Minnesota," Susan returned without hesitation.

"Completely unfamiliar."

"You're not as unfamiliar as you think. You remember the treadmill video? The band who did one continuous shot while performing mild stunts on treadmills?"

Michael's memory hiccupped, then landed where it was supposed to: "Right... Yeah. Yeah, I remember that. Couldn't hum a melody, though."

"Well," Susan continued, "that's OK Go, and I saw them in the middle of nowhere, Minnesota, and it was great."

"Because they were up and coming, and you saw them before they got big?"

"The opposite, actually. I saw them after they were famous, but they were asked if they'd play this tiny town called Worthington. They said yes, even though they were already selling out places like The Metro in Chicago and First Avenue in Minneapolis. To be honest, when I saw they were going to Worthington, I had to look it up; I figured it was a suburb of Minneapolis. But nope. Just a farming town off the interstate that runs across Minnesota. I-90, I think. I drove five and a half hours, because they weren't coming anywhere closer. They played a 750-seat community auditorium in a 'city' of only twelve thousand people. And because it was a community center? The community came out. There were kids around six and seventy-year-old farmers in overalls. I guarantee they weren't all fans; they were just curious locals turning out to see a show. And it was fantastic. Best concert I've ever seen, easy."

"Well then, fair enough."

"You say that a lot."

"Fair enough. I'll stop."

Susan laughed.

"My turn?" she asked.

"It is. And even if it wasn't, you are technically the boss..."

"OK, sticking with music: most overrated song."

"Stairway to Heaven. Do I even need to justify that?"

Susan smiled, "No. I'm with you there. I also would have accepted Free Bird, or anything by Kanye."

"Hey now, Kanye is a genius. He says so himself." Michael wagged a scolding finger, but he wasn't serious. "Your turn," he continued. "Most underrated song."

Susan's phone buzzed before she could answer; it was an incoming text. She glanced at it, and her demeanor shifted to a more professional mode.

"OK," she explained. "We're getting some information, so no more questions. Here's me in a nutshell: I've always been told that respect is something you earn. After hearing that my whole life, I started to disagree. As a woman, people have made me earn their respect, because they have this false idea policing of any kind is a 'man's job.' Here's how I operate: I think respect is given, not earned. It's given immediately and freely, because I don't care that you're young and raw, I respect what you did to get here, to get into the agency and on this plane, and on this case with me. The catch is that respect is easy to lose, and once it's gone, it can take a lifetime to re-earn."

Susan paused to allow her words to sink in.

"Fair enough?" she asked.

Michael digested everything. He'd never really heard that sort of take on respect, but he liked it. He'd gone through some of the same things— having to earn respect, eyes on him wondering if he'd been given placements because of affirmative action or similar programs.

Michael looked at Susan. Her straightforwardness was refreshing.

"Absolutely," he said. "Absolutely fair enough."

Susan smiled. She was still in professional mode, but "all business" didn't mean "not human."

"Here's what I've got," Susan told him. "It was a janitor, confirmed. Evan Francart, white male, age fifty-seven. Our point of contact with the local PD will be... looks like they've brought out the biggest of the big from behind his desk, Police Chief Matthew Dalton. You look up Evan, I'm going to give Chief Dalton the once over."

Michael was confused.

"Are we investigating him?" he asked.

"No..." Susan explained. "But it's best to go into every situation with as much information on *everyone* you're about to interact with as possible."

Michael nodded, digesting the information.

Susan's phone vibrated again; her eyes flicked back and forth as she read the screen.

"Find as much as you can on Evan, because I just got his address," Susan explained. "A collection team is going to the bombing site, and we're going to his house. We'll meet Chief Dalton there, and we'll be the first ones inside."

Michael nodded.

This was it; no more simulations. He was in the field.

Chapter 5

The Drive

The rest of the flight was spent mostly in silence.

New information popped up on Susan's phone randomly, which she would read or forward to Michael. They would each take notes, be they mental or written, and began constructing the pieces of this particular puzzle.

When they landed, Michael was again impressed by how wonderful it was to fly private. There was no standing in the aisle waiting for people to get their oversized bags out of the overhead compartments, no one jostling or elbowing for better access to the exit... just him and Agent Chamberlain standing up and walking down the stairs and into the airport.

Their rental car was ready and waiting for them, which was another perk. Agent Chamberlain flashed her ID, signed one form, and they were on their way.

Michael drove.

As they approached the car, Agent Chamberlain had tossed him the fob and said, "I'll be on my phone too much to focus on where we're going, so I hope you have a valid driver's license."

Michael did, and enjoyed the fact he was being treated like an equal, not relegated to the back seat or not taken seriously.

Before throwing her bag in the trunk, Agent Chamberlain opened a side pouch and pulled something out. Michael didn't see what, exactly, but when they got in the car, he discovered that Chamberlain came prepared. She had grabbed a clip-on phone holder for the rental.

"Remind me to grab this when we leave," she told Michael. "I've bought three in the last year, and Amazon doesn't sell them in bulk."

"I'll do my best," Michael nodded as Susan attached the device to the dashboard.

"Put your phone on it and pull up your GPS," she said.

Michael did just that and entered Evan Francart's address into the map.

"OK," he said, looking the route over. "It's about twelve miles from Des Moines International Airport to his house, and that translates into..." Michael paused. "Jesus, twenty minutes. Thanks, traffic."

"Where are we going?" Susan inquired.

Michael started the car, turned on the lights, and pulled out of the stall as he answered: "Johnston. Suburb of Des Moines. North."

Susan's thumbs tapped away on her phone.

"OK," she read. "It's an upper-middle class neighborhood. Average home cost is $350,000."

Susan paused.

"Something is off here," she said haltingly. "One, this is not where you usually find domestic terrorists. People with money don't blow themselves up easily. And two, this is not a neighborhood you find a janitor in. No way he bought that house on his salary. This doesn't make sense."

Michael started running numbers in his head.

"If a house is two seventy-five in Iowa," he mused, "what would it be in Chicago? A million?"

"Probably."

"Jesus, it pays to live in places no one wants to live."

Susan laughed. "Hey, we did just land at an international airport."

"We did, because I'm sure there are multiple directs to Shanghai daily."

Michael turned slightly serious.

"He's not a janitor," Michael explained, the thought coming to the forefront of his memory. "His backstory... Like you said, he worked there for two years, but before that he was a professor. He taught economics at Drake University."

Susan's forehead scrunched instinctively as she thought.

"Well this just makes no sense," she said. "Was he fired from the university? Did he have a relationship with a student?"

"Nope. Walked away of his own accord. At least according to the quick file I read. If there's something dark underneath that, it's hidden away."

Susan looked out the window: concrete, strip malls, apartments, homes. Flyover country took flack for not being on the cutting edge of culture, but she could be anywhere. In America, a city was a city was a city.

"Tell me about his family," Susan probed.

Michael flipped his signal on, looked left-right-left, and pulled into traffic.

"No kids, one wife, but she passed away... wait, shit."

"What?"

"She passed away two years ago. Look up the dates, I don't have them memorized."

Susan pulled up the document she'd been sent.

"Jesus," stated as she read. "Jennifer Francart died two years ago, like you said. It was after a long illness..." Susan paused to read forward a couple sentences. "Evan took a leave of absence from the university several months before she passed, ostensibly to take care of her..."

Susan paused once more.

"And he started working at Glenback Pharmaceuticals last October."

"Does it say what she died of?"

"I'm scrolling..." Susan drifted off, continuing after reading forward a little. "She had leukemia, but her death was a suspected assisted suicide. They didn't have enough evidence to bring him to trial for it, though. Jesus..." Susan sighed. "We just entered Alexander Hamilton territory."

"I don't follow."

"Sorry, sometimes I make sense only in my own head. 'The World Turned Upside Down.' It's one of the songs in the musical. Nothing makes sense; the unexpected happened."

Michael began digesting all the information as his phone chimed, "Stay right to merge onto I35 north." He threw on a turn signal, and before Michael realized it, a conclusion was forming in his head.

"But it actually does make sense," he offered.

Susan arched her eyebrows; the look said "continue" without her having to vocalize it.

Michael watched a car cross two lanes without signaling in order to make its exit. He shook his head lightly in disapproval as he continued his line of thought.

"You've got a guy hammering out a paycheck as a professor. It's a dignified position. His wife gets sick. She dies, and there's nothing he can do about it. He's grieving, angry, and wants to lash out. Glenback becomes his target. They're local, which makes it easy, and look at the specifics: he didn't take any hostages or make any demands. This was a revenge attack. Something Glenback did to his wife made Evan Francart blow up their executives."

Susan was impressed, and just a wee-bit embarrassed. The way Michael spelled it out made it seem so easy it could have been a connect-the-dots puzzle. But she was no peach and didn't bruise easily. If her ego took a hit, it was a minor one. Michael had drawn the conclusion and should be recognized for it.

"I think we're gonna be sleeping in our own beds tonight," Susan told him. "Because you just Scooby-Doo'ed the shit out of this mystery."

Michael laughed.

"Well, now all we have to do is prove that," he reminded her.

"True. But we can't get too fixated on that solution, because then we'll just work toward that, not the truth."

Susan's phone buzzed. She glanced at it and gave a slight eyeroll.

"Chief Dalton wants to know what our ETA is," she explained. "Apparently he's tired of waiting and wants to go inside."

"Locals don't like it when we show up, do they?"

"It's a mix and depends on the ego of the person involved. Sometimes they're happy to have the mess off their hands. That allows them to point at us and tell the press, 'Ask them what's going on.' It's especially useful when a case goes unsolved to blame those above you. Other times... yeah, they want to do it all. Whatever happened, happened in their back yard, and they want to clean it up themselves."

Susan took a look at Michael's GPS, and texted the corresponding information to Chief Dalton.

When they turned on to Evan Francart's block, they didn't need to read addresses to figure out which house was his; Chief Dalton's car was parked right out front. Dalton himself was leaning with his back against the car, arms crossed. An agitated look rested comfortably upon his face, as if it was effortless for him to be annoyed but took some doing to be relaxed.

Dalton looked exactly as his file had described him: white male, sixty-five years old, salt and pepper hair in a crew cut, military style. He wasn't exactly athletic in build, but Dalton wasn't slovenly out of shape; if anything, he was "stout." Dalton had been policing for a long time and was described as being old school and no-nonsense.

As they parked, Dalton checked his watch as if to show impatience.

Next to the police car was a locksmith's van: '*Locked out? We'll let you back in*' was painted across the side. Susan appreciated the thoughtfulness; Chief Dalton was a man of action. Even if the orders were for locals to stay out, that didn't mean they couldn't be ready for action.

"That's it?" Michael asked. "One cop car? No police tape? No gawking civilians or media vans?"

"I forget this is your first real field assignment," Susan mused with a smile. "All that comes later, if the place becomes a crime scene. Before that, we like to keep everything low key."

Michael nodded in understanding, and had the thought, *never base your expectations on television or movies, because they forever get it wrong.*

Michael pulled into the driveway. No one was going to be coming home and needing to get into the garage, after all.

As Michael and Susan exited their vehicle, Dalton made his way to the duo.

"First time I've had to wait for feds in order to search a house in my district," he began.

Susan took note. There was no "hello," no extended hand, just a light puffing of the chest to let his displeasure be known. She rounded the car to greet Dalton, but he was already focusing on Michael.

"I've got the front door open," he continued, speaking to Michael. "I kept the guy here in case there were any locked doors inside."

"Do you mean the front door is physically open, or just unlocked?" Susan interjected.

Dalton directed his answer at Michael: "I mean it's open. Unlocked and open. You said I couldn't go in, but you didn't say I couldn't get the ball rolling."

"Thank you," Susan offered. "But considering we're dealing with a bombing, was there any thought given to the idea doors and windows might be booby trapped?"

Chief Dalton showed a momentary surprise, but however briefly his face betrayed his confusion, it immediately returned to annoyance.

"Well," Dalton mused to Susan. "I guess we got lucky."

He turned his attention back to Michael. "Are you two the only two coming? Doesn't the government like to send as many people as possible, so they can get on all the news channels and be seen doing whatever it is you do?"

"Officer Dalton," Susan began, but was cut off.

"Chief Dalton," he corrected her.

Susan paused while she did a quick assessment of the situation. Normally, agitating the local help wasn't the best way to start a case, but it looked like a recalibration was in order.

"I apologize," Susan continued. "Chief Dalton. To answer your question, a task force has been sent to the bombing site to collect evidence. Agent Godwin and I will be the only two people representing the government at this location. Now, feel free to address your comments, questions, and concerns my way. I am the ranking agent on this case, and Agent Godwin is working under me today."

This time, Chief Dalton's face betrayed a scowl before returning to its "agitated-neutral" phase.

Susan waited to see how far he would push it; was that statement enough to put him in line, or was he going to throw down?

"Well now," Dalton began. "I guess it's my turn to apologize."

Only it wasn't an apology; the words were spoken with a sneer.

"I'm sorry I assumed you were the assistant, because I figured when part of the job involves kicking in doors and chasing down perps, the senior officer would be the person built to do just that. The stronger one, if you will."

Susan sighed internally. She had hoped it wouldn't come down to a pissing contest—a confrontation to see who could be the bigger asshole—but that's where they were.

"Chief Dalton," Susan began. Her voice was level. It contained no hint of anger, or emotion. She wasn't going to let him get to her, but she was going to squash him like a bug. "I read your file. You're lactose intolerant, correct?"

Dalton was legitimately confused as he asked, "What does that have to do with anything?"

"Well," Susan continued, "my body was designed to grow, carry, and give birth to life. Yours can't even handle a glass of milk. Who is the weaker between us?"

Chief Dalton would have responded, but he was taken too sideways by the verbal assault. If he'd been expecting an attack, it wasn't along these lines.

"Now wait a minute..." he managed, before Susan started back in.

"No, you wait a minute. I'm sorry you are unhappy with the arrangements, that this is currently a federal case and that I am a woman. But you do not get to express that displeasure by belittling me, or my partner. I bleed like you bleed, and I want to get to the bottom of this like you want to get to the bottom of this. If you continue with the attitude, then I'll file a report that states you ran out on the investigation because there was yogurt in the fridge and that made you feel unsafe. Got it?"

Chief Dalton was fuming, but he knew better than to continue. Once everything went up the chain of command, the social justice warriors would label him a "woman hater" and he'd be reprimanded.

"You know what?" he finally asked. "Go ahead. Do your thing. I've real work to deal with back at the station."

And with that, he turned on a heel and started walking back to his patrol car.

"Chief Dalton," Susan called after him.

Dalton stopped, but didn't turn back to her. He wasn't going to give her the satisfaction of a face-to-face.

"Thank you for the locksmith," Susan concluded.

Dalton gave a half-wave as he resumed stride. The thanks sounded genuine, so he had to acknowledge it somehow.

Michael had watched the exchange carefully and wasn't sure what the proper protocol was moving forward.

He finally broke the silence with, "Always read the file, you say?"

Susan nodded wearily, tossing in a slight eyeroll of frustration for good measure.

Chapter 6

Evan Francart's House

The door was indeed wide open; Chief Dalton got credit for that.

The locksmith himself was sitting on a chair on the porch, playing a video game on his phone. Susan asked him to wait in his van.

"This is technically a crime scene," she explained. "Plus, it might not be safe. Go relax while you earn a couple bucks."

The locksmith shrugged. He didn't care what he did, so long as it increased his paycheck.

As the locksmith sauntered off, Susan reached into her tactical bag.

"Gloves on," Susan ordered Michael. "Flashlights out."

Michael did as he was told. The blue latex sliding over his hands was Goldilocks; not too tight, not too loose. Just right.

"How many searches have you done?" Susan asked as they moved into the entryway with caution. "This your first?"

"This is my first..." Michael confirmed, his voice trailing off at the end.

"How well do you remember your training?"

"I got high marks, but I'm always up for a refresher. Especially one in real time."

Susan smiled, though Michael's attention was elsewhere and he didn't see it. She liked the fact he came off like a sponge. He was willing to absorb, to learn. There was nothing worse than a cocky young subordinate. More often than not, the problem with youth was that they thought they knew everything. Youth meant passion, and passion meant arrogance. Michael deferred to her, which was a plus.

"Well," Susan began, her flashlight moving around the room and her eyes following the beam. "Like I told Chief Dalton, we're dealing with a bomber here. This whole house could be rigged. Don't flick any light switches. You have to open doors millimeter by millimeter, looking for wires or listening for clicks, and only doing so after checking hinges and jams. We're bulls in a china shop, and anything we break could kill us."

"That's the one thing I remember most from training," Michael mused, as if the thought were entering his head as the words exited his mouth. "That searching is nothing like the movies, where you see overturned rooms with furniture and clothes strewn everywhere."

"Nope," Susan agreed. "It's meticulous, which means monotonous, which means boring. You have to keep your senses heightened, because you don't want to destroy evidence."

She paused a beat.

"Or, I suppose, die. But I already said that."

Michael was scanning the ground as he inched forward. He wasn't paranoid in the belief a tripwire was waiting for him, but he didn't want to dismiss the notion, either.

After a brief pause, Susan spoke again.

"That scene with Chief Dalton..." Susan began. "That isn't how I wanted our first encounter to go. That's not how I wanted you to see me interact with local law enforcement."

Michael nodded.

"I figured that. But he did push you."

"Exactly. It's best to give people the benefit of the doubt. Especially those you might need to rely upon for help, or information. But you also have to stand up for yourself when push comes to shove."

"I understand."

"Good. It's not how you go out; it's how you greet someone that's important. The first impression matters, and if they don't accept you off your hello, then do what you gotta do."

By now, they had moved through the entryway and into the living room.

"Do we split up, or stay together?" Michael asked.

"Every team develops their own methods," Susan answered. "But for now, let's keep you by my side."

She paused.

"You OK with that?"

"Absolutely. I'm here to learn."

The house was tidy; so much so Michael thought it felt like a museum. The furniture was bare; there wasn't even a throw pillow out of place. It was as if a cleaning crew had come in and sterilized everything. Like the place was for sale and about to be shown to perspective buyers.

Susan noticed as much herself, and made the mental note, *even the trash cans are empty.*

A pair of closed glass doors were past the living room; it looked to be a den, or office.

Michael gestured to Susan, who nodded in response.

They eased their way to the doors, then directed their flashlights through the glass and into the room.

Built-in bookshelves lined two of the walls; books aplenty covered those shelves. In the center of the room was a desk, and on that desk was a laptop. It was open and positioned to ensure anyone looking in would see that the screen was dark. In the middle of the screen was a sticky note with '*PRESS ENTER*' written in crisp, easy-to-read handwriting.

"Well," Susan mused. "This just got interesting."

She paused, then said: "OK, check the right door. Look for anything and everything out of place. Wires, a blinking light, a sensor of any kind…"

Susan herself set about examining the left side of the double doors; her flashlight traced the door jamb top to bottom. Looking through the glass, she examined as much of the room as possible while Michael did likewise on his side.

"Looks clear to me," Michael offered.

"Yeah," Susan responded. "It does."

She paused again, and after a beat exhaled the words, "Well, no time like the present."

Placing one hand on a door handle, Susan pressed downward ever so slowly while listening for a click. If there was a bomb, and it was pressure-sensitive, she might be able to hold it in place; triggered, but not detonated. Hopefully Michael could then get the bomb squad to rescue her.

If, that is, she could hold the door handle just right while she waited.

Susan wasn't the uptight type, but neither was she a robot; the prospect of dying got her nerves up a bit. Though Susan gave no outward appearance of fear, internally she relaxed as the door eased open silently.

She examined the floor in front of her; nothing seemed to block access to the desk. There were seemingly no traps waiting, but she still motioned for Michael to wait as she entered the room alone.

Cautiously, Susan made her way to the desk, then got down on one knee in front of it.

PRESS ENTER.

Susan stared at those words, the question, *Right, and wake the computer up, or blow the house up?* running through her head.

She examined the floor around the desk and saw nothing. She scoured every millimeter of the laptop and found no extra wires or anything out of the ordinary. Just a simple laptop with a power cord.

For safety, she traced the power cord to its outlet.

Everything seemed legit, so she motioned for Michael to join her.

When he was by her side, Susan gave him an *it's now or never* look and reached one index finger to the enter button.

"Here we go," she muttered before tapping it.

Chapter 7

The Message

The computer woke up quickly.

So quickly, in fact, Susan made a mental note to buy the brand the next time she was in the market. Her computer took at least 45 seconds to figure out what was going on every time she jostled it out of sleep mode. She likened it to trying to wake up a teenager for school; the thing was groggy, and non-responsive.

On the screen was a web browser, but no webpage was showing; the screen itself was bright white.

Michael spoke first.

"The URL..." he noted. "We are one hundred dot com."

"Does that mean anything to you?" Susan asked.

"Never heard of it." Michael thought a moment.

"Refresh the browser. That should bring up whatever he wants us to see."

Susan nodded. That made sense.

Using the same gloved finger, Susan used the touchpad to move the cursor up to the browser's "refresh" button. Once the cursor was centered over it, she clicked.

As quickly as the computer woke up, it refreshed the screen. A black background faded in, and over that background was a scrics of whitc-outlined boxes, five across.

"I'm guessing they go twenty deep," Michael offered.

Susan looked at him quizzically.

"We are one hundred... Five across, twenty deep. One hundred."

Susan chided herself silently for not catching that, but didn't dwell on it.

Inside every box was a deep red question mark. Susan didn't recognize the font, but each question mark had blotchy edges and the color ran as if wet and being pulled down by gravity. The font appeared to resemble spray paint.

Or blood, Susan thought.

As they watched the website load, one of the boxes—seemingly random, as it wasn't the top left, which is where you'd start if reading a sentence, and it wasn't the top right which is where the human eye naturally drifts when working on a computer—changed.

The question mark faded out, and a man's face replaced it.

"That's Evan," Michael explained.

There was no emotion betrayed by the picture; it looked like a driver's license, even if it wasn't *actually* his driver's license photo. There was no smile, no anger, no anything. Just Evan, staring into the camera, his face devoid of any clue as to what was going through his head.

Both Michael and Susan waited for something more to happen.

"Try hovering the cursor over some of the boxes," Michael offered. "Especially Evan's."

Again using the touchpad, Susan moved the cursor around the screen. None of the question marks were clickable, but when she hovered over Evan's face, it showed a link was available.

Susan double tapped the touchpad.

Evan's face expanded into a video player, and he began talking from beyond the grave.

"Hello," he began.

His voice was like his picture: monotone, matter of fact.

"My name is Evan Francart, and this is my confession.

"I am responsible for the death of Michael Dexter, CEO of Glenback Pharmaceuticals. I'm sure there were several other board members on hand when I completed my task, but as they are not innocent souls, my conscience is clear.

"My story is no different from that of many others; the more you dig into my past, the more you'll put the puzzle together and understand the reason for my actions.

"The fact of the matter is that people are suffering and dying. If politicians aren't going to protect or help us, then it's time for we the people to stop depending on our elected officials and take matters into our own hands.

"The sad truth is, I know that the most likely result of my statement will be that other corporate executives will just tighten the security they have around them, not change the way they do business. It's easier to hire another guard than it is to do what's right.

"What is right?

"People before profits. It's that simple.

"I get that corporations need profits to survive, but how much is enough? Millionaire, multi-millionaire, billionaire, multi-billionaire... at what point do you realize money is less important than being a decent human being?

"Michael Dexter never had that epiphany, and unfortunately never will.

"Will Glenback change their ways going forward? I have no idea. Will anyone else out there see what I've done and decide to take a more humanistic path than the one they're on? I have no idea.

"But what's done is done, and there are ninety-nine statements left to make. Only you can make yourself a target. Be good, and you'll be left alone.

"Otherwise? Godspeed."

The video player collapsed, and where a question mark once resided in Evan Francart's box, a red X now covered his face.

Silence hung in the air as a tangible presence for several moments before Susan exhaled deeply.

She was about to speak when four more question marks turned into pictures.

"Holy shit," Michael whispered, stunned. "So much for sleeping at home tonight."

Chapter 8

Cassandra

Josh Hodges heard a ding.

He was in his kitchen, filling a glass of water from the dispenser on his fridge. Cool water always seemed to refresh him more thoroughly than room-temperature liquids.

The ding had come from his laptop one room over, and though Josh acknowledged the noise internally, he did not turn to the sound. Instead, Josh nodded thoughtfully; the website was live. The authorities were in Evan Francart's house, and they probably believed Evan was the mastermind behind "We Are 100."

Which is exactly what Josh wanted.

Oh, he knew that one of them had to play chess and would soon realize that the king doesn't move first, pawns do. But the ball was rolling, and now it was just a matter of seeing how far momentum would take it.

Having four boxes go live at the same time was certainly a good ruse. Evan was the big one; he'd draw the most attention. But once they realized that several one-off crimes from the past several weeks were actually part of the bigger picture? Goodness, the authorities would be scrambling.

The way Josh saw it, the system was like a Rube Goldberg machine; everything had to happen in order.

Wait, no. Not really.

It worked *best* if everything went in order, but there were redundancies set in place should one piece of the mechanism fail. Hell, even if the whole thing fell apart, the sheer idea more were out there would keep those in power frightened.

The key was in expectations: if you worked as hard as possible, and put your best foot forward, you had to be happy and accept the outcome no matter what. Go in a perfectionist; exit a realist.

And that's what Josh was: a realist.

Even if only ten or twenty of The 100 succeeded? Well, this was the first time anything like this had been attempted, and the chips had to fall where they may. One team always loses the Super Bowl, and if he were to lose then at least he tried. At least he made it to the championship round.

This wasn't about starting a revolution, or even changing anything, really. Going in thinking he'd make a difference or inspire people, that was nonsense.

Life moves in increments, not leaps and bounds.

All Josh wanted to do was nudge the needle. Maybe start it on a slightly new course, so that while almost invisible to the naked eye, movement could be seen years down the road. Maybe one senator, or one corporate head... One person deciding to do right by humanity. That's all.

Put the fear into everyone; change one person.

Oh, sure, most in power would just double down on security and remain status quo: I've got mine, fuck you and yours.

Which was fine.

It was the idea it *could* happen; the knowledge people were frustrated with the way things are and frustrated with business as usual, that's what mattered.

With the plan and several executions of it finally public, how many followers would follow through, and how many would back out? How many would contact authorities when the eventual reward for information was offered?

Josh had hedged his bets; run the numbers and looked into an over/under. This was gambling.

Most of them would do their part, he believed. Especially if the first case started getting attention. The idea they would live on in infamy was a powerful motivator; the worst thing the media ever did was to name murderers. It made them famous, and if there's one thing people love, it's fame. They want to be remembered; to be known as *someone* who did *something*.

Especially something they believed in, even if that "something" put them on the same fame list as Ted Bundy and John Wayne Gacy.

Those two lived on in the minds of the American public better than the Las Vegas shooter. Sure, that guy had the biggest body count—at least as of now, Josh mused—but horrific events happened so often these days that it was hard to stand out.

Josh had given one hundred people a chance to be a part of the greater good. To get their thought, their belief out into the world. And, instead of being an isolated incident where they would soon be forgotten, they would be forever known as part of a movement.

To that end, Josh wondered how many realized they would be forgotten, but the institution remembered. ISIS was a brand; individual martyrs remained anonymous.

Josh frowned.

The comparisons with a terrorist organization were going to be inevitable. Those who didn't understand, or who refused to understand, would label him, and his followers, as evil. He'd probably be called some form of Jim Jones or David Koresh.

The thought made him simmer, but he soon brushed the negativity aside. Josh wasn't evil; he was going out of his way to have his people target the guilty.

Again, he was actually *trying*, and that's what was important.

So many people don't even try. They accept. They resign. They slump their shoulders and move forward in a daze, taking control of what they can, which was usually nothing more than the remote control.

Almost worse than the apathetic were those angry over everything, especially anything inconsequential. Mob warriors on the internet.

"I'm going to show the world how outraged I am by tweeting! There, mission accomplished. Now I can eat ice cream a hero."

Plus, with everyone angry about *everything*, there was no focus.

You want to know why the powers that be remained the powers that be? Because while you were yelling about how *this* actress shouldn't be allowed to play *that* role, those at the top were consolidating power. While you were enraged because a comedian made a joke or a random person posted a meme you didn't like, those in power were crafting legislation.

Josh had considered buying change, like the Koch brothers did every election cycle. He certainly had the money to be "legitimately corrupt," as he put it. Buying politicians was legal, but that didn't make it moral.

Which is why he took a different approach. If you're not going to be "moral," why not go all out?

Josh was rich. Maybe not Warren Buffett rich, but rich.

In school, he'd been a math prodigy. In college, he started playing the stock market; he examined the ins and outs of futures, short selling, commodities...

By the 1990s, Josh had a decent portfolio going. He wasn't obscenely wealthy yet, but he was already making more than, say, a specialty surgeon. Even though he took his skills to Wall Street, growing up in Seattle meant he liked investing in businesses back home. He invested in a local coffee company, and an online bookstore. Those two decisions gave him everything he ever wanted and more, but the kicker to his fortune came in 1997. That's when Steve Jobs returned to Apple, and Josh decided to throw some money into the computer industry. Even he didn't realize how valuable that choice was going to be when the iPod and subsequent iPhone came to fruition within the next decade.

In 2007, Josh noticed what was taking place in the housing market and decided to short a handful of stocks. That move took him from rich, to the so-called 1%.

Now he had F-you money.

Money that allowed him to live on the cusp of Central Park, in an apartment over one of the rare green expanses in an otherwise concrete jungle.

Josh smiled wistfully as he looked out a window and saw Summit Rock. He was going to miss this place. But, with the wheels in motion, it was probably time to move to the warehouse. Had to stay one step ahead of law enforcement in a game like this, after all.

Anyway, yes, he was rich to the point he could have purchased reform, but that didn't appeal to him. Voting a corrupt politician out of office didn't change anything. If anything, the former politician went on to become a well-paid lobbyist. Removing an executive from power just gave that executive his golden parachute early.

No one was ever held accountable for their actions, and that offended Josh.

From Enron, to the savings and loan scandal, to the perpetrators of the financial crash in 2008 he himself had cashed in on... no one ever got held accountable.

Cassandra was going to change that.

Josh's good mood returned at the thought of Cassandra. He liked the name, and the mislead.

Once the authorities figured out Evan wasn't behind anything, they would eventually discover Cassandra. They had to. Even though Josh had covered his tracks meticulously, he wasn't insane. The idea "I'm smarter than everyone" never crossed his mind. He knew the authorities would use all their resources against him, and though he had plenty of resources himself, they were nothing compared to the weight of the United States government.

Cassandra was basically a somewhat-commercial version of Watson, the AI supercomputer that had supplanted Deep Blue. Deep Blue played chess, Watson won on *Jeopardy!*, and the IBM Power System AX955—which Josh named "Cassandra"—was a version of those computers on steroids.

Cassandra was able to process language, and use automated reasoning to make decisions, which meant the obvious use for her was to overpower the stock market. Human traders were nothing but figureheads these days anyway. Computers watched for patterns and bought and sold shares as they deemed necessary. So it wasn't unusual for Josh to buy such a powerful entity, it's just that he never intended to use it for monetary gain.

Moralistic gain, well, that was another thing.

With no one being held accountable for their wrongdoings, Josh wondered if anyone out there felt like he did; if anyone out there ever longed for a cause. Did people long to act, or were they content with just stewing and shaking their fists?

That's when he realized: he could weaponize tragedy. People who suffered tragedy, or in the least, *the right kind of tragedy,* wanted revenge. If people felt wronged, attacked, or let down, they wanted to lash out.

Josh knew this from personal experience. Not a day went by without the memory of his old life.

Josh broke his life down in three segments: B.B., W.B., and A.B. It was a play on the Gregorian calendar, where you had B.C. and A.D. Only instead of 'Before Christ' and 'Anno Domini,' Josh's life was sectioned by 'Before Beth,' 'With Beth,' and 'After Beth.'

After Beth had taken up five years of his life so far, yet Josh still struggled with accepting the fact it would also be the segment he spent the rest of his days inside. She was gone, and gone is eternal.

Josh decided that if he was going to live 'After Beth,' he needed to make it worthwhile. He needed to use his resources, his wealth.

Which is why he bought Cassandra. Josh bought a supercomputer and she set up shop online. Cassandra monitored the news, and more importantly, online support groups.

Those groups were integral to Josh's plan.

The members were desperate people; those who either couldn't afford a traditional, $100-an-hour therapist, or who didn't want to go public with their grief. Online support groups provided anonymity. You didn't have to go into a church rectory or a community hall, sit on a plastic folding chair, and stare someone in the eye while spilling your guts—your pain—into the world while holding a Styrofoam cup full of stale coffee. You could send your avatar into those places. The emotions would be real, but no one had to know it was *you* having them.

In those groups, Josh found desperation.

Though it was, Josh admitted, cruel to use these people, they were the ones most willing to join him.

Cassandra scoured the internet for support groups, ran scenarios, crunched numbers, and decided on targets. Once a potential was named, they were researched.

Thanks to the wonders of social media, this could all be done from afar. The thing with social media sites is they're always interested in money. All you had to do is present yourself as an advertiser; you were selling a product. Then, like the Russians in the 2016 election, you started getting specific. Who fits your profile? Who do you want to advertise to? What are you selling? Most importantly: who do you want to ensnare in your web?

People thought data mining involved using information for marketing or advertising. But you could also manipulate people in pain, those who had suffered loss.

Because even more important than "Who suffered loss?" was the question, "How did they respond to it?"

In short, *who could be manipulated?*

Cassandra was meant to study information, and hypothesize. That meant it made sense for her to analyze social media profiles. Sure, you could figure out who was most likely to buy a certain brand of shoes, but you could also suss out the kind of person seeking revenge. And if someone wanted revenge, all you had to do was help them achieve it.

Once you found those people, then you had your army.

And once you had an army, you could change the world.

Chapter 9

Seattle

Freddy Broe wasn't nervous.

It wasn't that he was calm, exactly. He was conditioned. He'd run the scenario in his head 1,000 times and physically performed the action twenty times, albeit test runs in an imperfect setting.

Freddy knew that no amount of running drills could compare to real life, but drills put you in a certain mind frame. He learned that playing football. He never went pro, but he made it through college on a scholarship, and that in and of itself was a pretty good accomplishment.

At six-foot-three and 230 pounds, he'd played safety. Sure, the twenty-five years since then had changed his physique, but not much. Freddy still had a good frame, even if his belly had gone from six pack to slightly paunchy.

Either way, in any organized sport, you ran drills. They prepared you for the game, and that's where Freddy was now: game time. He knew the drills, and now he was ready to enact muscle memory and play to win.

To that end, Freddy began running through his checklist as the numbers on the elevator flashed higher and higher.

Outside, it was beautiful.

As it was dusk, the city was just coming to life. It wasn't clear enough to see Mount Rainier, but knowing it was out there provided a bit of comfort to Freddy. Comfort, with a slight hint of tension. Freddy found it exhilarating, living next to a piece of nature that could kill you in an instant.

He chuckled, but the laugh was barely audible. If only the volcano would blow it's top, then he'd be off the hook and wouldn't have to go through with everything.

Yeah, his mind followed up almost immediately. *But then how many people would have to die? Tonight, it's just you, and him.*

Freddy nodded, though no one else in the elevator noticed. This was his fight, and there was no need to involve anyone else, much less an entire city full of innocent kids, pets, and grandparents.

Pets.

That was an odd thought to have. But, then again, who didn't love the purity of a pet? An animal that loved you unconditionally. A dog that wagged its tail uncontrollably when you walked in the door, or a cat that purred so loudly you wondered if it could get kitty laryngitis.

Focus, Freddy reminded himself. *You're drifting again.*

Drifting... that's what Freddy's life had felt like since it happened. He had two modes: in pain, and lost. He'd either be completely distraught, fully aware of the pain consuming his entire being, or he'd snap out of a fog and realize three hours had gone by without his even noticing.

Freddy was determined to remain clear-headed and *get this one thing done.* He began to take in his surroundings.

Freddy had been to the Space Needle several times; twice as a kid on field trips for school, and then once to propose to his wife.

His wife.

His ex-wife.

Shit.

Freddy didn't want to cry; he couldn't afford to be distracted. Not now.

Their union had ended the way many do; it couldn't survive the loss of a child. Specifically, their only child. Their daughter.

Knock it off, Freddy thought. *Get off this topic.*

He had to be mentally prepared for what was about to happen, and thinking of the reason he was here wasn't going to help him.

There were less than ten seconds left on his ride.

Shit.

Shit-shit-shit.

He needed to re-calibrate.

Freddy took a deep breath and decided to get a quick drink at the bar. Sure, he was breaking protocol, but in reality, it would allow him to scope the place out. Instead of walking in and having to wander through the restaurant looking for his target, he could take the edge off with one drink and observe his surroundings.

Then he'd beeline it to the table and carry out his objective.

There was no need for speeches or delays; give no one an opportunity to jump in and prevent him from completing his plan. His video would explain everything.

A thought crossed Freddy's mind as the elevator came to a stop: *his plan.* Was it really his plan? Or had Cassandra come up with it? Did it matter?

Everything was muddled in his mind. The drink would focus him.

One drink, he promised himself. If he had two, or three all would be lost. He'd be back on the path that helped his marriage deteriorate.

When the elevator doors opened, Freddy let everyone exit before him. They stepped off and to the maître d', who would alternately seat them or tell everyone to wait. Did people still grease palms to get a better table? Did they ever? Or was that just something you saw in the movies?

Freddy's thoughts were scattershot; he needed that drink.

Waving the host off, Freddy made his way to the bar. He didn't need a table, or a menu. Just a…

A what?

What would be his poison for the evening?

A cold beer would go down smooth, but then he'd want a second, or a third. He needed something harsh. A drink with bite, that wouldn't lead to his becoming sloshed and incapacitated.

Scotch.

That would do the trick. No one drank scotch for pleasure. At least, not anyone with working taste buds.

Freddy walked over to the bar and remained standing. If he sat down, he'd relax.

The bartender greeted him amiably, and when he asked what he could get Freddy, Freddy paused to reflect. He'd never gone all out in his life. His family was never poor, but they never had enough to be truly extravagant.

"What's your highest-end scotch?" Freddy asked.

"We have Glenmorangie Pride, 1974," came the response. "But due to the price, it's only sold by the bottle."

"What is that price?"

"I have to look..." the bartender explained, grabbing an iPad from the counter behind him.

Technology, Freddy chuckled as he shook his head.

"The bottle is $8,000," the bartender finally said, eyeballing his iPad.

Fuck it, Freddy decided. *It's not like I'm going to have to pay the bill.*

Freddy reached into his pocket. His hand brushed past the gun weighing down that side of his jacket, and grabbed the wallet resting beneath it. He pulled the wallet out, and then retrieved a credit card. Mentally, he crossed his fingers. He wasn't wealthy, but he paid his balance on time and believed his limit was high enough.

"Run this," Freddy said, holding his card between two fingers. "Make sure it clears."

The bartender took the card and swiped it on an attachment on the iPad.

Freddy shook his head again. *What happened to cash registers?*

"It cleared," the bartender explained with a smile. "Should I retrieve the bottle?"

Freddy nodded, tossing in a thumbs up for good measure.

When the bottle and glass were in front of him, Freddy paused to enjoy the moment.

So this is what it feels like to live high on the hog.

Freddy turned away from the bar to sip his drink and eyeball the room. That's when he saw Charles Hoover.

Everything snapped back into place. He wasn't here to spend money he didn't have or to get drunk. He was here for the city prosecutor. Charles Hoover. The man who repeatedly decided not to prosecute rapists.

"He said, she said," Charles would tell the press. "Insufficient evidence."

There was always an excuse.

And when he did "prosecute," they never went to court. He always took a deal. No jail time, usually a form of rehab... "Let's not ruin *two* lives," he'd say.

Because, right, a rapist having to pay for his crime would "ruin" his "innocent" life.

Charles was having dinner with friends; three men Freddy didn't recognize, but like Charles were sharks in suits. Predators.

Freddy's daughter, Heather, was seventeen when it happened, and after that only made it three more years.

Like so many stories before her, Heather had gone to a party, had a drink, felt woozy, and woke up with a member of the college football team on top of her. A star player. A local hero.

Having lived among them, Freddy knew the type. They'd been told their whole lives they were different. Special. They deserved to have whatever they wanted, because they were athletes. They passed classes they never attended; they were given gifts outside the scope of NCAA prying eyes.

Freddy had never been like that, but he saw it in a handful of his old teammates. He knew that they felt above the law, and time and time again, the law let them believe it.

Sometimes.

Sometimes the law let them believe it, but not this time. Not on the policing side of things, anyway. The detective assigned to Heather had been great. Detective Mills told Heather she did everything right. Once she got out of the frat house, Heather called a friend for a ride, went directly to the hospital, had a rape kit exam done... Heather had even gotten her rapist to admit what he did on a recorded phone call with Detective Mills listening in.

"I'm sorry," the boy had pleaded. "I was just drunk and horny and thought you liked me, too!"

"Then why did you drug me!?" Heather shouted.

There was a pause in the recording, and then the rapist said, "I was just trying to get you to lighten up. To relax."

The thought made Freddy want to vomit. Or maybe it was the scotch. Jesus, people drank this on purpose? If this was $8,000 scotch, what did bottom-of-the-barrel shit taste like?

Anyway, the rapist had confessed. Said flat-out he had drugged Heather, but Charles didn't want to take the case.

"He can always say he was pressured into that confession," Charles explained. "Confession under duress. His attorney will get it tossed. Plus, she was drunk, so her memory of giving consent could be blurred."

Except she hadn't been drunk.

It was one drink that had sent her down; it had been spiked.

Plus, being too incoherent to walk, talk, or stand meant she was unable to give consent.

Charles shrugged; nothing he could do. Juries were "fickle," he explained. Especially when it came to their star athletes. If the quarterback got a good lawyer, and they *always* got a good lawyer, then the lawyer would create confusion in the jury. Did they do a tox screen at the hospital? Did they test her blood alcohol level?

"If they missed even one step, that leads to skepticism. Skepticism leads to doubt, and doubt leads to acquittal," Charles explained.

Freddy didn't like that and did a little research. Turns out, the Seattle police were diligent in their approach to rape. They gathered evidence, ran an investigation, and made referrals: "We believe there is sufficient evidence to make an arrest, and prosecute a case."

Problem was, Charles Hoover almost always disagreed with the referral, and declined to prosecute.

But only in cases of rape.

Burglary? Sure, arrest him. Murder? Well now, that's a horrible crime. Gotta get murderers off the streets.

But rape? Too dicey for Charles Hoover.

The more he looked into Hoover's records on rape prosecution, the angrier Freddy got. He hated the "What if?" game, but he had to play it: What if Charles had prosecuted the quarterback? What if he had gotten a conviction? Would that have provided any solace to Heather? Would that have given her closure?

As it stood, knowing her rapist was walking freely among the public terrified Heather. After the attack, everything scared her.

Heather couldn't sleep; she became afraid of the dark. The thought made Freddy want to cry. The idea his daughter, a woman, suddenly afraid of the dark. As a child she hadn't needed a nightlight, but as an adult she had to have a lamp on.

She'd tried every pill available to sleep, and the more she took, the more she needed. The more she needed, the more she took. It was a merry-go-round.

Finally, one day she combined the wrong two pills, and like many a celebrity before her, Heather went to sleep and didn't wake up.

Only Heather wasn't a celebrity, she was just another statistic in an ever-growing epidemic of pharmaceutical cocktails gone wrong.

Before Heather was born, Freddy heard that having a child was like having your heart walk around outside of your body.

He agreed, because after she was gone, Freddy's heart was gone. It was just... gone.

He withdrew into alcohol; his wife just withdrew.

One day Freddy cracked open a beer, and one year later he woke up unemployed and divorced.

After that, Freddy looked into Charles' history. He was sickened to discover the man prosecuted roughly 1% of all rape cases brought before him. One. Fucking. Percent. There was no way that 99% of the rape cases in Seattle weren't prosecutable. The man was making a concerted effort to let rapists walk.

A message had to be sent: if prosecutors weren't going to do their job, they were going to be eliminated. Not voted out of office, where they could just return to private practice, *eliminated*.

That, Freddy realized, had absolutely been Cassandra's idea.

She found him online. They'd become friends, even though they never really met. Maybe when the internet was in its infancy, that might have bothered Freddy, but not now. Now, knowing someone intimately and never actually shaking their hand was normal. People shared things online they would never share in person. There was a comfort in being alone with your computer in the middle of the night; the cold screen in front of you allowed you to type out thoughts you'd never verbalize. It was a better confessional than the Catholics had in their churches.

Cassandra had been a sympathetic ear. She had consoled him, supported him... Cajoled him? Manipulated him?

The last two thoughts had bothered Freddy from time to time. He didn't like thinking he could be controlled, or made to act as a puppet.

But he did want to do this, didn't he? He wanted to make Charles pay, yes, but he wanted to send a message: if the powers that be wouldn't do their job, then the people would rise up and act. Maybe it wouldn't change the past, but it could damn well change the future.

"If you eliminate Charles Hoover," Cassandra explained, "the next person to do the job will do it better, because they'll understand there are consequences. Actual consequences. Not bad press, not lose your job, but life and death consequences."

Freddy liked that.

Consequences.

For every action, there was an equal and opposite reaction. *That Newton was a goddamned smart physicist,* Freddy thought. *But I bet he never saw anything like me in his laws.*

Freddy looked at the glass in his hand.

This is disgusting, he decided.

Freddy put down the scotch, reached into his pocket, and took hold of his gun.

He wouldn't pull it out until the absolute last second; there was no need to give anyone cause for alarm before it was necessary.

Freddy had stacked the bullets exactly as he'd been told; there were fifteen rounds in the magazine, and one in the chamber. The first three bullets were hollow points, meant to expand upon impact. They would weaken the glass dramatically. The next three bullets were armor-piercing; the hope was they would poke holes in the glass and start the shatter. Following that, the rest were all Winchester PDX1 rounds. Fat and tough, they would hit hard and make sure whatever remained was in such a weakened state he and Charles would smash through it like breaking open a fortune cookie.

Freddy hoped any bullet that made it through the glass didn't stray too far and hit some unfortunate passerby below.

To that matter, Freddy hoped he and Charles didn't land on anyone.

Well, Freddy thought, *it's not like God will forgive me for this act, so any other sin on top of it is to be expected, I suppose.*

Buying a unique mix of ammunition took time. Freddy bought slowly, one box every so often, and always at the shooting range. He'd shoot most of the box, and then just save a couple rounds at the end. Freddy was cautious; he didn't want to end up on an FBI watchlist and get interviewed and caught.

Cassandra, then, had supplied the armor-piercing rounds.

Any purchase of that kind of ammunition that came with questions, forms, and scrutiny, three things Freddy didn't need during the planning phase of things.

Freddy stared hard at city prosecutor Charles Hoover.

He and his crew were laughing; they'd probably won a case earlier. They ate here at least twice a month, always celebrating a victory. Justice didn't matter to them, winning did.

Freddy eyeballed the window next to them. Charles and his team always had a window table, one that overlooked the city they pretended to care about, but neglected when things got difficult. Protecting a winning record was important, prosecuting the guilty somewhat less so.

The glass looked thick, but he was thankful they weren't on the observatory level. That glass was near-unbreakable.

Freddy knew from practice that he'd clump the first three rounds, then expand the radius slightly with the next three, and the rest were gravy. After that, his 230-pound frame—combined with whatever Charles weighed— should do the trick.

This was it; his moment to shine, or walk away having done nothing. "Go big or go home," just like it read above the tunnel to the football field.

Go big.

Freddy grabbed the glass with his free hand and downed the rest of the scotch with a gulp. It burned, but Freddy was beyond noticing.

He kept a hand on the gun and kept the gun in his pocket as he marched across the restaurant toward Charles' table.

The quartet barely looked up from their drinks and appetizers; it wasn't until the first shot was fired that anyone actually noticed Freddy.

He squeezed the trigger quickly, but methodically.

Boom, everyone flinched. *Boom*, they covered their ears and hunched up. *Boom*, people started screaming.

If anyone at the table was confused and thought he was a really bad shot, it only took a few seconds to realize Freddy was not, in fact, aiming at them.

Just as Freddy had hoped, the window began to weaken. Spiderweb cracks came first, and by the fifth bullet, it started to shatter.

Freddy kept firing.

Neither Charles nor his companions had thought to run; they were all ducking and throwing their hands over their heads. In part it was to shield themselves from the shards of glass, but it was an odd instinct to cover your head at the sound of gunfire, as if the flesh and bone of their hands and arms could prevent a bullet from reaching the skull.

When the clip was empty, time stood still. One, maybe three seconds passed. To Freddy, the moment felt like an eternity.

No one moved; no one jumped Freddy, and the restaurant was silent.

People had initially shouted in fear, but as the shooting stopped, so did the screaming.

All eyes turned to Freddy; he stared back.

"Charles Hoover," he said. There was no question in his voice, it was a statement.

Freddy thought about saying something clever; a quip you'd hear in a movie right before the good guy took out the bad guy. In the end, he decided it was too corny.

Instead, Freddy looked at Charles with sad eyes and in a very plain voice quoted Rose Fitzgerald Kennedy: "It has been said, 'time heals all wounds.' I do not agree. The wounds remain. In time, the mind, protecting its sanity, covers them with scar tissue and the pain lessens. But it is never gone."

And with that, Freddy stepped into Charles Hoover, lifted him out of his seat, and with the energy only an adrenaline rush (or PCP) could muster, lunged as hard as he could and slammed the two of them into the weakened window fifty stories above the city of Seattle.

Less than six seconds later, both lay bloodied and broken on the pavement.

Online, a red question mark turned into a photo of Freddy.

Chapter 10

Setbacks and Speculation

Susan and Michael watched the four new videos and took notes.

They didn't speak during or between viewings; each absorbed what they could from their own point of view. Opinions and observations would be shared during their dissection of the videos, what they gleaned from each.

The stories contained elements of similarity and difference, with one wild card.

The people were: Donny Lin, who rammed his car into that of a rising star in the NRA. Donny had cracked open a couple beers and left them open on the passenger seat, making the incident look like a drunk driving accident. In his confession video he explained that he had actually been stone cold sober and knew exactly what he was doing. Donny lost his son in a school shooting, and though a former member of the NRA himself, couldn't believe the organization balked at the most common-sense regulations. His target had led the fight against biometric trigger locks—guns that wouldn't shoot unless the correct person was holding them—as well as any form of background check or waiting period.

Donny hadn't worn a seatbelt, all but ensuring that when he hit the other car at a speed of eighty-seven miles per hour, he wouldn't survive.

He didn't.

Travis Stevens took out a lawyer that pitted states against one another for tax breaks. The lawyer had gotten $20 million in incentives for one of his clients; the loss of revenue had devastated local schools, libraries, and public works. Worse than that, five years later, the company up and left; the lawyer had found a new state willing to give even more if they moved and "created jobs."

Travis became unemployed, and got angry.

While local papers had covered the incident, no one had ever suspected it was anything more than a disgruntled client with an axe to grind. The fact Travis committed suicide after shooting the lawyer was chalked up to "realizing the enormity of what he'd done and not being able to deal with it."

No one suspected he was covering his tracks.

Brody Morgan Jr. killed a local pharmacist in his hometown of Williamson, West Virginia. The pharmacist had become wealthy by selling opiates to anyone and everyone who asked, and then in turn many people who hadn't. Williamson had a population of fewer than 3,200 people, but in ten years 21 million painkillers made their way into the city. Williamson was considered ground zero for the opioid epidemic; a bullseye that showed drug makers were only in it for the profits, not healing. From Williamson, the pills made their way all across the country, destroying families and killing hundreds.

Brody lost his wife to opioid addiction and knew which pharmacist had supplied his wife's dealer. It looked like an easy case—angry husband commits murder and then suicide—but with this video everything took on new meaning. Brody had acted alone, but he was part of a bigger picture.

His act was meant to send a message to dishonest pharmacists.

Finally, there was Tom Lucas.

Tom shot two white supremacists while on a hunting trip in Idaho. The racists both had long rap sheets of harassment and vandalism; they had broken the windows of a local Thai restaurant and spray-painted Swastikas on Jewish tombstones. Tom figured the world would be a better place without them, so he sat in a tree stand at the edge of their property, and one day when the duo was shooting squirrels, Tom took aim. Once he was sure they were dead, Tom took his own life.

Tom was the odd duck out, as he hadn't lost anyone or suffered any outside tragedy. Tom had been diagnosed with cancer and wanted to "do something good"—his words—with his life before he died.

Of the four, three were white, while Donny was Asian.

For the record: yeah, that meant Tom Lucas was white. A white guy with, again, his words, "a conscience. Someone who knew he could get close enough to the other hunters and take them out before they realized what was happening."

He said as much in his monologue.

By the time Susan and Michael had finished the final video, other agents—a collection team and numerous other staffers of various specialties—had shown up to sweep the place for anything Susan and Michael had missed in their limited once-over.

This group included the FBI's computer technicians; people who could dig up deleted files and scour the hard drive for any and every bit of history it had. They could figure out what websites it visited even if the browser history had been deleted, and most importantly, they could discover who Evan Francart had been in contact with.

As the tech team took control of the computer, Susan and Michael retreated to the living room to compare (and contrast) notes.

"So," Susan began. "First thoughts?"

"They're being coached," Michael responded. "They received instructions on how to record their goodbye."

Susan responded nonverbally; her nod was enough to show she was both listening, and curious about Michael's line of thought.

"The videos are similar in style," Michael continued. "Everyone made sure their phone was horizontal in order to provide that "movie theater" look. If someone doesn't tell them to do that, most will hold their phone vertical and record a square video, creating those stupid blur-bars on the side."

Susan half-laughed. "That's an odd take."

Michael smiled.

"Well, yeah. Not knowing how to hold your phone to shoot a video should have ended over five years ago. It's annoying people still don't get it, but it also means they had a guide. That means there's a leader, a figurehead to the one hundred."

"Evan?"

"I doubt it," Michael responded hesitantly. "You're not going to find too many sixty-year-olds who are technologically savvy."

"But as a professor, he does have the brainpower to research everything. He did put together a working bomb. That's not easy. Most people either blow themselves up in the process, or they push the button and nothing goes boom. It's why bomb makers in terrorist organizations are held in such high regard. It's also how they get caught. They all have a signature style, which is what investigators focus on."

"That's why it's interesting that only one person has blown themselves up," Michael countered. "Maybe Evan didn't make his bomb. The head of this snake could be the bomb maker and doesn't want to reveal himself too quickly. Which means Evan got the only explosive device... *so far.*"

Michael's emphasis of the final two words sent a chill down Susan's spine. A series of suicide bombers would put the country into a panic.

"OK..." Susan thought aloud. "Everyone else has used conventional methods, true. But look at the way this was all stacked: Evan went out to get attention. The others, they all did so in a manner that suggested either accident or one-off crime. Evan became the glue to the other four. There's no way they would have been linked otherwise. The question is, what happens from here on out? Do the attacks get bigger and bigger? Or do they remain quick, seemingly random hits? And, Jesus, what will the frequency rate be now? Are we going to tear through 95 people in a week, or will this play out over years and years?"

"That's the goal of any terrorist organization," Michael said pointedly. "To keep you guessing, and to keep you in fear."

"Terrorist organization..." Susan mulled the words over. "I wonder if that will be the official take?"

"I don't see how it could fall any other way."

Susan didn't like what she was hearing, but couldn't disagree. This smacked of terrorist attack, and given that there were multiple people, it was organized.

"OK," she stated. "New approach. Say it is a terrorist cell. How do you find people willing to do this and organize them?"

Without hesitation, Michael shot out, "The internet."

Again, Susan let him continue.

"The internet was supposed to break down all the walls between people, and information. We were all supposed to get smarter, and this would usher in a new age of enlightenment. In reality, all the internet did was make it a thousand times easier for crazy people to meet and befriend one another."

Susan arched an eyebrow. "Crazy people?"

"Think about it. Back in the day, if you were a racist, you had to know a secret handshake or have a code to discover other racists. It took effort, and you generally kept your mouth shut until you knew you'd found a kindred soul. Now you have chat rooms and online social groups that make no secret of their beliefs. All you have to do is log on and look."

"This doesn't seem to involve race, though. Aside from the guy..."

Susan looked at her notes. "Aside from Tom."

"Right," Michael agreed. "Because it's not limited to race; that was just one example. It doesn't matter *what* you believe. There are seven billion people out there, and some of them are going to believe the same nonsense you do. That's how we end up with flat earthers, moon landing or 9/11 'truthers,' or people who say that vaccinations cause autism. It doesn't matter how stupid your belief is, someone out there thinks like you, and the internet made it easier for everyone dumb to circle their wagons and feel not so alone in the world..."

Michael trailed off, and after a beat, Susan picked up where he left off.

"All you'd need then is someone to take advantage of them. To focus them; to weaponize the belief. Once you do that, you can do anything. Make money, be elected to office..."

"Right," Michael agreed. "Only in this case, the person behind this wasn't weaponizing 'stupid,' he weaponized grief. He took people in pain and unleashed their rage and confusion."

"All they needed was a nudge," Susan mused. "A manipulative ear to explain that all the anguish they had should be focused. He gave them a target."

"Or," Michael countered, "they already had a target. What they needed was permission to act on their feelings."

The two shared a moment of silence. Though it went unsaid, each felt the bond one feels when two people click and the quiet is comfortable, not awkward.

Eventually, Susan broke through the silence with an ugly thought; "What happens as this website goes viral? 'Breaks the internet,' as the phrase goes."

"You're going to get a lot of ordinary people supporting what's happening," Michael responded. "And maybe a few copycats."

"Which is probably what the person behind this is hoping for."

"Exactly. Which is why it's scary. When you have people acting in their own best interest as opposed to that of the collective…"

Michael thought for a moment.

"People have different ideas of what's right and what's wrong," he continued. "If violence, actively killing someone you have a beef with becomes the norm, society doesn't stand a chance."

Susan shuddered.

"Hopefully that's worst-case scenario," she offered.

Susan and Michael took a moment to digest everything they had discussed. As if blessed with perfect timing, one of the tech specialists, Kristen Richardson, approached them during the break in their tête-à-tête.

"So," Kristen started. "Do you want the bad news, the bad news, or the really bad news?"

"Well that's not promising," Susan stated flatly.

"I know," Kristen continued. "Here it is: the computer you found? It's new. Like, brand new. Your guy took it out of the box, turned it on, set the browser to the website you found, and that's it. There are no files on it, it hasn't visited any websites… There's nothing on it to give us any evidence as to how your guy planned this or if he has any associates out there. It's basically a blank chalkboard."

"Well shit," Michael said, then looked at the other two apologetically for swearing.

"Shit indeed," Kristen said of Michael's face, letting him know his interjection was fine. "Except like I said, that's not the only bad news."

Susan raised one hand, palm up. The gesture signaled, "OK, give it to me."

"We found his actual computer, and we're not gonna get anything from that, either. He opened it up and took a nail gun to the hard drive and circuit board—I guess he did the circuit board for good measure—and then he bought a half-dozen car batteries, cracked them open, and poured the acid over the components. I'm guessing that one had a ton of useful information on it, because he made sure the thing was toast."

"Which means we have no way of using Evan to figure out who's behind the other ninety-five question marks," Susan said matter-of-factly.

"Not from what we've discovered. Did he have an office, or a work computer off property?"

"If he does," Susan offered, "we haven't heard about it yet."

Michael had a thought.

"Is there a way to use his IP address to determine what kind of traffic went in and out of here? Could we subpoena his provider? See where he went and who he talked to?" he asked.

Kristen had an answer at the ready: "They have it, but they're not always interested in turning it over. Even with a subpoena. They'll push back, fight it in court... It's why getting ahold of old emails is such a pain in the butt. Corporations love collecting your data and selling it to advertisers, but they're less interested in turning over the same data to the government or law enforcement."

"That doesn't mean we shouldn't try," Michael said, trying to sound upbeat. He turned to Susan and asked, "Who do we know in Iowa? Do we have a favorite judge?"

"I'll call Sumner," Susan responded. "Diplomacy, politics, and courting favors is his department."

"Cool beans," Kristen said happily. "I'll probably start digging tonight, but let me know when we get the go-ahead to make it official. There is one more angle... Have we found his phone?"

Susan and Michael exchanged a glance; though they weren't outright embarrassed, each realized they had forgotten about a possible treasure trove of information.

"Even if it's locked and we can't get anything out of his carrier," Kristen continued, "I just need to figure out what apps he downloaded. Most people don't turn off location services, and their phone tracks them 24/7. If he so much as has a weather app, we can see exactly where he's been."

"For how long?" Susan asked.

"Depends on how long the particular company stores data, but probably for the length of time he's had the app. Some developers have their system ping every minute, so we can pinpoint everywhere he's been and see if anything jumps out. We can examine his pattern of life pretty extensively, and possibly figure out who he's been talking to, and where."

"Jesus," Michael chimed in. "We always thought Big Brother would be the government keeping track of people, but in the end, it turns out it's big business, and we welcome it."

"Yup!" Kristen said cheerfully. "It's a statisticians dream. Even if he destroyed the phone, we can probably figure out how he used it, and that will help us see where he's been. From there, we can see if there are security cameras, old footage of him and who he talked to..."

"Time to cross our fingers, I guess," Susan said.

"Cross them toes, too," Kristen replied pleasantly. "Hope and optimism always help."

With that, she turned and headed back to her team. As there wasn't much else for them to do at the house, they decided to call it an early night.

"So..." Michael began. "What now?"

"I'm thinking we'll probably get called back KC," Susan mused. "We're first on the case, so as these boxes start turning from question marks into people, the agency will want a central location for all information to flow to. It's doubtful they'll want us flying all over the country, chasing ghosts. Whatever happens next will get the once-over by the nearest agents. Unless they find someone for us to interview here, we'll be on our way."

As Michael was nodding in understanding, Kristen called out from the other room: "Guys! You're gonna wanna come in here... There's a new picture on the screen!"

Nearly 2,000 miles away, Freddy Broe had just hit the pavement below the Space Needle, a city prosecutor named Charles Hoover wrapped in his arms.

Chapter 11

Day Two

Michael swirled a spoon in his coffee, but it was only to cool the beverage down; he hadn't added any milk or sugar.

He and Susan had watched Freddy Broe's video, gone over their notes again, tried to find any connections between the perpetrators, couldn't, and determined they were all independent contractors who didn't know one another.

"With no tie that binds," Susan sighed, "the case is going to need a miracle in order to make any decent headway."

They'd found a motel back by the airport, crashed for a couple hours (which basically constituted a nap, not a good night's sleep), then woke before dawn for an early—non chartered—flight back to Kansas City.

"That's the beauty of the bureau," Susan explained. "They'll get you to the scene of the crime ASAP, but they're not overly concerned with bringing you back home."

The jet they'd flown in on was off carting other agents to other, more pressing, destinations.

Their flight was at 6:15 AM, hopefully. Being the tickets were last minute, they were flying standby. The plane was technically full, but they could cross their fingers and hope.

"Maybe someone will snooze their alarm too many times," Susan mused.

"Right," Michael countered. "Like anyone is going to miss an opportunity to leave Iowa."

Being unaware of how smaller airports operate, Michael and Susan had shown up dutifully two hours early, only to discover nothing was open. There were no lines, no crowds, no one elbowing for a better position at security.

"I guess we could have slept in," Susan offered, staring at the desolate terminal.

"I didn't really sleep at all," Michael countered. "I stared at the ceiling for about two hours, and when I finally *did* fall asleep, I crashed so hard that when I woke up I asked Alexa to turn the lights on three times before remembering where I was."

Susan laughed.

At 5AM a snack shop turned on their lights, and the two bought coffee. Susan grabbed a banana, while Michael frowned at the overpriced energy bars.

"These things are $1.98 at my grocery store," he said, holding up one with a $5.50 tag on it.

"You own a grocery store?" Susan teased.

Michael rolled his eyes, but caved due to his growling stomach and bought the overpriced snack anyway.

Twitter had broken the story, and it immediately became the number #1 trending topic worldwide. Once traditional media got involved, they tackled the subject using the traditional media playbook: sensationalize, sensationalize, sensationalize.

"Gotta get clicks to keep the advertisers happy," Susan sighed, reading a particularly attention-grabbing headline on her phone.

The airport terminal televisions were all tuned to the 24-hour news broadcasts, and each one had live remotes set up at every location they could find. Teams had flown out overnight in order to put reporters in front of houses—"This is where Evan Francart lived! This is where he grew up!"—and harass neighbors—"What was Donny Lin *really* like?"

(As if anyone actually knew the inner workings of anyone else's mind.)

Michael's favorite story was one that involved the questions, "Where will they strike next?" and "How many more are there out there?"

Michael showed the headline to Susan as he laughed; "How many more are there? I guess that reporter can't subtract."

Susan shook her head as she smiled, and then got down to business.

"By the time we get back to the office," Susan said, changing gears, "we'll have files to go over. First thing this morning, agents are going to be calling the local PD at every scene. They're going to ask about computers, phones, what was found, what was destroyed... Now that we know these cases are all tied together, we have to hope that one person slipped up; that one person left behind one crumb of information we can use to figure out if there's a central figure, and who that central figure is. If we can get our hands-on phone data, we can see if they all pinged a central number. If they did, we're on our way."

"Even low-level drug dealers use burners," Michael countered. "You don't think anyone able to organize something this big would cover their tracks?"

"Even if they did, we have to try. El Chapo used burners and layers of protection, but they found him through cell phones."

As if mentioning a phone reminded her of her own, Susan grabbed her device and thumbed away at it.

"I had this sent to me last night," she continued, opening an attachment on an email. "The website is registered to a dummy name and was paid up through the next ten years. They used a throwaway credit card loaded up by transferring money from a bank account that has since vanished. We can't trace the name, and we can't trace payment. Oh, and the website itself is being hosted in the Ukraine."

"And the Ukraine isn't too friendly when it comes to sharing information, are they?"

"Not traditionally, no."

"Well," Michael said thoughtfully, "technically, we're no worse off than when we started. This isn't a dead end, it's just a stalled beginning. All we need is one spark, one clue to send us down a path, and we'll be off and running.

"True, but all we have now is speculation."

"OK, who goes first?"

Susan liked Michael's attitude. He wasn't being defeatist, this despite the opportunity to throw up hands and say, "I give up!" They had no evidence, and at this point their only option seemed to be ambulance chaser; jumping from attack to attack without any clue as to what was going to happen next.

Susan didn't like playing clean up; she liked being out in front of problems, attacking them head on. The fact Michael was willing to spitball ideas impressed her.

"I," she said, ceding the floor to him, "am all ears."

"Well," Michael began, "so far, all but one of our perps have been white men; whoever has done this really tapped into the white anger everyone says fueled the 2016 election. I think we should assume a white male is behind everything."

"Not a bad assumption," Susan agreed.

"But we shouldn't count out anything, no matter how far-fetched, right?"

"Correct."

"So what if this is bigger than one person? We've had other governments—Russia—interfering with our elections in order to sow discord, what if they want to really stir the pot?"

"OK, that's a stretch..."

"A plausible one," Michael interjected. "The website *is* registered in the Ukraine."

"But unless you're on the Crimean Peninsula, you're probably not too big a fan of Russia." Susan countered. "We can put it on the perp board, because I'm not discounting anything, but I don't think we should go all Jason Bourne without exhausting a few other angles first."

"Fair enough," Michael stated, before laughing off Susan's look. "I know, I say that a lot. Anyway..."

Michael paused for thought.

"OK, we believe, at the moment, our mastermind is tapping into white anger. What if it's a Black man?"

Susan was intrigued. "I'm not sure where you're going with this, but I'm listening," she offered.

"We're dealing with revenge, right?" Michael said, sipping his coffee and setting it aside. "What if this whole thing were a double-revenge? A joke, or an attack on the system itself?"

"What do you mean?"

"You were around for the OJ verdict, right?"

Susan winced. "Yes, but just because you're a kid doesn't mean I'm a grandmother," she joked.

Michael laughed as he continued, "Look at the difference between the way white and Black America reacted. White people were stunned; Black people cheered."

"OK..." Susan said hesitantly.

"Do you think that underlying anger in the Black community has gone away? We see the difference in sentencing; a Black kid has a little pot and the book is thrown at him. A white kid rapes a girl at Stanford and is barely slapped on the wrist. It breeds resentment. So, what if this is a Black man getting white America to turn on itself?"

Susan took a moment to clarify her thought before responding, "You like to cast a wide net, don't you?"

Michael smiled; he wasn't offended.

"I'm not going to shoot you down," Susan continued. "The idea goes on the board, but it's an area we have to tread with caution. You studied the Atlanta Child Murders?"

Michael nodded.

"I did, too. It was a little before both of us. The point is, when Black children started disappearing from a Black neighborhood in Atlanta, the FBI said, 'It's probably a Black man doing this.' Logic told them a white person would stand out like a sore thumb in those areas, but passion trumps logic, and the Black community was incensed. They felt they were being singled out and blamed, even if studies show killers generally stick to their own."

Michael digested Susan's words.

"My point is, we have to be very careful what we discuss with the media. Negative press can kill a good investigation. Now, I'm not saying it's a Black man; I'm still leaning toward white male. But, and this is just an educated guess, I bet that the person behind this has suffered. Evan lost his wife..."

Susan began looked over her notes as she spoke.

"Donny lost his son; Brody lost his wife... We're dealing with pain-based reactions. Fundamental emotions. That's the common thread between our first six participants, and I bet it's the tie that binds them all to the lead figure. The difference between a citizen and a criminal is opportunity. Ever run a red light at 3:00 AM? You pull up and the road is wide open. The light should be flashing yellow or red, but the city doesn't have its shit to-gether, so it's still cycling green-yellow-red. And you're sitting there, staring at that empty street, glaring at a red light, so you run it. Opportunity. These people had the desire; someone gave them the opportunity."

Michael absorbed the information. He liked that Susan gave him the chance to offer his ideas, but when she spoke? Goddamn, she was smart.

At 6:00 AM, they were told the flight was full; the next one south was at 9:45 AM, but again they'd be flying standby and could be bumped again.

"That's three-and-a-half hours sitting here doing nothing," Michael noted. "If we start driving now, we'd be back in KC before the flight even leaves."

"Let's get a real breakfast and call in," Susan countered, having noticed an actual restaurant opening for the day. "Sumner will tell us what to do—wait for the plane, or drive home."

"You ever return a rental to a different location?" Michael asked. "Man, they do *not* like that. Price goes through the roof if you take a rental one way."

The two ate as good a breakfast as one can eat in an airport restaurant, and were finally told to hop in a car and drive back.

They'd made it a little over an hour when another text landed in Susan's phone. She read it aloud.

"Situation in Peoria. Agents en route. Join them there."

Susan re-programmed Michael's Waze, which told them to take US-34 east across the bottom of Iowa all the way to Illinois.

Chapter 12

Peoria

Matthew Kimsey loved his hometown.

Born and raised in Peoria, Illinois, he was always slightly disappointed that the city prided itself on being the birthplace of Richard A. Whiting—writer of the song "Hooray for Hollywood"—while simultaneously brushing legacy Richard Pryor aside.

Of course, "Hooray for Hollywood" was family friendly; Pryor's time in Peoria—growing up with an abusive grandmother in the brothel his mother worked—well, that was less flattering. Even if Pryor was widely respected in the comedy world, he'd used the N-word quite often in his career. In a time of snowflakes being upset over everything and never examining context, it was all too easy to see why Pryor wouldn't be the top local celebrity to champion.

Thus, on Peoria's Wikipedia page, Whiting got a full paragraph. Pryor was given a mention.

But, what can you do? It wasn't Matthew's style to cause friction, or be angry. He'd always just taken note of the world around him and accepted it with contemplative resignation.

"You can't change the world, but you can change yourself," his father Ben had told him. That made Matthew a proponent of being the best person he could be. Self-help tomes filled his bookshelf, and positive, life-affirming messages adorned his desk and walls.

Ben had been a blue-collar, salt-of-the-earth man who came home sweaty and tired every evening. He wanted his son to work using his mind, not his hands. Ben knew hard labor was destroying his health, and believed education was the way to escape the world they lived in.

By the time he was sixty, Ben's body had started to betray him. First it was arthritis in his hands, then the cartilage in his knees. By the time he died he was nearly bedridden, but he was still proud. Ben lived long enough to see Matthew embrace the white-collar world. Ben watched as Matthew did well enough in high school to get into the local college, Bradley University. Once there, Matthew focused on business; from undergrad to his master's, he was all business, all the way.

Matthew had remained in Peoria his whole life; he never felt like living anywhere else. He was comfortable, and that's the best life has to offer, right? Joy is an extreme, and sorrow is an extreme. If you were comfortable, then that was actually pretty good, all things considered.

Matthew went to work for the local behemoth, heavy equipment maker Caterpillar, in the late 1980s. He was considered bright and unafraid of a challenge. Before long, Matthew had risen to a management position and had a team of people working under him.

For over twenty years he worked his way up the chain, until finally deciding he liked where he was and—like a man who never moved from his hometown—settled into the comfortable-enough life of upper-middle management. No, he wasn't a CEO or CFO or anything with an acronym, but he made good money and didn't have to wear a public face. It was like perfect: not too much responsibility, not too little responsibility, it was comfortable.

Then came the economic crash of 2008, which became the global recession of 2009.

Caterpillar's sales dropped from $51.3 billion, to $35 billion. Facing a loss of $112 million in one quarter alone, the company laid off 22,000 employees.

Matthew Kimsey was one of them.

There he was, forty-seven years old, out of work, and no one was hiring. No one.

Even worse, after the economy came out of its tailspin, anyone hiring was looking for young up-and-comers who could be hired on the cheap. The people not on any corporate radars? Those would be middle-age men like

Matthew, people who needed medical insurance and had bills to pay—bills like a mortgage, and his son's tuition.

His son was a good kid, but he'd come along at a cost.

Matthew and his wife, Valerie, had struggled with infertility. Her eggs, his sperm, yada-yada-yada... He wasn't too sure on the specific medical issues; he just knew the attempts to get her pregnant cost a lot of money. Insurance in the 1990s didn't quite understand or care about infertility, so he footed the bill and several rounds of in vitro fertilization later, success arrived in the form of a son. The money spent wiped out their savings, but it was worth it.

Matthew let Valerie name their child, because she wanted to honor her late father. Vernon wasn't very modern, but Matthew figured the boy could always go by his middle name, Maxwell—or more likely Max—if he wanted to.

Matthew took pride in being a father, and wanted Vernon to have all the benefits and opportunities he himself had had. Just like his father before him, Matthew wanted more for his son than he'd grown up with.

Which is why when the recession hit, things became difficult. Vernon had to take a semester, and then two, off from college.

Matthew felt like a failure, like he was letting his son down.

Then things got worse. Even though they had always lived within their means, the bank seized their house. Matthew hadn't missed any payments, this despite being unemployed, but one day a foreclosure letter arrived. Knowing it was a mistake, Matthew fought and fought, but couldn't compete with the overwhelming resources the bank had. They ignored his calls, left his emails unanswered, and buried him in paperwork and lawyer's briefs.

The foreclosure had ruined Matthew's credit score, which made it near-impossible to get a job when the economy started improving. It was the most frustrating thing he'd ever experienced; "Oh, we'd love to hire you and give you money, because you have experience and a great resume...but it looks like you're not good with money, which means we can't trust you."

Matthew couldn't believe such a vicious cycle existed; you have no money, so you need a job. But no one will give you a job, because you have no money.

He couldn't even go back to his old company, because they had "restructured," meaning his position had evaporated into the ether. It was like they discovered, "Hey, we can get along just fine without you!" Which is never a good feeling for those being disposed of.

Everything he had worked for was gone.

Matthew eventually took a "layover" job at a hotel, but before long he realized it had turned into a permanent position. Which was fine—work is work—but Matthew believed he deserved better.

More than anything, he felt he had let his son down. Vernon had eventually returned to school, but had taken out massive loans in order to graduate. Sure, everyone borrowed, but Matthew didn't like seeing his son in debt. If there was one thing his father had instilled in him it was that you took care of your family. Matthew wasn't doing that, and it made him feel like a failure.

Then, ten years later, came the kicker. It turned out that the foreclosure *had* happened due to a bank error; Matthew had been right all along. Which is what he'd tried to tell them at the time, but back then no one would listen. Well, lawyers would listen, but they'd explain they couldn't take the case on commission. Since Matthew couldn't afford to pay a retainer, he would be shown the door.

Matthew joined a class action lawsuit; those who lost their homes unjustly were banding together to sue the banking company that had screwed them. The problem was that those things took years to work themselves out, and money couldn't make everything right in the end. Money couldn't make right the neglect he'd felt when trying to work everything out in the first place.

The bank had ignored his initial pleas when first taking his house and they'd ignored him for years after the fact. Now they were going to negotiate to lessen the financial repercussions of their mistake. Instead of apologizing, they were going to nickel and dime their way to the lowest settlement possible.

It was too much for Matthew.

Quietly, without telling Valerie, or anyone, really, he'd started visiting "therapy" groups online. Matthew couldn't afford conventional counseling, and wasn't sure he'd attend even if he could. Sitting in a circle, discussing his feelings... that didn't sit right with him. But being online allowed him a bit of anonymity. He could empathize with others going through the same thing he was facing, yet not expose himself entirely.

Plus, when it came to having to get up off your keister, getting into the car, driving somewhere, finding parking... all that versus just logging on? Logging on and finding similarly afflicted people was much easier.

Some of the sites he visited considered themselves emotional support groups, while others were just places to vent. Initially, Matthew had been looking for hope. What he discovered was the promise of action.

One day, Matthew tossed his father's quote into a discussion: "You can't change the world, but you can change yourself."

After he'd posted it, he discovered a private message in his inbox. A woman in that group, one of the places people vented more than they discussed getting over their problems, was reaching out to him. Her name was Cassandra.

At first Matthew wondered if this was an attempt at an online romance—he may be down and out, but he still loved his wife and wasn't about to cheat on her—but that turned out to be his ego getting ahead of him.

In reality, Cassandra was interested in the quote—if Matthew really believed it, and if he really thought one person couldn't make a difference.

Cassandra became a sympathetic ear that was more in tune with him than the rest of the group. She always responded to messages no matter when he sent them. So quickly, in fact, Matthew once wondered if she ever slept. Then he realized she might be thinking the same thing about him.

Over the course of several months, Matthew realized he was harboring a slight crush on Cassandra. He laughed it off, because he wasn't interested in romance, and he still wasn't about to cheat on his wife. But Matthew realized and admitted that he liked having Cassandra in his life. Even if he didn't know exactly who "she" was.

Matthew added the quotes around the pronouns "she" and "her" whenever he thought about Cassandra, because he wasn't dumb. He'd read about catfishing and knew that just as he held back certain information while online, it was just as easy for others to be fibbing, too.

Cassandra asked Matthew how financial destitution had affected his attitude toward life, if he still believed in positivity. Matthew had looked around his desk at all the faded, upbeat stickers clinging desperately to his computer.

Lead by example. Be the best you *you can be.*

He'd spent his whole life focusing on the positive, and look where that got him. He'd always wondered what it would be like to actually speak his mind, just once, to a boss, or someone who parked like an asshole in a crowded lot... but he'd always kept quiet.

Well, he'd kept quiet, except for once.

The restaurant.

That hadn't worked out well at all.

Cassandra told Matthew he could make a difference; that if he were to take action, others would notice. That sometimes being the "best you that you could be" involved taking charge when everyone else was standing still.

Matthew liked that.

She asked him, "Why are you holding back? Do you think nice guys succeed, or do they finish last?"

The question gnawed at him. Why should jerks be at the top of the success pyramid? If someone with power wasn't acting according to what was best for the whole, then why not knock them down a peg or two? Push back against the powers that be, make their lives as miserable as they had made his.

Cassandra spoke of a movement, a movement where ordinary people stood up and said they'd had enough. If the elected representatives wouldn't listen, then "the people would damn well make themselves heard."

Matthew was skeptical, but he listened.

Then, one day Matthew woke up and it was all over the news; everything was taking place just as Cassandra had said it would. People in power were being punished. No one innocent was being hurt. Since no one was looking out for the little guy, the little guy was taking action, and he was making his voice heard.

And now it was Matthew's turn to step up to the plate.

He'd been in the batter's box warming up, but now it was go time. He'd get back at those who had made him fail as a parent, and prevent them from doing it to anyone else in the process.

Which is why Matthew Kimsey found himself on a chilly autumn morning, waiting for the local branch of the bank that had screwed him.

Matthew checked his watch; five to nine, an exact one-eighty of the popular song.

When the doors were unlocked, he was going to walk in, show everyone the bomb he was wearing, demand to see Jessica Decker, the branch president, and walk into the vault with her.

Together they'd empty all the cash onto the floor; hundreds of thousands if not a million or two dollars.

And together they'd blow it all up.

Well, technically *he'd* blow it all up, but she'd be right there next to him to go "boom" with the money.

Sure, however much was at that specific branch was a small amount to the bank overall, and yes, the bank would get that money back via insurance. But goddamn if drastic action wouldn't send a message to those that needed to hear it.

"It's the only way to be heard," Cassandra assured him.

As crazy as it sounded, Matthew knew she was right.

He'd tried to get someone—anyone—to listen to him. For years he sent letters and made phone calls. He'd tried scheduling appointments; he did everything but stand on a desk while waving his arms in the air and shouting, "I need help! Someone please help me!"

All he got was form letter responses and transfers to different departments.

"That's handled at a national level," he was told. "We don't hold the loans, we just process the forms and send them on to corporate. You're going to need to fill out form two six dash five four H."

And so on.

No one ever helped. They pushed the problem off on someone else, they shuffled Matthew around. Matthew wasn't a person; he was a nuisance. A non-person.

Anger rose in Matthew's blood as he thought about the bank, and Jessica Decker. The indifference toward his plight was frustrating. Infuriating.

After losing his house, he had looked up Jessica's financials. One year out of the meltdown, she was given a raise and a bonus, all because she had protected the bottom line of the bank. Sure, she had done so at the expense of hardworking families just trying to make ends meet, but the bank remained solvent, and that's all that mattered.

Matthew had tried meeting Jessica in person. After numerous attempts to schedule an appointment hadn't worked out, he'd approached her in a restaurant.

It didn't go well.

Though he had rehearsed what he wanted to say, he had grown nervous. Customers started staring at him, and when he was asked to leave Matthew started shouting. The police were called, and Matthew was forcibly removed, which was a polite way of saying "thrown out." Jessica filed a restraining order against him.

What's funny is that the bank didn't terminate his account. Matthew found that oddly amusing. "Sure, you're not allowed in here, but your money is."

The incident cost him the hotel job he'd resigned himself to.

And that was that.

Matthew, the ever-positive member of the "you can change yourself" club decided to finally change. Only this time, he wasn't going to force himself to be "better," he was going to stop being a doormat. He would stop allowing everyone to walk all over him.

The way the bank took his house, and how it all turned out to be an error... The fact they needed "years" to make things right... the fact he had to be a part of a class action lawsuit to get justice where it should be given freely by the offending party... That was too much.

Oddly enough, it was one of his own lawyers that became the final straw on Matthew's fragile back.

They had been discussing the eventual settlement. The law firm would take sixty percent, and forty percent would be divided among those affected.

Matthew had asked if that seemed fair, and the lawyer responded, "It's not about the money, it's the principle of it all, right? Don't focus on the money. Money can't buy happiness."

"But..." Matthew responded, "money takes away worry. If you're not worried about your bills or if you're going to be able to pay rent next month, then you can work on being happy."

The lawyer had no response to that, so Matthew decided to take the man at his word and focus on the "principle of it all." To Matthew, that meant making a statement.

Just like Cassandra said he should.

Matthew again glanced at his watch. 9:05 AM. He had gotten lost in his thoughts and was slightly behind schedule.

Whatever, no worry. Five minutes wasn't going to change anything.

Matthew took a deep breath to steady himself, and then walked into the bank. He made his way over to the closest customer representative, smiled, and stated, "I'm here to see Jessica Decker."

The clerk smiled in response and asked, "OK, and do you have an appointment?"

Matthew opened his coat to expose the wires and small gray blobs wrapped around his chest. He hadn't asked Cassandra how she was able to get her hands on C4—weapons-grade plastic explosives—but she had sent it to him via a private courier when he'd asked how he could best make his "statement" to the world.

"Let me repeat myself," Matthew said. "I'm here to see Jessica Decker. Now."

The fact the woman didn't scream was good, but Matthew wouldn't have minded if she had. His mission wasn't one of stealth; he didn't care who in the bank knew what he was up to, because they would all be leaving immediately. Matthew wasn't interested in hostages; he was interested in justice.

The woman behind the counter picked up an office phone and nervously punched a single number; Matthew could hear the phone in an adjacent office ring. It was answered immediately.

"Miss Decker," the clerk said hurriedly, "I need you to come out here. We have a situation."

Matthew laughed as he shook his head.

"A situation." That's what he was. Interesting terminology. He wondered if it was code, and if President Decker would be dialing 911 as quickly as she could. To that end, Matthew wondered if the teller had tripped a silent alarm. Again, not that it mattered. The police wouldn't rush in; they'd set up a perimeter to prevent the getaway. By the time they figured out what was up—that this wasn't a robbery, and he wasn't going to try and escape—it'd all be over.

Matthew turned and spotted branch president Jessica Decker striding out of her office. She looked concerned, but not alarmed. Even when she spotted Matthew, her expression didn't change. Either she was great at poker, or she didn't remember him.

Jessica walked up to Matthew with the confidence of a person who had been battle tested in the boardroom and who usually bested her opponents; you don't become the president of anything, even a small bank, by being shy.

Jessica looked at the teller, and then Matthew: "How can I help you?" she asked.

"You," Matthew said plainly while holding open his jacket, "can begin by opening the vault, and then sending everyone home."

Jessica's demeanor went from concerned, to confused.

"But..." she began, saying the only thing that came to mind. "I just became a grandmother."

And with those words, Matthew froze.

Chapter 13

The House of Cards

Josh was on a treadmill when a *Breaking News* icon flashed across every television in the gym.

The stations tuned to 24/7 news were a little ahead of the curve; stations showing game shows and soap operas needed a couple minutes to get anchors behind the desk before interrupting their scheduled broadcasting.

Matthew Kimsey had fallen short of his goal.

Josh scowled for a second, then returned his face to a more neutral setting.

Well, he'd expected this. He just hoped it would have come later, rather than sooner.

It had taken him a couple minutes of listening to figure out who exactly Matthew was; he didn't have each member of The 100 memorized. Sure, he recognized names, and had a few backstories down pat, but if given a pencil and paper there was no way Josh could write down all the details of each member of his tribe. There were just too many moving parts, too many stories.

Josh wondered what he could have done differently—maybe vetted Matthew a little better and made sure he wasn't going to wimp out so easily.

Matthew was supposed to send a message to the banking industry.

A small message, yes—the death of a branch president in a small Illinois city wasn't going to right all the wrongs the banks had been perpetrating— but still, a small message is better than nothing.

Plus, Josh realized he had to instill action where he could. If Josh had tried to fly Matthew across the country to kill the head of Bank of America or another huge institution...

Well, first of all, the logistics would have been insanely difficult. And second, the idea that little nobodies in the middle of nowhere America were going to have to pay, too, was the point: this can happen *anywhere*.

Anyway, not only had Matthew failed his task, he'd turned himself over to the police.

That meant he'd be in FBI custody soon, and they'd start grilling him.

Best case scenario, Matthew had wiped his phone and computer that morning before his attempt. Sure, they'd get information out of him, but only what he could tell them. There'd be no actual evidence, physical, digital, or otherwise.

The real question became: was this a tipping point? Would Matthew's defection begin a trickle, or a torrent, of others refusing to follow through with their objective? More importantly, did it mean Josh should start preparing for the end?

As he slowed the treadmill from a jog to a cool-down walk, Josh believed it did.

The best way to handle a problem was to stay out in front of it. Instead of waiting until the authorities were hot on his heels, he'd start moving forward now. Josh hoped he'd have time to make his contribution to The 100, but if he didn't, he'd just leave the country outright.

Josh had several identities waiting for him; he'd been purchasing passports on the sly for over a year. Sure, he could just go to a country that had no extradition agreement with the United States and flaunt what he'd done, but Josh didn't want to be public. Being public made him a target. Even if law enforcement couldn't get to him legally, individuals were another matter. Hell, a billion-dollar company like Glenback could easily hire the right people to make sure he went to bed one night and didn't wake up the next morning. If shit went south and he couldn't fulfill his own obligation, it was best to remain anonymous.

Josh's mind turned to his task. It was supposed to be the final act before the curtain fell, but now Josh mused that while his contribution to the cause was big enough to look like the finale, it didn't necessarily mean it was the final act. Actually, the more he thought on it, if others started backing out,

Josh showing the world what he'd lined up could revitalize the movement. Maybe it would inspire some of The 100 on the fence to come down on the right side of it.

The thought made him smile.

Josh started running through the steps he had to take. He had something special lined up for his video and wanted all his ducks in a row before acting.

While Cassandra was plucking lost souls from social media, she was also scouring the dark web for something worse: pedophiles. While Josh wished he could get to them all, he had to focus on those closest to him, those living in New York City. There were more than he'd expected, but that wasn't saying much. Josh had long ago come to terms with the fact that humans had the capacity to be downright evil.

After researching everyone Cassandra found and winnowing the number down to ten, Josh started planning.

It was scary how people who wanted to hurt children found ways to be around them. Every once in a while a machinist or drywall contractor liked his girls a little too young, and that was disgusting. But pedophilia meant the creeps became teachers, priests, and daycare providers. Positions with access to children.

That's who Josh focused on. After he was done, the police would get files on every pervert he'd discovered, but he needed the ten worst-of-the-worst all to himself. They were going to act as his shining example to the world.

Everything had taken over a year of preparation, and it began small. Josh discovered who they were, and started placing very specific advertising on their social media pages.

"Win a trip to Thailand," the ads whispered.

"Win a ten-day, all-expenses-paid vacation to the Philippines," another offered.

The locations were chosen carefully.

The targets would have great interest in areas like that; places known for the sex trade. A person with distinct, disgusting sexual needs could find their thirst quenched in countries like those.

What the targets didn't realize is the banner ads were specialized to the point they were the only people seeing them. Such was the beauty of the internet. Unlike a TV commercial, designed to get as many eyeballs as possible, social media marketing could narrow down recipients to a microscopic section of society.

These men weren't impulsive, so the ads were subtle, and ever-present.

Josh wasn't stupid, either. He didn't just offer up a trip the instant someone clicked a link, he played it slow. More often than not the targets didn't even fill out the form required to "win," but they kept clicking. Josh could see who was taking what bait, and how long they lingered on each website after clicking. He tweaked both ads and the website depending on the responses he got.

Nothing happened all at once; no website gave all the information immediately. You had to do a slow roll when laying a trap. There was an ebb and a flow to everything. Once a mark finally entered their information, they didn't receive an email telling them they'd won. They actually learned (after an appropriate waiting period, of course) that they'd lost.

But, the email promised, *you've been automatically entered in the next drawing!*

They were never asked to buy anything; the contests couldn't look like a marketing scheme. "Buy now, win later!" was the quickest way to lose a mark.

Finally, after two rounds of "Sorry, maybe next time," all ten pedophiles "won."

Not the grand prize, no. They'd won the second place; a runner-up offering: an evening cruise on an exclusive yacht. Dinner, drinks, and everything else was included. A "booze cruise," as it was commonly known.

In a way, it was a bit of a "staycation." You didn't have to pack for overseas travel, you didn't have to request off of work... the logistics of trying to get ten people to travel to Thailand on the same week of the year? Nightmare. But getting ten people to board a 400-foot super yacht for a night, one that launched from their own city? Easy-peasy, yo.

The cruise was scheduled to take place one week from... Josh glanced at his watch to snag the date. Yesterday. The cruise was scheduled to take place one week from yesterday. Six days, to those who could do the most basic of math.

He'd timed everything in the hope a good chunk of the other 99 participants would have completed their tasks. Now it was a matter of waiting. You couldn't just tell someone, "Hey, you won a cruise! Tonight only!"

You also couldn't change your plans last minute: "Hey, I know this was scheduled for next Tuesday, but the ship sails tomorrow."

No, the date of departure was set in stone.

He needed to give all ten "winners" enough time to finalize whatever plans they needed to make in order to get their butts on that big boat. Now it was a matter of avoiding detection long enough to put his piece of the puzzle into place.

Josh began to pack up for his move from the apartment to the warehouse.

Best case scenario, all would still go according to plan.

Worst case, he'd make a quick getaway and be gone before anyone could get their sticky fingers on him.

Chapter 14

Interviewing Matthew

Susan and Michael arrived in Peoria a little after 1:00 PM, having made decent time driving across the forgotten parts of America: wide swaths of nothing followed by small towns in rural Iowa and Illinois. These were places dismissed by the outside world, whose citizens are generally made to feel inferior because of the twin sins of not existing on one of the coasts, and not being diverse enough for the people who lived on those coasts.

Michael took note that the countryside was a sea of sameness. In fact, if they hadn't crossed the Mississippi River, he wouldn't have even realized they'd transitioned from one state into the next.

Susan and Michael had gotten to know one another a little better on the trip, as people trapped in a car tend to do. Even if focused on a specific subject—and for them it was work—you can really only discuss that subject for so long before doing so becomes rote.

At first, the two had played a round of "worst case," but it was lopsided as all get-out.

As Michael was still a rookie of the highest order, his only "bad" case involved wire fraud. An elderly couple had been scammed out of their life savings by someone in India claiming to be the IRS.

"I didn't understand why we had to pay all these fees using gift cards, but the man on the phone was insistent..."

Michael admitted to having been an equal mix of sympathetic and annoyed when talking to them. Yes, they'd been duped, but by an obvious scam. It boggled his mind people fell for it.

Susan...

Susan had actual bad cases in her filing cabinet.

"Missing kids," she stated matter-of-factly. "Missing kids are always the worst, especially when they don't end well. I had one where a couple worked in tandem. There was a mom at a park with a dog, watching her child play... one of the kidnappers scratched the dog's ears, and unhooked the leash. When the dog bolted, the mom took off after it, and the partner nabbed the kid."

Susan felt like throwing up at the memory of it.

"What happened?" Michael asked, dreading the answer.

"To the perps, or the kids?" Susan responded.

"The kidnappers."

"Death penalty."

Michael looked out the window. He wasn't a huge fan of the death penalty, but in situations like that, he understood its value.

Susan had no qualms about the worst of the worst being removed from the planet. She had a generally strong constitution, but adults hurting children pushed her to the brink.

"Do I want to know what happened to the child?" Michael asked.

"No," Susan said flatly, the memory eating her up inside. "No you do not."

After an appropriately uncomfortable silence, the conversation shifted. Fortunately, with nothing but windshield and road in front of them, they had plenty of opportunities to bounce across topics without getting too attached to any single one of them.

Personally, Susan learned that Michael was "between girlfriends," as he put it while shrugging.

"I think when you get married too young," he explained, "you end up getting divorced anyway. Sure, the whole 'high school sweethearts' thing is great for movies, but in reality, your twenties are meant to be lived exploring life."

Michael said he wanted to get married "sometime in his thirties."

Conversely, Michael discovered that even though Susan had never been married, she thought she was close, once.

Michael noticed Susan's faraway look as she spoke of her past. She was watching the road while she drove, but wasn't really seeing the pavement in front of her. Susan was actively feeling the old relationship as she talked about it.

"Turns out I was a rebound," she explained. "I didn't realize it at the time, but he just needed a vine to hold on to while he swung from tree to tree; a stop gap to fill the void. I'm pretty sure I loved him, but I don't think he really understood what love is. He just used the word because..."

Susan trailed off a moment before continuing.

"He used the word 'love,' because that's what people do. They've heard everyone else using it, so they do, too. Before you know it, 'love' has no meaning; 'I love you,' 'I love this movie,' 'I love my new car...' I think he liked me, but like isn't enough to make a relationship last."

She paused one final time before concluding her tale. When the final words exited her mouth, it was as if she were speaking to herself; coming to terms with old emotions that still haunted her from time to time.

"It's weird," Susan began. "It's weird when you've been planning to spend the rest of your life with someone, only to realize they've been taking things one day at a time with you."

Michael saw vulnerability in her, and while that didn't make him uncomfortable, he was happy when Susan broke the slightly awkward tension by seeing a sign for Knoxville and making a dumb joke about them being lost in Tennessee.

(In fact, it actually took Michael a second to realize there was a Knoxville, Illinois. The blink-and-you-missed-it thumbtack of a town existed where they left the rural highway that had brought them across Iowa, and connected them to the wide (and 75 mph-speedy) lanes of Interstate 74 in Illinois.)

They stayed on I-74 all the way to downtown Peoria, specifically to the "State of Illinois Peoria Adult Transition Center." Michael was amused to learn the facility had been reviewed on Google, and laughed at the angry 1-star offering as he read it to Susan. Apparently being a prisoner hadn't sat well with the guest, and he wanted to let the world know that "Not every offender is a bad person!!"

Michael noted that double exclamation points meant serious business. He was, in fact, a little surprised the review wasn't in all caps.

"I wonder why he's in a transition center," Susan wondered aloud. "County jail is where he should be."

As it turned out, the police were trying to stay one step ahead of the media.

When the press found out a living member of The 100 was in Peoria, they would descend upon the city like a plague of locusts. The first place they'd go is the county jail, so the police were playing an advance version of whack-a-mole by keeping Matthew hidden from view.

"This place has locks on the doors and bars on the windows. He ain't going nowhere," their liaison, Officer Ninmann, explained.

Michael was happy to discover their experience with the police chief in Des Moines had been a one-off. Where Chief Dalton had looked at them through eyes of suspicion, in Peoria the FBI was welcomed with open arms. Not only did the police not want the hassle of dealing with a domestic terrorist, they actively hoped Susan and Michael would remove him from their quiet city.

"Ever been part of a media circus?" Ninmann asked as he escorted them through the lobby. "A kid murdered his parents over at Bradley University. Got the media all excited and was a pain in our collective ass. And that was small potatoes compared with this."

Matthew Kimsey was waiting for them in a windowless interview room, Ninmann explained. "We don't have interrogation rooms, because everyone here is already guilty and awaiting their final destination. Some'll go to a county prison, others federal... it all depends on what they did."

That meant Matthew would be wearing arm and leg chains the whole time, as opposed to being handcuffed directly to the table in front of him. Basically, he was mobile. He couldn't move quickly, and had limited dexterity, "But you don't wanna get too close to him, because he can grab you," Ninmann cautioned.

Susan took note of the warning, and while she didn't dismiss it or even really lower her guard upon seeing Matthew, she did realize that the person on the other side of the two-way mirror wasn't a hardened criminal in the slightest.

Matthew Kimsey was shorter, maybe five foot ten. Pale complexion, sandy brown hair, and an average build. By that, he had a 'dad bod.' He wasn't fat, but neither was he ripped. He was just your run-of-the-mill fella.

His face wore a combination of exhaustion, and acceptance. It struck Susan as odd. More often than not, speaking with a suspect meant seeing anxiety or fear written into the creases on their skin. Or, failing those two, anger and arrogance. Criminals were either looking for a way out—a way to cover their tracks—or they thought they were above the law; that their lawyer was going to loophole their way through the courts.

Basically, criminals had two tells: they were either too confident, telling the authorities to go fuck themselves, or worried they were about to go to jail for a very long time.

By comparison, Matthew seemed not only at peace with what was happening, but relieved. He had gotten in over his head and was happy to be done with it all. Even if being done with it meant prison.

"What do you see?" Susan asked, turning to Michael. She wanted to know what he had gleaned from his thirty seconds of observation.

Michael was thoughtful in his answer. He didn't rush it, like a student trying to impress a teacher; he responded methodically.

"He's not fidgeting," Michael said. "That's the first thing I noticed. He's not nervous, which means he's OK with where he is."

"Well recognized," she confirmed. "Anything else?"

"Just that he doesn't look like a terrorist."

Susan smiled and stifled a small laugh.

"They never do," she explained. "Don't buy into the preconceived notion of 'this is what a criminal looks like.' Terrorists, murderers, kidnappers... they take all shapes and forms. Do you know what the difference between a criminal and an honest man is?"

Michael shook his head.

"Opportunity. Remember the red-light scenario? Same thing, higher stakes."

Susan allowed the lesson to sink in. Once she believed Michael was on board, she asked gamely, "Ready to go in?"

Michael half-shrugged and raised his arms slightly. *This is your world, I'm just living in it,* he signaled.

As the lead agent, it was natural for Susan to take charge of the interview. She wasn't an interrogation expert, but she'd definitely been around the interrogation block a handful of times.

"We're not going to be playing games," she explained. "There's no good cop/bad cop here. I've found that the best approach is to be honest. If they ask a question, answer it. If they ask something that cannot be answered, tell them so. You want to create trust, and once you tell a lie, you have to re-member that lie and get it right every time. Also, I find it easier to just allow the interview to flow and see where everything takes you over trying to force it down a specific path. If someone is talking, you don't want to get in the way of what they have to say."

Susan paused, then redefined her words.

"Which doesn't mean you shouldn't nudge the conversation in certain directions, you just don't want to end up with information that's inadmissible in court because you pushed a suspect too hard."

"Basically," Michael said, "it's a tightrope act."

Susan nodded. Michael continued to impress her.

"If you're ready to go in," Ninmann started, "You'll check your weapons here. If a weapon goes into an interview room, it's because it's drawn. I'll be the man on the door; if I hear anything out of the ordinary, I come in. Otherwise, a loaded gun is something every perp is waiting to get their hands on."

Though she didn't believe Matthew Kimsey was going to make a play for her sidearm, Susan wasn't about to argue protocol as a fish in someone else's pond. She motioned for Michael to turn over his Sig, and did so herself without complaint.

Upon entering the room, the first thing Susan and Michael noticed was how polite Matthew was.

He didn't look at them with suspicion or fear, but instead greeted them with a half-smile and a genuine "hello."

They exchanged names and had the usual pre-interrogation pleasant-ries—"Would you like something to drink? Coffee? Water?"—and Matthew chose water.

"Caffeine makes me restless," he explained.

Once everyone settled in, Susan began the process of extracting infor-mation. It was easier than she expected; Matthew was as willing to talk as his body language suggested.

"So," Susan asked, pulling out her phone and firing up a recording app. "I understand you've waived your right to an attorney. Do you have a state-ment to make, or would you like to start answering questions?"

"I've been sitting here several hours," Matthew began slowly, "and I've yet to come up with any rhyme or reason for what almost happened."

Susan made note of the "almost." Matthew was sharp. He was slyly (or accidentally) pleading his case; stating that he realized that while he'd committed a crime, he hadn't gone full Keyser Söze.

"And what almost happened?" Susan asked.

"I almost killed someone," Matthew explained. He paused, and then, as if saying the words out loud made it real to him, repeated himself. "Yeah... I almost killed someone."

Susan and Michael exchanged a look before Susan continued.

"Who were you going to kill?"

"Jessica Decker."

Though he maintained his composure, Susan saw a hint of anger in Matthew's eyes when he said the name.

"Why her?"

Matthew took a deep breath, and then let it all out. From the loss of his job to the loss of his house, the way everything had built up. She was going to be an example, an example for other bankers. Deal with your customers honestly and humanely, or you'll end up like Jessica.

After Matthew finished his monologue, Susan digested the words carefully.

Now they had Matthew's backstory, and it matched—in emotional experience, if not to the letter—those of The 100 that had already gone through with their act. Loss, anger, a sense of powerlessness, and the desire to take it all out on someone.

Now came the real work: figuring out who the rest were, and how to stop them.

"OK," Susan began gently. "I hear you. You've been through a lot, and it sounds rough."

Michael made note of Susan's words: *I hear you.*

In a world where all people did was talk over everyone, he realized how intelligent it was of her to say that—to validate Matthew, to let him know someone was listening.

"How did going through that lead you to being a part of The 100? How did you meet them?"

"Oh," Matthew said, slightly surprised. "I don't know any of them."

Though she made no external show of disappointment, Susan thought *well shit.*

If all 100 were independent of one another, then Matthew wouldn't be able to offer up any names or locations of those still remaining.

"How did you become involved with them?" she offered, deftly changing gears.

"Well," Matthew said hesitantly. "I didn't know there was a 'them,' really. I mean, I knew there were others, but I didn't know there was an actual number. I was just told I was going to be a part of something big. When I saw the news last night, I realized what I was involved with."

Susan gave him space to continue, and when he didn't, she gave Matthew a verbal nudge.

"And this morning," she began, "you got up to carry out your piece of the puzzle, but stopped. Why?"

"Because of what Jessica said," Matthew said without explaining.

Susan raised her eyebrows and gave a gentle look of expectation. Though she didn't say, *continue*, it was written across her face.

"Oh," Matthew started, catching the drift. "She said she had just become a grandmother. That was enough..."

Matthew trailed off and became somber.

"I'd never looked at her as a person before that. She was always just a figurehead. She was the one in charge, the one officiating over all the evil that befell me..."

Matthew's voice became quiet.

"It's probably easy to kill a 'position,' to say, 'I'm going to shoot the bank president.' It's not so easy to kill a person."

Susan gave Matthew a minute to breathe. She didn't want to push him too hard; he was talking, and that was important. She just had to get him on a path where he discussed his recruitment.

"You know what that means?" Susan asked rhetorically. "It means you're human. It's a good thing. It shows good judgment."

Matthew nodded to himself, but didn't make eye contact for a moment. He was still trying to come to terms with everything.

"Yeah..." he finally continued, "all's well that ends well, I suppose."

Now Matthew looked at Susan directly.

"I'm going to prison, aren't I?"

Michael made note of the term 'prison.' Most people used 'jail' in circumstances like this. Matthew was smart enough to know the difference between the two institutions.

"That's not up to me," Susan answered honestly. "What happens now is that detectives will gather evidence. They'll present it to prosecutors, who will then decide whether or not to bring charges against you, and what those charges will be. Then you plead, and depending on how you plead it either goes to trial, or before a judge for sentencing."

Susan leaned in for effect and placed a hand on Matthew's knee.

"I do know this: how you act from here on out will help determine what happens next. The more you help us, the more you're likely to get a lighter sentence, or even counseling over hard time. You committed a minor crime. Your intent was a major crime, but you held yourself in check. That says a lot. But the more you help us, the more you help yourself. If you can tell me how you got involved with The 100, even if you didn't know what it was called or who they were, if you can tell me everything you know, I can testify on your behalf and say you were very forthcoming and accommodating."

Susan pulled back her hand and leaned back into her chair.

She's giving him space to talk, Michael realized. *She's not in his personal space, intimidating him.*

"Her name is Cassandra," Matthew began. "She found me online. Said she could help me get back at those who wronged me, and that I'd be preventing others from having the same kind of problems I did…"

A thought struck Michael when Matthew said Cassandra. He reached for his phone, pulled up Google, and did a quick search.

Matthew spoke for about ten minutes. Susan asked a question here and there but mostly just listened.

While he was talking, a series of very interesting words exited Matthew's mouth. Words that caused Susan and Michael to look at one another in surprise.

"If you'd like, I can show you our messages," he stated plainly. "They're all online."

"Online?" Susan asked. "You didn't wipe your computer?"

"No," Matthew explained sheepishly. "It's my wife's, and I couldn't do that to her. But I don't even need it. The messages are all online. I just need any computer, and I can log in to my ChatApp."

Susan perked up. ChatApp conversations were one thing, but if his computer was still intact, that could be a windfall of information.

"That would be very helpful," Susan explained, reaching for her phone. She turned off the recorder milliseconds before a text came in: Director Sumner's plane just landed in Peoria.

He'd be at the transfer center within twenty minutes, ready for a briefing.

Chapter 15

Michael's Moment

Director Sumner was on his phone when he walked into the building.

Susan rubbed her thumb and first two fingers together in the gesture referencing money, suggesting Michael needed to pay up. She bet that Sumner would be attached to his cell when he arrived, and was surprised Michael played along and took the counter position.

Oh well, she mused. *He'll learn to never bet against someone with more experience than you.*

Once he finished his conversation, Sumner was to the point.

"We have two more confirmed, and a copycat," he started, shoving his phone into a pocket. "The confirmed are Patrick Novak and Paul Brandmeyer. Patrick killed a doctor who botched four surgeries in Texas, crippling two and killing two—one of the two dead was Patrick's wife—yet was allowed to keep his license and hurt three more people via surgery-gone-wrong in Florida. Patrick's message was, 'any incompetent doctor who keeps practicing after destroying families is now on notice.' Brandmeyer found a guy—Mike Garland—who set up fake GoFundMe sites after tragedies. He collected donations after Hurricanes Sandy *and* Harvey. He pretended to have lost a kid at Parkland..."

"Jesus," Michael whispered.

Susan gave her agreement by giving him a look that said, *You're right, that's pretty disgusting.*

"Yeah," Sumner said. "Garland is one shitty human being. And he covered his tracks well, too. We don't know how Brandmeyer found him, but he tied him up, and lit his house on fire. It burned down with the two of them inside."

Susan and Michael were both stunned silent, causing Sumner to explain without prompting.

"Brandmeyer lost his family in a fire. Which was bad enough, but then Garland cashed in on it. He set up a site that said he was raising cash for the funerals, but it was a lie. Garland kept the money. Brandmeyer shot himself and let Garland to burn to death. In his video, he said he didn't have anything to live for anymore."

There was a moment of silence while Susan and Michael digested the information, then a synapse fired inside Susan's head.

"What did the copycat do?" she asked.

"The copycat was arrested after spraying the front of a gang house with bullets," Sumner explained. "Fired twelve rounds into the house and then turned himself in, citing 'The 100' as inspiration."

"He's lucky he didn't get shot in the process," Michael noted, mostly to himself, but Sumner picked up on it anyway.

"Nah, he did it at 6:00 AM. Took him less than twenty seconds. The bangers had all probably barely woken up from the first couple shots before he high-tailed it outta there. Point is, shit is gonna get out of control fast the longer this goes on. I need good news. Is Kimsey singing?"

"Yes, and we have a name, Cassandra." Susan began. "Even better than that, he has correspondence for us."

"And he wants access to a computer," Sumner correctly surmised. "Not sure that's a good idea. Is he looking to get online in order to send instructions or make contact with someone outside of these walls?"

"I don't think so, no," Susan responded. "And even if he is, we can restrict and control his access while online fairly easily. He doesn't even have to touch the keyboard; we'll get the password from him and then look through everything on our own."

"We don't have that password yet?"

"He's not dumb. He wanted to hear from you about what sort of recommendation for leniency the FBI will be making on his behalf."

Sumner muttered something under his breath.

Even though Susan didn't catch exactly what it was, she knew he wasn't happy about the idea of a tit-for-tat involving information and clemency.

"OK," Sumner continued after his expression of displeasure. "Who is Cassandra, and what did he tell us about her?"

"Best we can tell," Susan explained, "Cassandra is in charge of The 100. She reached out to Kimsey online, fed him the idea of revenge, sent him the bomb, told him he was right to be angry at everyone at the bank... We're guessing she's behind the others, too. It's all speculation, but if we're right, she probably sent Francart his explosives, too."

"Do we know who or where she is?"

"We hope to glean that information from the messages Mr. Kimsey is going to provide for us."

Sumner nodded, and glanced at his phone; it had begun vibrating in his pocket. He pushed a button that sent the call to voicemail as Michael injected himself into the conversation.

"Can I say something?" Michael asked, half-raising a hand as if in school.

Both Susan and Sumner turned their heads; Susan's expression was inviting, Sumner's less so.

"I've been thinking about this," Michael continued, "and I'm wondering... what if Cassandra is just a name?"

"You mean a false identity?" Susan asked. "I think that's assumed at this point."

"No," Michael offered hesitatingly. "I mean, what if it's not just a false identity, but a sort of clue?"

One word exited Sumner's mouth: "Explain."

Michael took a deep breath.

He didn't feel he was putting himself on the line with this, but offering any theory, especially to the big dog, called for some nerves.

"We've been thinking that the person behind this is a white male," Michael offered. "It makes sense, and falls in line with the basics of profiling. White men make up the targets, and a white male knows how to speak to his own, how to trigger them. The idea it's a woman doesn't really fit. Sure, women can manipulate men, and have done so to take advantage of them—think of all the things men do for beautiful women—but Cassandra... that's not a name that pops up pretty much anywhere."

"If you have a point," Sumner stressed, "get to it."

"In Greek mythology, Cassandra was the daughter of King Priam and Queen Hecuba. She was given the gift of prophecy by Apollo, and could see the future. But he also cursed her, in that no one would believe her. She saw the coming of Helen and the eventual war, and she told Priam not to allow the Greek gift of a wooden horse into the city of Troy, the infamous Trojan Horse. After she was taken by Agamemnon, she foresaw his murder by his own wife. She told everyone how to avoid tragedy every step of the way and was ignored at each turn."

The room went quiet for a beat. Michael wasn't sure if he had over-stepped his bounds, or if they were going to believe him or understand where he was going.

Finally, Sumner broke the silence with a curt, "Jesus Christ, Godwin... have you ever even *kissed* a girl?"

Michael was stunned, but relaxed as Susan laughed, which in turn caused Sumner to break into a smile himself.

"What you're saying," Sumner began thoughtfully, "is that we've got an angry nerd out there who feels like no one is listening to him. He's all-knowing, but since no one pays attention to his wisdom, this is his way of venting his frustration."

Michael nodded.

"Yeah," he said, relieved. "Pretty much, yeah."

Sumner mulled it over, then tossed a "Thoughts?" to Susan.

"Well," she began carefully, "it actually makes more sense that we're dealing with Ted Kaczynski two, Electric Boogaloo, than a woman named 'Cassandra' in today's day and age."

Sumner nodded, then admitted, "Goddammit, I hate that that does make sense. OK, what's the next step?"

"We're looking for a needle in a haystack," Michael explained. "Who-ever this is, they've probably written blogs, or letters to an editor, or opinion pieces. They've put their ideas out there, and this is their way of saying 'Stop ignoring me!'"

"Great, all we have to do is find someone online with a strong opinion," Sumner muttered, the frustration clear in his tone. "That should be easy. Check Facebook for, I don't know, every single user."

"I know," Michael sighed, partially defeated. "It's near-impossible. But if we take the messages between Cassandra and Kimsey and are able to dig up communications between her and the others, we can get a sense of her style of writing. After that, we cross-reference everything we've come across so far—lawyers, bankers, pill-pushing pharmacists—we might be able to find a couple articles that reference all of them. Sure, everyone is angry about something. We're looking for someone who's angry about everything."

"Point taken," Sumner acknowledged. "I'll have Richardson put a couple people on that after we see the messages. Hopefully whatever profile or IP address Cassandra is attached to can give us a decent lead."

"Except," Susan interjected, "she's not mad about everything. At least, not yet."

Sumner didn't respond verbally, but his look suggested Susan should continue.

"I know we're only a day in on this," Susan began, "but Michael and I have been keeping tabs on public opinion. We just spent four hours in a car watching Twitter and reading the comments on news websites. I wouldn't say *everyone* supports what's happening, but The 100 already has a fanbase."

"Yeah," Sumner agreed, irritated. "We've been picking up on that as well."

"Look at who the targets are, and aren't. One, everyone hates politicians, but we haven't had anyone go after one. From as big as a senator to as small as a mayor, they've been left alone. And if any politician was a target, they would have been an early one, because the window to get at one of them is closed. Their security was heightened and tightened after the first video dropped. Two, there's an unfortunate segment of society that hates law enforcement. But no one has gone after a cop. Whoever Cassandra really is, she's playing the PR. game perfectly. It's easy to write an editorial denouncing the police, but when an officer gets killed, public sympathy immediately swings toward law enforcement. 'Cassandra' wants public opinion on her side, because she wants copycats. This isn't just about The 100, this is a call to arms."

"When the government is no longer by the people, for the people," Sumner nodded, "then the people rise up."

"Exactly," Susan confirmed. "And if you want the people on your side, you have to choose targets that are..."

Susan trailed off for a moment while she tried to find the right words.

"To a degree, non-controversial," she concluded. "Whether or not you support the idea of violence against them, you can't say people will be sympathetic to drug company executives or lawyers who screw working people over for the benefit of the rich."

Sumner nodded again, but Michael wasn't sold.

"I... disagree," Michael countered. "Somewhat."

Susan and Sumner gave him the floor, allowing Michael to continue.

"Swaying public opinion is easier than you think. Outrage is controlled by information, and I don't mean that in a conspiracy theory way, I mean it more like we've all got ADHD, and *everything* is a shiny object. The second-largest outbreak of Ebola, *ever*, took place in 2018. Most people don't know that, because it wasn't in the news all that much. Compare that to the Ebola coverage of 2014. People with absolutely no reason to fear infection went nuts. It was on every channel, every night. The difference between the two outbreaks was only a couple hundred people, but the news amplified one, and ignored the other. And the public went along with each accordingly. In 2014, they were afraid. In 2018, since no one was hyping the outbreak, no one noticed what was happening. Africa didn't suddenly change in location to us, but in 2014 you'd have thought Ebola was knocking on America's door. In 2018, Africa was again a far-away continent most people couldn't find on a map."

"How does that tie in with what we're dealing with?" Sumner asked.

"Look at the first of The 100—the first person we became aware of, Evan Francart. Compare Ebola to Martin Shkreli, Pharma Boy. He bought a pharmaceutical company and raised the price on one medication through the roof. It went from something like a hundred bucks to twenty-some thousand dollars. People complained, the media got wind, and the story exploded. But other drug companies raise prices constantly, they just don't do it all at once. Look at Francart's target, Glenback. They were smarter about what they did. I read up on them, and they took one drug and bumped the price from $10 a pill, to $100 a pill. It gave them good profits, but more importantly, it kept them out of the news. Two years later, the same pill cost $250. They didn't explode the price, they just kept inching it upwards, slow and steady, forever the tortoise and never the hare. Everyone was mad at Pharma Boy, because he made the news. since no one reported on Glenback, no one knew about them. But Francart had skin in that game, and took action. The interesting thing about Cassandra is that she's pulling back Oz's curtain. She's bringing the unknown stories into the light."

Susan furrowed her brow in thought; something Michael said struck her, but she couldn't figure out what.

"You said..." Susan began haltingly. "You said 'the first we became aware of,' regarding Evan Francart. Do we know who, technically, went first?"

"We do," Sumner offered. "I don't have it memorized, though."

"If we go off the premise that Cassandra is mad at everyone and everything, that's fine. But people usually go after their personal gripe first. Everything after that is just gravy."

Both Michael and Sumner caught on at the same time.

"There were, what?" Michael asked. "Four or five that popped up after Francart's video played?"

Sumner looked irritated.

"Donny Lin was one of the first," he growled. "If the M.E. had done his job in Pittsburgh, he would have discovered Lin didn't have any alcohol in his system during his 'drunk driving' accident. We wouldn't have pegged him as part of a huge conspiracy, but we would have realized the hit was on purpose."

"True," Susan agreed. "But we can't get involved with a game of 'maybe' or 'what if?' We have to go down the path in front of us."

"Right," Michael concurred. "But I think you're on to something with the 'who was first' angle. That could reveal Cassandra's personal reasons for going on this crusade.

"OK," Sumner said, resigned. "Richardson should be here with a team within the hour. We have people at Kimsey's house. Now it's a matter of Richardson going there, or her coming here, getting Kimsey's password, and starting the research on Cassandra's messages. You two pull up the first four popped up after Francart and see if we have dates on them. Then we'll start with Michael's path of looking for that needle of anger that's the haystack of the internet."

Sumner gave a half-shrug.

"These are our ingredients," he said. "Let's make a meal out of them."

Chapter 16

Preparations, Examinations, Evaluations

Josh was inspired by the Winchester House.

He didn't know when he'd first heard of it; somewhere in his childhood was all he remembered.

But he liked the house. More realistically, he liked the idea of it.

The Winchester House, or *The Winchester Mystery House,* if using proper names, was the brainchild of the widow to the Winchester Rifle fortune. Legend claimed she was told to build the place by a medium, someone who said those killed by her husband's invention needed a place where their spirits could find peace.

Construction began in 1884 and continued unbroken until 1922. During that time builders worked without any master plan or input from a proper architect. What you ended up with, then, was a hodgepodge of a house. Story upon story, with more rooms than you could shake a stick at, staircases that went nowhere, and doors that opened into walls.

Josh found the concept of the house intriguing as a child, but even after his initial interest faded, he saw the value in owning such a structure. Not for the oddity of it, but for practical reasons.

Or to be realistic, one reason.

Escape.

If the authorities were closing in, and by that he meant *physically* closing in, he needed a place where once he was inside, he became a ghost.

Which is why he bought the abandoned warehouse in Industry City.

Josh didn't go full on crazy with it; he didn't want to bring attention to what he was doing. In the age of the internet and Instagram, with contractors able to expose plans (even if accidentally), Josh knew he had to cover his tracks carefully.

First up, as always, was to use dummy corporations to hide his involvement. Josh played hide-and-seek with his name on ownership papers, because having it out there meant unwanted attention. All it took was paperwork; if you created enough, it was near-impossible to trace a purchase to its buyer.

The second step was to dream up something interesting. To this end, Josh decided an 'entertainment center' fit the bill nicely. If the contractors were building something crazy for the sake of crazy, they'd talk. But if they were building a structure that had a greater purpose—profit and neighborhood revitalization—then they might scuttlebutt on the merits of said idea, but they wouldn't raise any eyebrows via gossip.

Of course, the entertainment center never actually opened, which made Josh laugh embarrassedly.

The company he'd used to pay for it took a tax deduction on the loss, meaning that in a way, Josh was a criminal. Which technically meant he should have had one of The 100 target him, the rich guy taking tax breaks at the expense of the working class.

The hypocrisy amused him, even if he had to admit *he* was the hypocrite in this situation.

After the first construction company finished their work and the place sat vacant for a couple months, Josh used another dummy corporation to buy the bankrupted center. The second company built the living quarters. Nothing fancy, just enough to make it look like an eccentric dingbat wanted to live in a quirky environment.

It all went back to the idea of gossip: if he'd had a bedroom, bathroom, and kitchen in the original design, people would have talked. But having a second company add them later? That was just someone with too much money and no clue how to spend it. Because he was building living quarters in a sketchy neighborhood, the state-of-the-art security cameras being installed wouldn't be questioned. Home security is important, after all.

The final addition was the tricky one, and for that he'd turned to survivalists—companies that built panic rooms and underground bunkers for the end times.

Because they dealt in paranoia, those people were discreet to a fault. If you needed a getaway for when society fell and anarchy reigned, they'd do whatever you wanted. No questions asked. Not even if you paid cash. Since the survivalist companies believed the government was monitoring everyone, they didn't find anything odd. They wouldn't even blink if you needed a hole punched in the floor of your warehouse. A hole with a trap door attached that allowed you access to the sewers of Brooklyn.

In fact, the people building such a contraption would actually praise you for your clear-headedness.

"Good idea," the builder would say. "When government helos are targeting people on the streets, you *want* to be underground. We could probably build a bunker down there for you. One the city planners couldn't find too easily..."

He appreciated the attempted upsell, but Josh didn't want a bunker. He just needed access to the tunnels. It had taken thirteen months and probably $2 million, but if he needed to use the place to its fullest capacity, it'd be money well spent.

Josh clicked the touchpad on his laptop and looked over the map he'd drawn.

The warehouse was a half a mile from the garage, and the garage was only fifty yards from the docks. He wouldn't keep the yacht close to the warehouse, because it would draw too much attention. Especially in that part of town.

Instead, he left two inconspicuous getaways: in the garage, a 2004 Honda Accord. The second-most common car in America wouldn't gain notice in any situation, and for the most part, people liked having their expectations met. Since he was a billionaire, anyone looking for him would imagine him behind the wheel of a Porsche, or a Tesla X (if he were being trendy).

At the docks, Josh had a rowboat with an outboard engine attached. If the roads were too clogged with law enforcement, he would take that up to NYC proper, specifically the Chelsea Piers. That's where the yacht was.

The yacht.

That was another case of meeting expectations. He couldn't tell the contest winners, "Hey, head on down to Industry City to board your luxury cruise!"

Even the dumbest of the dumb would sense something was wrong with that scenario. He kept the yacht where people assumed such a luxury liner would be. Josh would board at the Chelsea Piers and then float down the Hudson to the bay. From there it was into the high seas.

And once he was in that vast, blue expanse?

Then everything would take shape and he'd finally make his contribution to the overall plan.

Josh smiled.

It was one thing to have others do your bidding, but it was going to feel good to actually be a part of it himself. Like the difference between buying a tomato from the store and eating one grown in your own garden. Having skin in the game made life all the more meaningful.

Success was tethered to planning, though. To that end, Josh went over a mental checklist of what could go wrong, and how he'd respond.

He wouldn't be leaving the warehouse for the next week, just to be safe. No one would be able to catch him standing in line at Starbucks or grab him on the way to the subway. Of course, those scenarios came under the assumption they'd even figure out who he was within the next seven days, which was doubtful at best.

But Josh didn't play to the odds; he was meticulous. Even a slim chance was a chance, which meant he covered all his bases.

If his identity was discovered, the first thing law enforcement would do would be to put him under surveillance. Which means they'd be watching his apartment. Since he wouldn't be going back there, big whoop.

If by the grace of God they were able to trace him to the warehouse, well, they were more than welcome to watch it, too. He was good to go for over a month if need be. Food, water, clothes... Josh didn't need to leave the property, period. But since his go date was close at hand, waiting a month wasn't necessary.

Even if no one was actively closing in—even if he didn't see a S.W.A.T. team on his monitors—he'd exit through the garage anyway. It was best to be careful than to end up in the middle of a chase. Chase scenes looked good in movies, but exiting out the garage meant he'd be able to skedaddle completely unseen.

If it looked like he could drive away without being noticed, great. If not, he'd hike it on foot for a few blocks, and then hop into a nice, anonymous cab. Sure, people loved ride share apps, but those traced you from pickup to drop off. Anyone monitoring his credit cards would get an alert the instant he requested a ride.

Realtors were about location; Josh was about planning. Over-planning. Leaving no detail unexamined.

As those words crossed his mind—*leave no detail unexamined*—Josh had another thought.

Kimsey hadn't gone through with his act. Did that mean he hadn't gone through with the *complete process* of his act?

Specifically, had Kimsey wiped his computer and destroyed the components? Everyone on the list had been given specific instructions on how to wipe their computers clean. Not just factory reset them, wipe them and dismantle the hard drive.

Just looking at the law of averages, Josh figured that one or two or even ten might not follow through. Even when you have nothing to live for, it's still difficult for people to destroy their property. The act makes what you're about to do too real. If you had that second thought, "Oh, shit... I'm *really* going to kill myself," it might halt you in your tracks. The alcoholic's "moment of clarity," so to speak.

Was Kimsey like that? Did he have second thoughts that morning, before entering the bank? If Kimsey didn't wipe his computer, then it would still be active.

And an active computer could be very helpful to Josh.

Cassandra had sent each participant an encryption program. As far as The 100 knew, the program gave them two things: one, access to a bank account created in their name. Yes, it was a bribe, but it was also practical. Money gave them freedom. Some—like Freddy in Seattle—used that money to buy guns. Others used it to pay rent and buy food. Evan had been instructed to use it to buy his new laptop.

Two, encryption made it difficult for anyone *else* using the computer to know what members of The 100 were up to. After all, some of them undoubtedly shared a computer with a significant other. This extra layer of protection made sure that person couldn't see and therefore thwart any plans.

What none of them knew, however, was that the encryption program had very special malware attached to it, a Remote Access Trojan. The RAT gave Josh complete control of The 100's computers; access that gave Josh the ability to monitor their interactions both on and offline.

Online, he could see everything they were doing, who they were corresponding with, and what they were discussing. Josh could monitor their social media interactions, shopping habits, and discover (should he find it interesting) any fetish they might have if they visited porn sites.

Even better, the RAT allowed Josh to keep an eye on The 100. Literally, keep an eye on them. Once Josh had access to their computers, he had access to their webcam. Josh programmed those to remain on 24/7. More importantly, the cameras were on without the computer display *saying* they were on.

Facial expression recognition software watched as each user interacted with Cassandra. What did their faces say while they wrote to her? What did their faces show when they read her messages? Were they nervous? Hesitant? Confident? Every moment was analyzed, and reports were drawn up automatically.

Even when members put their computer to sleep or turned them off, Josh could watch them. The RAT allowed him to let users think their computer had shut down, when in reality the camera was still on. Who came into their house? What did they talk about?

Josh was frustrated by the fact that even with all these safeguards in place, he'd missed whatever warning signs Kimsey had given. Something had to have suggested he wasn't going to go through with his task; that he was a weak link.

But, since he *was* a weak link, it created the possibility he hadn't wiped his computer.

And if that was the case, the RAT would still be intact.

Which meant he could still look through Kimsey's webcam.

Which meant he could see whoever was searching Kimsey's house and poking around on his computer.

Josh stared at the screen in front of him. Checking Kimsey's computer was a risk. Was it worth the possible rewards?

There was only one way to find out.

Josh opened a folder on his computer. Once the contents were revealed, he double-clicked a spreadsheet. Listed were The 100. Every name, every tragedy.

Josh scrolled to the row marked "Kimsey" and clicked the link within it.

Chapter 17

Interaction

Matthew Kimsey's wife Valerie had left by the time Susan, Michael, and Sumner got to the house.

She'd undergone preliminary questioning by the first agents to arrive, then wanted nothing to do with the people searching her home. Valerie wasn't interested in watching anyone manhandle her property and resented them being in her house.

Valerie's mother's name, phone number, and address were written down—Springfield, Illinois, was only an hour away—and she was allowed to retreat there to escape what was about to be a media hell for her and her neighbors.

After receiving assurances Sumner would draft a letter on his behalf for the eventual trial, Kimsey had given up his social media credentials. Kristen Richardson arrived a little before the Susan/Michael/Sumner trio and began examining it straightaway.

(Sumner had grumbled a little about the trade—passwords for a referral—but was ultimately a pragmatic man and knew the information they were receiving was more important than throwing the book at someone who had *almost* committed a horrible crime.

Plus, Kimsey had initially asked for a court appearance by Sumner to testify on his behalf, which, in Sumner's words "wasn't fucking happening." A letter on Kimsey's behalf was an easy and acceptable middle ground for both of them.)

Kimsey lived in a modest (and that was putting it politely) home in West Peoria. Michael looked it up on a real estate website that ranked housing areas in any given market, and the neighborhood showed up on the lower end side of things. It wasn't a slum in the traditional sense of the word, but the homes were smaller and less well-kept than you'd find in an established middle-class area. Where there were sidewalks, they were cracked; many driveways were gravel, and garages were detached, and single car.

Overall, no one was surprised when they pulled up to discover the neighbors had a lawn full of plastic pink flamingos and an old-school, rusted-out swing set.

"That's a tetanus shot waiting to happen," Susan observed.

"He went from upper management to this?" Michael asked while looking around the neighborhood. "That's a hard fall."

"You judging these people?" Sumner questioned.

"No... this is pretty close to how I grew up." Michael responded. "Not exactly, but kissing cousins. My parents probably earned maybe $10,000 a year more than these people, and that's the difference between a clothesline in the backyard and a dryer in your laundry room. I'm just saying that if you've never experienced this kind of life, it's gonna be a shock to your system."

Sumner nodded understandingly.

The three entered the house to find a plethora of agents doing their work with routine precision. Sumner wondered if they were always so professional, or if this was a bit of theater since they knew he was going to be on site.

Eh, doesn't matter, he decided. *As long as it gets done correctly.*

Kristen was in an upbeat mood when they found her; Kimsey kept his computer in the dining room. Space was limited in such a house, so he had used a section of the dining room table for his monitor, and the tower sat on the floor.

"Good news, better news," Kristen greeted them. "The computer hasn't been cleared, and the messages from Cassandra are still there."

"Goddamn," Sumner offered happily. "It's like my birthday, only without vanilla cake and off-key caterwauling."

"We had an office party for him once," Susan explained to Michael. "*Once.* And he hasn't let us forget that he prefers chocolate since."

"Or that having a tin ear is apparently part of the FBI entrance exam," Sumner said offhandedly.

Michael arched an eyebrow at Susan, then all three turned their attention to Kristen.

"Does us having their correspondence mean anything?" Susan asked. "Specifically, does it mean we can trace her messages to their origin, to the sender's home base?"

"Doubtful," Kristen answered. "We'll be able to get an IP address off them, but I'm going to go ahead and guarantee it's a fake."

"I mean," Sumner jumped in, "even we use a Dynamic IP address that changes randomly."

"Which means hunting them all down to see if a single one of them is accurate," Michael sighed, "is pretty much like having a bottle of scotch and a dartboard."

"That would be our best-case scenario," Kristen explained. "I could trace a shifting address. I'm guessing whoever sent these used Tor, which runs an IP address through thousands of untraceable routers. It's like a safe with a thousand number combination."

"So, we're fucked," Sumner grumbled.

"It's classic cat and mouse tactics" Kristen said. "The oldest game between cops and criminals."

"A literal Tom & Jerry, where the police are 'Tom,' and the criminal mouse 'Jerry' runs circles around us," Susan sighed, resigned.

"Sometimes yes, sometimes no," Kristen countered. "Yes, we're bound by rules and regulations, and they're bound by nothing, which makes it difficult. But there are ways of getting information no matter how adroitly it's hidden."

"Did you just use 'adroitly' in casual conversation?" Michael said, impressed.

"Check out the big brain on Brad," Susan exclaimed. "Or Kristen, in this case."

"Big Kahuna Burger," Michael offered. "I got that one."

Susan gave Michael a wink and a finger-gun: *Bang-bang, good on you young'un.*

"If we could focus here..." Sumner muttered.

"Right," Kristen said, centering herself. "We have the messages, and I've been going over them. Basically, Cassandra played on his emotions. He was angry, so she told him it was OK to be angry. She was like a therapist, validating his feelings. And then validation turned into exploitation, and that's how we ended up here."

"Can assume this is how she operated with all of them?" Michael asked.

"I'd say that's, as you like to put it, fair game," Susan concurred.

"I say fair enough," Michael countered.

"Shit, right."

* * *

As the agents bantered, Josh watched and recorded everything from the safety of his hodgepodge living quarters in the Industry City warehouse.

Cassandra had already identified Kristen Richardson.

Within seconds of her having logged on to Kimsey's computer, Cassandra had begun combing the internet, using facial-recognition software to ferret out matching pictures. It had taken fifteen minutes, which was exceedingly speedy given what little she was given to work with.

Now Cassandra was working on the identities of the latest arrivals.

Pictures would provide names, which would provide social media accounts, college transcripts, work histories... all things Josh could use to determine how best to approach this new development. Because the more you knew about your pursuer, the better you could evade them.

(And, fingers crossed, you could possibly find something to use against them.)

Josh was a combination of amused and annoyed as the agents chit-chatted over their approach to finding Cassandra, and therefore (and unknowingly) him.

If one of them would just say another person's name, he thought, *it would make things so much easier...*

But real-life conversation was nothing like movie dialogue. In the movies, or at least, poorly written ones, names were always being tossed about: "Hey, *Bob*, what do you think of this?" "I think it's great, *Jerry*! Just great, *Jerry*!"

In reality, people say, "Whaddya think?" and "Great!" Names rarely get used in everyday conversation.

When name overuse happened on the big screen, Josh was annoyed. But now he wished one of them say, "Hey, Agent *Sherman*..."

Having any name, first or last, would speed things up.

As Josh had the thought, Cassandra shot him an alert on another tab he had open. She'd been scraping anywhere and everywhere across the web for Agent Richardson, and was building a profile on her. Josh stole a glance at it and didn't like what he saw.

Kristen Richardson was whip-smart.

She'd been a hacker in her teen years, and was accepted into the online hacking community *Cult of the Dead Cow* in 2006 when just sixteen years old. She was also a hacker in the purest sense of the word. Kristen Richardson wasn't interested in disruption; she enjoyed learning. She broke into systems to see if she could, and to see how they worked; Kristen Richardson didn't steal data or credit card numbers.

Her skills caught the attention of a former member of the group, a hacker known as Mudge. Mudge was one of the most prolific technophiles of the 1990s, and he befriended Kristen, showed her how she could use her skills for good. Mudge explained that if she joined the right side of the law, she'd never have to worry about various agencies knocking on (or breaking down) her doors and confiscating her computers.

(As had happened to Mudge several times during his escapades across the fledgling internet of the boy-band decade.)

Kristen took Mudge's advice, got a full-ride scholarship to Stanford, and then was accepted into the FBI academy. That's who was chasing Josh, and it was no surprise she'd been put on such a high-profile case immediately.

It didn't make him nervous, per se, but it also didn't instill confidence that he was going to skate through this experience unscathed.

Josh was getting lost in his own head when a voice came through his computer's speaker. The agents in Peoria were discussing tactics, when one of them said, "She has to have seen the news, right?"

The words caught Josh's ear, and made him wonder what the agents were thinking.

* * *

Michael's question hung in the air a moment, and then Susan finally answered.

"I mean," Susan began, "it's the biggest story out there."

"The 100 is," Sumner countered. "Kimsey isn't. Yet."

"It was all over Twitter while we were driving here," Michael said.

"But we don't know her daily habits," Sumner cautioned. "Look at the Unabomber; he was completely isolated from the world. We know she's into apps, but we can't make any assumptions as to what she does and doesn't know."

"So she might not know he hasn't gone through with it?" Kristen inquired.

"We can't say one way or another," Sumner responded. "Look at it this way..."

Sumner paused to chew things over in his head a moment.

"I'm guessing that every member of The 100 is working independently," Sumner continued. "Cassandra is someone in a pickup truck stopping by Home Depot for a few day laborers. They only know what they're told to do, not the master plan. And we don't know what sort of instructions they were given, be it a specific time and day to carry their mission out, or a timeframe to act within, or maybe they were told to just do their thing... whenever."

"Which means if Kimsey wasn't scheduled to act today," Susan realized, "then Cassandra might not know he backed out."

"You don't think they check in the night before or day of?" Michael asked, playing Devil's Advocate.

"They probably do," Susan agreed. "But we don't know that for certain. Right now, we should play whatever angle we can."

"By angle, do you mean..." Kristen inferred, trailing off.

There was another moment of silence as everyone in the room exchanged a glance and realized they were all on the same page. Susan looked to Sumner, who nodded ever so slightly.

That was all the go-ahead Susan needed.

"Do it," she told Kristen.

"It won't be admissible in court," Kristen cautioned.

"We're not looking for evidence," Sumner explained. "This is a lure. We're fishing, and don't need anything that might be said here. This is about capture, not building the case."

Kristen nodded, then turned her attention to the computer in front of her. She sat quietly a moment, staring at the screen and taking deep breaths, and then rested her fingers on the keyboard.

"Am I doing this solo?" she asked. "Or do we want to committee this?"

"You get started," Susan coaxed gently. "We'll chime in as necessary."

Kristen nodded, and took one more breath all the way down to her diaphragm. As she exhaled, she began typing.

Cassandra... I couldn't go through with it. I need help. I need to know what to do next. Can we talk?

She paused and looked around at the others.

"Good start," Michael enthused. "What's next?"

"Wait," Susan said quietly, holding up a hand. "I don't think there needs to be a 'next.'"

They all looked at Susan expectantly, so she gathered her thoughts and continued.

"We don't want to write too much," Susan explained. "We don't know how Kimsey writes. We don't know their relationship. We just want to open a dialogue."

"Maybe we should get Kimsey himself?" Michael asked.

"No," Sumner shook his head as he spoke. "He'll want another goddamn leniency trade, and I'm done with that."

Sumner leaned in and re-read the phrase.

"Chop the back half off," he concluded. "Tell her he couldn't go through with it. If he asks for anything unusual it might scare her away. Let's see how she responds to something short."

Kristen turned back to the computer and deleted the tail end of her message. Once she had, she rested a finger over the enter button.

One final time, they all exchanged glances.

Cassandra... I couldn't go through with it.

Kristen locked eyes with Sumner.

"Consider this authorization," Sumner told her.

Kristen's pinky finger tapped "enter," and a whoosh sound signified the sending of a message.

"Now what?" Michael asked.

"Now we wait," Sumner responded.

Susan opened her mouth slightly, and then thought better of it. She had almost said, "Ah, the waiting game sucks. Let's play Hungry Hungry Hippos," but at the last second decided that not everything in life needed to be a Simpson's reference.

(Just most things.)

* * *

Approximately two seconds after Agent Richardson hit send in Peoria, Josh's computer dinged.

Message received.

The two-second delay was due to the fact that the message had to go through a series of dummy networks, land in Cassandra's inbox, and then a copy of the message was peeled off, put back through the series of dummy networks, and ultimately sent to Josh.

Fuuuuuck.

Josh leaned back in his chair and absorbed what was happening. He didn't see this coming, and it was huge.

Would Cassandra respond?

The problem with computers, even super-computers programmed to learn from their mistakes, is that they don't have human minds. A computer would have to be told, 'read the news,' it wouldn't just do so for fun. And even if Cassandra had come across a story about Kimsey turning himself in, she didn't have the capacity to tie that to the Kimsey protocol she was running and realize things had gone awry.

Cassandra didn't know what it meant to not fulfill an obligation, or that Kimsey was supposed to be dead, or even what death was. Cassandra responded to prompts, and this was one she hadn't encountered yet.

Josh's mind began to race; should he log in and quickly program her to not reply? Should he reply *as* her?

"Christ," he muttered aloud, before finishing his thought internally: *why didn't I terminate the connection the instant he quit on me?*

For a moment, Josh thought about shutting Cassandra down outright, but then realized that others out there who hadn't completed their task might be looking to her for advice.

He thought he'd anticipated everything; Cassandra was prepared to deal with all the questions coming in from the concerned people waiting in queue for their turn. She was ready to deal with hesitation, and even do virtual handholding if necessary, but he hadn't anticipated this sort of attack on her system.

Because—and this was the fucked-up part—the FBI didn't realize they were tricking her. They thought they were writing to a person.

Anger grew in Josh. He didn't like being indecisive, and he didn't like over thinking problems. What were his instincts telling him to do?

Josh folded his hands and then leaned in, sliding his chin into his hands as he began counting to ten. He'd do whatever felt right when he hit that first double-digit number.

Counting calmed Josh, and when he reached ten he decided to log into Cassandra and delete the Matthew Kimsey protocol. Following that, he'd wipe Kimsey's computer himself. Even if Agent Richardson was clever enough to bring back deleted files, it'd in the least slow her down.

Josh was opening the necessary files to perform his task when he heard Agent Richardson say, "We've got an incoming message!"

Shit.

Those damned dancing dots at the bottom of a screen that showed up when someone was typing. Cassandra was formatting a reply.

He had to act quickly.

* * *

Cassandra's response was as truncated as the message she had received.

"That's unfortunate," Kristen read aloud, even though the other three were hunched in, looking over her shoulder. "Maybe you can complete your task tomorrow?"

"Well," Sumner stated flatly. "That was anti-climactic."

"And fast," Chamberlain added. "She must be monitoring incoming messages, but if she's online, how has she not discovered he's in custody? Has that not been released yet?"

"Maybe she thinks he's contacting her from jail?" Michael offered. "Everyone gets a phone call, right? Maybe she thinks you get access to a computer, too."

Susan shrugged, "People generally think what they want to think about anything, facts be damned."

"So..." Kristen began, hesitantly, "do I respond?"

Sumner frowned, but it was thoughtfully, not angrily.

"We've opened the door," he stated. "No point in closing it now."

"How far do I go with this next message?" Kristen asked.

"What are our options?" Susan asked in turn.

"Well," Michael began, "we can have him state he's done, that he's actually *not* going through with things, and see how she responds to that."

"I like that," Susan agreed supportively.

"Or, we could lash out," Michael finished.

"What would that do?" Sumner asked.

Michael turned his attention to his boss, but made sure to not neglect either Susan or Kristen.

"It'd be a very real response," Michael explained. "Soldiers are trained to go to war, and they still end up with PTSD. Here, we've got an ordinary civilian. A sad sack. And he's been put into a high-pressure situation: go to the bank and kill someone. Murder is a lot to ask of anyone, much less your average Joe. Most people won't back out casually, they'll freak out. They'll point fingers and lay blame. *You put me up to this! This is your fault!* That sort of thing. We could blow up at Cassandra and ask her to never write to us again, and see if that scares her out of hiding. If she knows Kimsey is a loose end, she might take action to deal with him."

Sumner digested Michael's words silently, but Susan and Kristen were impressed and showed as much in their faces. Each was offering a "thumbs up" look, even if they weren't giving one physically.

"OK," Sumner finally decided. "I'll go general consensus on this one. I like it, but if anyone has a problem or better idea..."

Sumner trailed off to cede the floor to either Kristen or Susan.

"I'm all in," Susan offered. "I think that's a solid approach."

Kristen nodded, signaling she was 'Team Michael's Idea' all the way.

"All right," Sumner said. "Let's do it."

Kristen moved her fingers into the necessary QWERTY position and whispered, "Here we go…"

* * *

Josh was conflicted.

On the one hand, he was still upset by the recent developments. He was pissed at himself for not vetting Kimsey thoroughly enough, and pissed at Kimsey for his impotence.

But, he had to admit that he was impressed with the FBI. If it wasn't his own ass on the line, he'd be interested in seeing what they did next.

Josh watched as Agent Richardson typed. She'd finish a line, they'd bounce ideas around, and then she'd type some more.

Though annoyed by the unfolding events, even Josh was forced to laugh when what looked to be the agent in charge asked about typing in all caps and received "Dude, are you fucking kidding me?" looks from the other three in response.

They seemed like a good group.

Josh liked their banter; they seemed at ease with one another. A team. A professional, smart, hardworking team. Under different circumstances, Josh felt he wouldn't mind hanging out with them...

Josh caught himself immediately. What the hell was he thinking?

These weren't his friends. They were actively hunting him down. There'd be no ball games or barbecues with these people; they were the enemy. If they caught him, they'd lock him up straightaway. The only time a cop was your friend was when he was trying to get a confession out of you.

Frustrated with himself for entertaining stupid ideas, Josh began typing forcefully.

Sorry Agent Richardson, he wrote. *I'm afraid this is where we end things.*

* * *

"Jesus Christ!"

Kristen Richardson didn't startle easily, but seeing her name pop up on the screen stunned her.

It had, in fact, caused all four agents to flinch.

Kristen's "Jesus Christ" was quickly followed by an "Oh, shit!" as the screen before her changed. A prompt had appeared: *Erase all files?*

"She's controlling this remotely," Kristen explained in a rush. "She's going to wipe the hard drive."

The cursor moved quickly to the 'Yes' box and clicked it.

Are you sure?

The cursor again moved to the 'Yes' box.

And with that, the screen went black.

Chapter 18

What Just Happened?

A coffee mug exploded against the wall.

Shards of ceramic flew everywhere, and the hot liquid the mug had contained left a chestnut-colored stain on the once-white plaster.

Josh had thrown the cup with the force of a major league pitcher. After witnessing the impact, the twin thoughts, *Shit, I should've gone pro,* followed by, *Wait, I never played baseball in high school, much less college* ran through his mind.

After the screen in front of him had shown 'Connection Lost,' Josh continued to stare at it for a full twenty seconds.

In reality, twenty seconds isn't that long a period of time. But when you stop and actually one-Mississippi yourself all the way there, it's longer than you think.

Upon hitting twenty-Mississippi, Josh had—in one fluid motion—grabbed the mug as he rose from his chair, planted one foot for balance, and spun and launched the coffee mug across the room.

He was in trouble, and it was his own fault.

His ego had gotten out in front of him, and now it might lead to his downfall.

That's what made him furious—the fact he had done this. There could be no blaming the failure on anyone else, no examining of what happened and realizing he had been outwitted by someone more intelligent than him. No, Josh had let his anger dictate his actions, and it had cost him.

All he had needed to do was wipe the computer, but he had gone and sent a message first.

He *wanted* them to know he was watching them. He *wanted* them to know he was smarter than them, that he was one step ahead, and that they were outmatched.

And it had blown up in his face.

Josh took several deep breaths and began to analyze the situation.

What in the ever-loving fuck should he do next?

Chapter 19

What Just Happened.

Sumner, Susan, and Kristen were stunned.

Their first lead and all the evidence contained within Kimsey's computer was gone. Just like that, in the blink of an eye.

As they began processing what had happened, Michael cleared his throat, the signal for, "Ahem. Please look at me, I'm trying to get your attention."

All three turned, where they discovered Michael standing, a power cord dangling from his left hand.

Kristen realized what happened first. "Holy crap... did you?"

Michael smiled and flicked his eyebrows proudly.

Susan caught on second, with Sumner a split-second later third place.

(Which, for the record, still got him on the podium.)

"When I saw your name, I knew she was watching us through the webcam, which meant she had control of the computer, so I grabbed the plug," Michael explained. "When I saw everything was about to be deleted, I pulled it."

"I guess we're lucky Kimsey didn't use a laptop," Susan sighed in relief.

"Yup," Michael acknowledged. "No battery backup on this."

"You know those times in movies where there's an inappropriate celebratory kiss because the mood is so joyous?" Kristen asked. "That's what this is."

She paused.

"But I'm not kissing you," Kristen concluded.

Michael laughed.

"That was goddamn good thinking," Sumner proclaimed, a tone of genuine impress in his voice.

"Thank you," Michael said, following that with, "I'll be putting in for a raise soon."

Sumner rolled his eyes, but did so while smiling. The kid's quick thinking really saved the day, and that deserved to be acknowledged.

"So..." Susan began. "What happens when we turn it back on?"

"She'll be angry," Kristen explained, "but it'll boot up. I doubt any files will be lost."

"What about the wipe Cassandra was executing?" Susan continued. "That's what I mean. Even if that didn't go through, won't she be able to assume control again once we turn it back on?"

"Nope," Kristen explained, still giddy because of Michael's reflexes and foresight. "Once we get this thing out of here and to our offices, we'll be fine. If it's not connected to the internet, Cassandra can't get at it, and since we have password protected Wi-Fi at the office, it can't automatically connect."

Kristen waited a beat, then switched gears.

"I doubt she was able to implement the factory reset in time. And, you know what? We have our ways of getting at computers that have been wiped, so I think we're good. And I think we owe Michael a high-five."

"Just not a kiss," he countered with a smile.

"Just not a kiss," Kristen confirmed, nodding and smiling herself.

"OK," Sumner began, bringing things back into the realm of professionalism. "What does this tell us?"

"Well," Kristen said thoughtfully, "we can assume she has, or had, control of all the computers being used by The 100. Those we know of, and any remaining. I bet... I have no proof of this, but I bet she probably used them as a network to hide her identity."

"How does that work?" Michael asked.

"OK..." Kristen said, and then paused. Her eyes drifted upwards—the act of a person trying to recall a memory, or searching for the easiest way to explain something to a novice.

After landing on a mental path, Kristen jumped in.

"The Russian hackers became known to the public because of the 2016 election, but we had people on them for years at that point," she began.

"There was a program, Gameover Zeus, that did what I'm describing. Consider the internet a chessboard. When Gameover Zeus took over a computer, it turned that computer into a pawn. The King was a hacker known only as Lucky12345, and he hid behind all the other computers—all the pawns. When anyone tried to trace anything to Lucky12345, they'd get lost in a web of the front-line computers. Instead of a trace going to the source, it would just bounce around all the dummy computers. Like an electronic hall of mirrors at a carnival. Does that make sense?"

Michael looked to Susan, who seemed very focused in her attempt to follow along.

"Sort of?" Michael said, hesitantly.

"OK…" Kristen tried, again. "Cassandra reaches out to someone. That's a peer-to-peer interaction. One-to-one, right? That person becomes a member of The 100, and Cassandra takes over the computer. You still have a linear back-and-forth. Then another member joins, and you have a triangle, then another person, and another—as those computers become inter-connected, they mask the location of Cassandra. Now instead of peer-to-peer, a linear interaction, you have a web of computers all hiding the location of one another. Tracing anything back to Cassandra will be exceedingly difficult."

"But not impossible," Sumner interjected, picking up on her last two words.

"No," Kristen said. "Not impossible, but if we find the first computer infected, that would help."

"With a smallish, 100-computer network, that shouldn't be too difficult, right?" Susan said hopefully.

"Two problems," Kristen explained, turning her attention to Susan. "What if the first computer infected is owned by the last person on the list?"

Susan muttered "Shit" under her breath.

"And we're assuming Cassandra limited herself to these specific computers. If it's an expansive program, it might have branched out to people not on the list. Friends and relatives of people on the list… co-workers…"

"Double shit," Susan said, this time loudly. "Wait, didn't I see this somewhere?"

"Do you watch Silicon Valley?" Michael asked. "This sounds like a version of what happened on there with refrigerators."

"Refrigerators?" Susan was genuinely confused.

"It was hilarious," Michael explained. "Trust me."

"If we had the time," Kristen said, returning things back to center, "we could treat it like a disease. Like we're searching for an antibiotic, so we purposely infect a computer and see how the malware works..."

Kristen looked frustrated as she trailed off.

"But that's if we had years and were watching a syndicate of criminals draining bank accounts or blackmailing corporations," she eventually concluded.

"Yeah," Sumner said, frustration clear in his voice. "We're a little more pressed for time here, what with people dying and all."

Sumner had been looking out a window when he spoke, but a second after realizing what he'd just said, he turned his attention to Kristen.

"That wasn't meant as an attack on you," he apologized. "Sorry."

Kristen nodded. She hadn't been offended.

"OK," Sumner concluded. "Let's pack this up and get it into Richardson's safe zone back at the office. She has Sherlocking to do, and the two of you have to get to finding out if there's any connections between anyone who's acted so far."

Susan didn't like the sound of that. It meant the real side of any investigation was about to begin: interviews. It was time to talk to anyone and everyone who had ever sneezed near a member of The 100. The questions were monotonous, and never-ending.

- "Did you notice anything unusual about him before he snapped?"
- "Was he spending more time online?"
- "Interacting with friends and family less?"
- "Did he ever mention..." followed by the name of every member of The 100 they knew of, with Cassandra's on top.

Gah, she sighed internally. *Why couldn't FBI work be like it is on TV and in the movies?*

Chapter 20

Recalibration

Josh allowed himself a moment of anger, and then went back to planning. By the time he was sleepy enough to go to bed, he was so over being upset with himself that he even had a good night's sleep.

The next morning, he cleaned up the shards of coffee mug and gave the floor a decent (if not meticulous) scrubbing. The wall? That was another matter. That stain had set, and there was no point in going after it with a washcloth or even fretting over it.

Josh discovered that, on the plus side of things, Cassandra had identified the three agents with Kristen Richardson. Gordon Sumner, director of the Kansas City office, Susan Chamberlain, a veteran with an impressive list of FBI accomplishments all her own, and neophyte Michael Godwin.

Having their names meant Cassandra could begin working the angles on each of them in search of a weak spot.

With his anger under control and the outburst banished from his mind, Josh went through a checklist of what was taken care of, and what needed completed. On the taken care of side of things, he confirmed payment for the pre-cruise actors. These were a mix of men and women given the role of "other winners."

Turned out you really could find anything online. He'd read about the guy who'd gotten drunk and purchased a yak on Amazon, but was still impressed when he discovered a site offering starving artists up as warm bodies to liven up parties. No wonder traditional shopping malls were going out of business.

The "party guests" were actors looking to make a few bucks while between gigs. Sometimes they were hired by groomsmen to crash a wedding
reception and liven things up, and Josh even found a description offering
mourners for an unpopular person's funeral. It was like hiring a clown for
your kid's birthday party, only without the makeup, oversize shoes, or eventual therapy costs.

(Given the trauma clowns inflict upon children.)

All these people had to know was two things: their role was that of "contest winner." They'd won a party on a yacht and were supposed to mingle
with the other winners. They could create any backstory they wanted: *I'm a
teacher, but at night I'm a stripper and no one was any the wiser… until the father of one
of my students saw me on the pole.*

Anything they wanted to dream up was fine. They just needed to seem
genuine, so the real winners wouldn't suspect anything was amiss.

The second bit of information was the big one: they were expressly for-
bidden from drinking any alcohol. The agent had it put in the contract: if a
bottle of alcohol is even seen in your hands, you don't get paid.

Josh had purchased a dozen of these actors to be extra "winners."

It was all for the appearance of normalcy. Ten sleazy dudes showing up
and being the only people on the boat would look suspicious. Josh had to
keep things on the up and up, after all.

He had also hired a few actors to play deckhands, and even several servers. Josh himself would be donning the Captain's uniform. He'd picked out
a head-to-toe outfit, but after trying it on realized the cap was a little over
the top and decided not to wear it.

The only thing he hadn't hired were actual caterers. Or a bartender. If
there were professional caterers onboard, then the food and drink would be
watched. Josh didn't want that; he made sure that all edibles and alcohols
would be delivered, designed nicely to the eye, and then left alone.

Before that start of the celebration, Josh would make his additions to the
beer he'd ordered. Each bottle would be opened, and then Josh would drop
a dose of Flunitrazepam—more commonly known as Rohypnol, and even
more commonly known as a roofie, the date rape drug—into each bottle.
They would all then be set in ice, ready for consumption.

That was the joy of targeting men: you could hoodwink them a little more easily. Women knew: *never accept an open drink at a bar or party. You don't know what someone put in it.*

But men?

Their radar was less powerful. They didn't sense danger, because to do so would shame their ego: *I'm a tough guy. No one can take advantage of me.*

If you set out an ice chest full of beer, each one pre-opened for convenience? Sure, one or two might grumble about that being a good way for the beer to go flat. But they weren't going to suspect something had been slipped inside it.

And if they weren't too into alcohol, Josh had several syringes full of liquid Flunitrazepam. If it came down it, he'd straight up jab someone and inject them.

If they put up a fight, all he had to do was lock himself in the bridge until the drug took effect.

Which, considering he'd made each dose high enough to knock down a 400-pound animal, wouldn't take long.

Josh did the math: best case scenario, everyone had a beer or two and fell asleep. Worst case scenario, he had to hit a couple guys forcefully.

Looking everything over, Josh had an initial crowd of thirty people celebrating on the yacht: twenty actors, and ten winners. Another five actors would work as pretend deckhands, and every hired hand would drift away slowly.

Josh had staggered their departure times. Some left at 9:15 PM, a couple more at 9:40, and the last few would leave around 10:35 PM, when the actual "winners" should have enough booze (and drugs) in their system to overlook the fact they were the only ones left.

After that?

Well, then things would get fun.

Josh would unmoor the yacht, float down into the bay, and beyond that was the ocean. When the ten "winners" finally woke up, they'd learn their fate, and the world at large would see the cherry on top of his power to the people sundae known as The 100.

The thought made Josh smile.

But only for a moment. Then Josh returned his attention to the task at hand and tried to imagine what other problems might arise before the final night.

The FBI knew Cassandra had control of the computers, which was problematic. They might be able to trace everything to her. In reality, that sort of search took months, but he had to be prepared for anything.

Which is why, even if they found her lightning-quick, they'd bust down the door of a vacant apartment in the Bronx.

That would probably throw them for a loop. A super-computer, sitting in an empty apartment, just doing its thing, connected to the fastest internet possible.

Josh was also slightly—ever-so-slightly—worried about piloting the yacht.

It wasn't the biggest boat out there—it had only cost him $2 million, and in the world of $65 million super yachts, that wasn't much.

Josh chuckled; the idea he found the thing by Googling "super yacht" amused him. It also made him a mix of angry and depressed. $65 million, for a boat. Imagine the good you could do with that money. The schools you could build. The children you could vaccinate...

The thoughts made his temperature rise, and he shifted his attention back to practice: had he put enough time in behind the wheel? Thankfully, technology—automation specifically—meant that steering a yacht was like playing a video game. You set course, pushed a button, and a navigation system did most of the work. All you had to do was gently nudge the thing left and right—or port and starboard, if we're being snotty—and the thing would practically sail itself.

Plus, it wasn't like taking your learner's permit onto the autobahn; he'd lazily drift toward the sea on a mostly empty river.

Sure, he could have chartered a boat and saved money, but that would have been a logistical nightmare. You can't tell a rental company, *no need for a captain or crew; I'll be flying solo on this one.*

By owning the yacht, he was in charge of the personnel. Or, as the case would have it, the lack thereof.

Josh would play Halloween and put on a captain's coat. He'd learned how to pilot the yacht on YouTube. It was insane how many instructional videos there were. Not just for yachting, but everything. Need to install a garbage disposal? Look it up. Want to put on a bow tie? YouTube'll teach you.

Anyone could learn anything today, which meant it was slightly surprising that society as a whole seemed to be getting dumber. You had all the world's information at your fingertips, and yet ignorance was championed as a virtue, and intellectualism was frowned upon or considered elitist.

Well, he wouldn't have to worry about such things for much longer.

Chapter 21

Four More

In the time since Matthew Kimsey's bowing out of The 100, four others hadn't been as squeamish.

In Miami, three real estate agents banded together and created a bank. The idea was: they'd sell a property, then loan the buyer the money needed for their mortgage. Smart, right? Well, they didn't really implement that particular business plan. No, they used the institution like their own personal piggy bank. The executives loaned *themselves* money, and then didn't repay said loans. This caused the bank to "fail," which meant the federal government—or, more specifically, taxpaying citizens, because that's who the government gets its cash from—had to bail them out. That meant the executives—the real estate agents who had founded the bank—won twice. They kept the money they loaned themselves, and then got a bailout, doubling their take.

That was too much for Edward Koch, who had lost everything trying to break into the Florida real estate market. He'd invested his life savings into starting an agency, so when a plucky young investigative reporter uncovered the bank hoax, Edward took out two of the three who profited before expiring himself.

(Edward had been en route to kill the third agent when a squad car lit up his rollers behind him. Instead of getting into a high-speed chase or taking chances, he pulled over to the side of the road and put his gun in his mouth. In his 'goodbye cruel world' video, Edward did state that he was hoping to take out all three, but that if he even nailed one to the cross, it'd be worth it. Having eliminated two left him feeling accomplished enough to end it when the police got involved.)

Stuart Walde watched his mother give everything she had to a prosperity evangelist. The minister was a small-time huckster—he had a show on local cable access outside of Mobile, Alabama. With every broadcast he preached the gospel of wealth; send him money, and Jesus would return that cash tenfold to the sender.

(Amen.)

Stuart's mom had drained her bank account hoping to buy her way out of poverty.

When his doctor found a spot on Stuart's lung, he decided to go out in a blaze of glory. Six to eight months slowly dying of cancer? Oh, hell to the no. Stuart grabbed the evangelist, forced him to open his personal safe, took him up in his single-engine crop duster, and made the evangelist watch as Stuart dumped a laundry sack of twenties over the Pleasant Hills mobile home community.

That's where his mother lived, and it infuriated Stuart that desperate people were always targeted by predators.

Once the sack was empty, Stuart nose-dived the plane into the Gulf of Mexico. When the bodies were recovered, the evangelist had a look of pure terror etched across his face. A pilot-induced plane crash wasn't the way he saw himself shuffling off this mortal coil.

Speaking of mobile home communities, Sean Poupard was in his early twenties when he decided to leave his parent's basement.

He didn't have enough money to buy a house, he didn't want to throw money away renting an apartment, and the availability of condominiums in his area was nonexistent. Which left a mobile home as one of his few remaining options.

Sean knew there was a certain stigma to living in a trailer park, but he also knew that life was what you made of it. If he had his own space and a little freedom, then the public perception of folks who lived in trailers didn't matter a whit.

Unfortunately, Sean's upbeat attitude didn't extend itself to thoroughly reading the contracts he was signing. Sean didn't realize what Ray Kroc figured out when building his McDonald's empire: own the land. Sure, Sean had a nice mobile home, but within several years the rent for the plot it was on skyrocketed. Sean fell behind in his payments and couldn't find a way out of his agreement.

Then he saw an exposé on mobile home communities.

Turns out, getting renters under their thumb was what many trailer park owners did. They'd bring in the desperate under questionable pretenses, raise the rent, foreclose on the land and kick the tenant out of their home, then resell it to the next unsuspecting victim.

Sean was angry, and he let the world know via Twitter. Someone deserved to pay. One day, a message appeared in his inbox from a woman who agreed with him: *someone did deserve to pay, but if Sean didn't do it, who would?*

So Sean went after the owner of his mobile home community with a baseball bat.

(Cassandra had suggested using ether, but Sean was into tactile pleasures, even if he wasn't familiar with the word tactile.)

Sean hit the owner several times, nearly knocking him unconscious. Then he used zip ties to bind the man's hands and feet, threw him in the back of his car, and drove the two of them to a set of train tracks.

The 10:15 freight out of Blackwell, Oklahoma, had just turned the bend when Sean parked his car on Peckham Road. By the time the headlights of the train reached Sean's stopped vehicle, it was too late for the engineer to stop.

The wreckage scattered 125 yards in every direction.

Sean filmed the oncoming train as it barreled down upon them and broadcasted it live on YouTube. The website removed the footage as quickly as they could, but by then it was too late. People worldwide had downloaded and saved copies of the footage, assuring the infinite life of the event online.

Finally, in Connecticut, a man named Brian Lowry pulled the pin on a grenade, opened the passenger door of a car, got in, closed the door, and opened his hand.

The car belonged to an executive at a student loan company.

Lowry had parked a few slots over and timed things perfectly. When the executive walked out of his place of business, Lowry got out of his car dressed his best in a Kenneth Cole Reaction suit. The executive probably didn't even look twice in Lowry's direction. Why would he? Normal-looking dude wearing a suit? That's not a threat.

Lowry casually walked toward the executive's car, head down, ostensibly staring at his phone like your average every-day American would. When the executive double-tapped his key fob, Lowry was in the perfect position to jump into the car a split-second later.

The executive had been too stunned to even react. Three seconds later, the explosion blew out all the windows and set off alarms on every car in a sixty-foot radius.

The executive in question had been profiled on a podcast investigating fraud; his company had a government contract and was in charge of helping people in debt navigate their student loans. The problem, however, is that the company was listed on the NYSE. That meant it needed to be profitable in order for its share price to go up, and the only way to be profitable when dealing with people in debt is to keep them in debt.

Instead of helping, customers were ignored. Advisors who could keep incoming calls to under seven minutes were given bonuses. Keeping call times down meant that anyone calling in for assistance received none.

The company refused to process applications for the Federal Student Loan Forgiveness Program. That program was designed to both reduce debt and increase public service. If you used your degree for public service—say a teacher or police officer—and you made regular payments on your student loans for ten years, at the end of those ten years your loans were forgiven.

The investigative podcast discovered that over 30,000 people who had applied for the program were eligible for debt forgiveness. In the course of a decade, the company processed 96 applications.

That left 29,904 pissed off people, and Brian Lowry was one of them.

It was actually a tweet that sent him over the edge. One day, while scrolling through his feed, he saw a tweet going viral.

The company in charge of his loan had posted, "We made it to the Fortune 500 list!!" A reply was catching everyone's attention: "Nothing like seeing your student loan company gloating about record profits while you can't pay rent."

Cassandra found Lowry in one of the many chat rooms dedicated to preventing suicide because of overwhelming debt. When Cassandra suggested, "If you're gonna do it, don't go out alone," Lowry listened.

"My act is a middle finger to anyone who profits off the unfortunate," he said in his video.

Naturally, the media loved it all.

Every 24-hour news channel saw a ratings bump, and websites dedicated to the latest information saw traffic shoot up by leaps and bounds.

Pundits pounded their fists in condemnation, and there were nightly debates on the merits of it all. Shows full of talking heads had pro-and-con people yelling at one another, further ratcheting up the drama and hype. Should The 100 be praised? Condemned? One side said they were heroes, the other called them criminals.

"Look at the difference between a mass shooter and these people," a commentator would argue. "They're surgical, not indiscriminate."

"What about Freddy Broe, shooting into the city through glass? He could have killed someone!" was always the counter-point.

And just as things got interesting: *We'll be right back, after a word from our sponsors.*

(Nothing got in the way of a commercial, after all.)

Then there were the copycats, and those who used The 100 as an excuse to unleash their inner asshole. Road rage incidents that once would have ended with shouting now turning into fistfights. The police would eventually arrive, and both parties would claim they were trying to make the world a better place, just like The 100. They were helping by beating the crap out of a "shitty driver."

The only problem, naturally, was that each participant believed they were in the right, and that the other person was the one ruining society for everyone else.

Everyone had an axe to grind, and The 100 gave people an excuse to sharpen the blade.

Chapter 22

Phone Calls and Paper Trails

"This is what happens when an idea goes too far," Sumner observed, looking over the daily reports. "The road to hell and so-called good intentions."

"I wish one of them would take out a robocall center," Susan mused wistfully. "I think I'm up to eight spam calls a day."

"Unfortunately," Michael said, a slight tone of disgust in his voice, "those work. If people weren't out there falling for scams, your phone would stop ringing."

Susan sighed wearily. She understood where Michael was coming from. The thing about being a member of law enforcement was that you saw the worst side of people. The criminals showed their lack of empathy for humanity in general, and humanity in general showed its inability to sense danger.

A quote from one of her training instructors flashed across her mind: "In life, you're either the fucker, or the fuckee. Which one do you want to be?"

Susan decided she didn't want to be either. She wanted to be a protector; she wanted to protect those who couldn't protect themselves. Which made this case all the more interesting. Here, the wolves were being attacked by the sheep. Fuckees had decided enough was enough, and they were pushing back against the fuckers.

But did that justify their actions?

She was jostled from her thoughts by Michael, who said, "Maybe we should be happy we've slowed from what could have been a torrent to a trickle. The first batch went bang-bang-bang, one right on top of the next. Four in two days seems almost manageable given how this started."

"I bet that was planned," Susan countered. "This way, the fear is perpetual. If people believe there are 90 suicide bombers still out there, never knowing where and when the next one will strike... shit, that'll keep you on your toes if you think you deserve retribution."

"Wouldn't it be hilarious if there were only twenty of them?" Michael laughed. "That'd be one way to keep the fear running. You get to number twenty, and everyone keeps waiting for the other eighty to do their thing, and it never happens."

The duo was back in Kansas City, having interviewed anyone in Peoria who felt they had something to say about Matthew Kimsey.

Generally, when a crime took place, talking to people allowed the FBI (or police, or whoever was doing the sleuthing) to answer questions: whose story kept changing? Who had a grudge? Who knew a little too much about what happened, even though that information hadn't been made public?

After the fact, interviews allowed them to build a character profile. When chasing a lead, those questions (and subsequent answers) gave you the most likely suspect. When headed to trial, the transcripts explained how they found the guilty party.

The problem with The 100 was that they gave up everything in their video. Identity, motive, and method. Which meant Susan and Michael had no real reason to talk to neighbors, co-workers, or the usual onslaught of anyone and everyone who claimed to have insight into a criminal mind. But, they had to do the interviews anyway. Heaven forbid anything be done outside standard procedure.

If there was one thing Susan didn't relish about her job, it was having to talk to someone who went to grade school with a suspect. Those old acquaintances went on at length about how they "always knew something was wrong with little Timmy." In reality, they wanted to feel important, and dealing with each one of those so-called helpers stymied any actual investigative work that needed done.

Once in-person interviews ended, Susan and Michael started taking phone calls.

"Considering how difficult it is to get your average, everyday American to do anything," Sumner had explained, "Imagine how many people you'd have to talk to in order to find 100 to do something insane. How many people did she have to target to get 100 takers? A thousand? Ten thousand? Your ROI isn't going to be high; it'd be like winning the Powerball every time you found someone willing to commit a murder-suicide. Even people at their wits' end usually pull out at the last minute. I bet Cassandra was dropping fishing lures into ponds everywhere."

His point was that there could be any number of people out there who had interacted with Cassandra—people who had passed on her offer to die at their own hands while taking someone "deserving" with them.

Sumner wanted to hear what those people had to say, so the FBI set up a call center. Like the auditions for American Idol, flunkies handled the initial onslaught of unwashed masses.

"How do you know it's a person behind it all?" one caller asked. "What if it's aliens?"

Those folks would receive a generous "Thanks for your input," usually accompanied by an eye-roll.

"Could be legit," Michael joked. "Berkowitz took advice from his dog, right?"

Susan shook her head wearily. Michael's joke hit too close to home; people would use any reason possible to call in with a tip.

When a screener heard a credible story, the call was passed off to an agent. At one point, Susan asked Michael if this is what he thought an investigation would be like.

"If you'd asked me that as a kid," he answered, "I would have said no. TV makes everything look like rundowns and shootouts. Once I started in the academy, though, I realized that most investigations involve talking to people and seeing if they trip up and change their story."

Susan nodded resignedly.

"The sad truth is, too many criminals are caught and too many cases closed simply because someone flipped," she explained. "Or we hear from an anonymous source, or someone walks through our door and gives us information we didn't previously have. Without that, many cases go cold."

"So we were lucky to land Kimsey," Michael concluded.

"Very," Susan agreed. "Even if he hasn't provided us with all that much to date."

Between what the screeners determined "legitimate" calls, Susan and Michael examined the motives of the first of The 100. The idea that crime is personal weighed heavy on the investigation, and they were determined to figure out whether or not Cassandra had a specific reason to set these wheels in motion.

"If you find a victim that's been stabbed twenty times," Susan said while eyeballing a file, "then it's like a bad movie sequel, *this time it's personal.*"

"Who is Cassandra *really* angry with?" Michael countered. "Because the first five are pretty disparate. Hard to glean where the personal grudge is there."

"I know," Susan sighed in response. "If it were all executives, that'd be one thing, but these..." Susan put down the file she'd been reading and picked up another. "They're just all over the place."

"There's been a wild card or two in there," Michael began, "but for the most part, everyone has faced loss."

Michael was silent a moment. When he picked up again, it sounded as if he were speaking to himself, the way one might when working through a problem.

"They faced heartbreak. Not teenage, 'oh, I got dumped, poor me' sadness, but actual sorrow. What's felt after having lived through tragedy."

"Great," Susan said sarcastically. She was looking over an information sheet, not really paying attention to Michael's tone. "Our main suspect is someone who has had something bad happen to them. That's, what? Everyone on the planet?"

Michael casually tossed the file he'd been reading onto his desk and exhaled tiredly, causing Susan to look up.

"Just trying to keep from gathering moss," he said.

Susan softened her tone in apology. "I know. I wasn't trying to shit on your point. I'm just frustrated."

Michael smiled as he waved her off. "Don't worry, you didn't hurt my feelings. I may be a Millennial, but my momma didn't raise no snowflake."

Susan laughed.

"Seriously, though," she said. "We've got nothing, and it pisses me off."

"We've got..." Michael began shuffling through sheets of paper on his desk, finally settling on one and picking it up. "Bonnie McClane, a neighbor of Kimsey's who said she knew he was up to no good, because, and I do quote, 'he thought people came from monkeys.'" Michael shook his head as he set the note back down. "Thank you, screeners, for letting that call through."

"They're fielding a ton of calls," Susan admonished lightly. "A few crazies are going to make it past them."

"I know, I know. On the bright side, at least the crazies break up the monotony."

With that exchange complete, each returned to their busywork.

As Susan and Michael alternately fielded calls and tried finding ties between members of The 100, Sumner handled the press. Sumner was the buffer between the big dogs in D.C. and the public's demand for information.

It was a position he accepted begrudgingly.

Younger people—Millennials and Xennials—lived to be in front of the camera, not Gen X. YouTube personalities, Instagram influencers... Sumner was too old for all that and felt his time could be better used working cases, not smiling for the cameras.

(Not that he actually smiled when being interviewed.)

Unfortunately, Sumner knew that raising awareness was an important part of any investigation. The more people you reached, the more likely it was a random John Q. Public might realize they had information that could help.

Sumner came across as gruff, but respectable, when dealing with reporters. His favorite responses were, "I have no comment on that," "We are attacking every angle of the investigation," and either "yes" or "no." While many reporters grew frustrated by their inability to get a decent answer out of him, the public at large appreciated his no-bullshit attitude.

Kristen Richardson, meanwhile, quietly and methodically delved into Kimsey's computer. She examined the malware that had allowed Cassandra to control it from afar, and more importantly, read each and every message between the two.

Crimes of a serial nature always have a pattern to them, Kristen thought, her eyes narrowing as she studied Cassandra's words. *What am I missing?*

Kristen opened a spreadsheet and started labeling the back-and-forths between Kimsey and Cassandra. She looked over the exchanges with a jeweler's lens and took meticulous notes.

Cassandra had groomed Kimsey over the course of several months.

It began, just as he had confessed, in an online support group. Kimsey was a unique combination of depressed and angry, and Cassandra had been a sympathetic ear.

She's like a bad therapist, Kristen noted. *She never really says anything important; she just keeps him going with a version of, "And how does that make you feel?"*

Luckily for her, Kimsey had a focus for his ire: Jessica Decker and her bank. Once that door cracked, Cassandra opened it wide. Jessica Decker and the bank became the focus of Cassandra's responses. If Kimsey ever tried to sway from it, Cassandra brought it back around.

"It's not your fault," Cassandra told him. "You did everything right. They took advantage of you."

They, Kristen noted. *They took advantage of you. Keeping the focus external never allows a person to come to peace with their past. He couldn't move through his problem with her continually reminding him it wasn't his fault.*

It was around hour nine and coffee four when she realized two things. First, that she wasn't going to be able to fall asleep that night unless she knocked it off with the caffeine.

The second revelation seemed so obvious, Kristen felt a little silly it wasn't the first thing she noticed. As she read the messages, a thought began nagging at the back of her mind. Kristen couldn't quite figure out what was wrong, but something was... *off.*

A puzzle was being pieced together in her mind, and on her third time through the messages, the incomplete picture began taking shape. When the idea hit her, it came crashing down like a ton of bricks.

"You've got to be kidding me," Kristen muttered to herself.

A coworker looked up from his computer two desks over and Kristen waved him off, slightly embarrassed.

Hey now, everyone talks to themselves sometimes, she thought as the man shook his head and returned to his work.

Kristen eyed her empty coffee mug and drummed her fingers on the desk in nervous excitement. She liked the path she was on, and didn't want to quit now.

OK, she decided. *Half coffee, half milk, no sugar.*

One more run through the messages would either leave her feeling confident enough to share her idea with the team, or throw it into question and force her to go home and start with fresh eyes tomorrow.

Ninety minutes and one bathroom break later, Kristen clicked open a new tab and pulled up her email.

I have something you need to see, Kristen typed up. *Second floor conference room, 8am tomorrow?*

The email was short, to the point, and hopefully eyebrow-raising.

Kristen clicked send, and within one-minute Sumner had responded.

Burning some midnight oil? he replied to everyone. *I've got a meeting at eight. Push yours to eight-thirty and I'm there.*

Susan confirmed five minutes after that, and Michael was last to chime in the next morning at 5:00 AM.

Now she had to pitch her idea, and cross her fingers they didn't laugh her out of the room.

Chapter 23

Examinations & Ideas

"I don't think Cassandra is a person."

Kristen was straight and to the point, and after making her declaration, gave her three-person audience a moment to digest the information. Even though that wasn't the message they had expected to hear, no one at the meeting was shocked. If anything, they were curious.

"OK," Sumner said, nodding slowly. "I'm listening."

Kristen took half a beat to gather her thoughts, and then gave Sumner, Susan, and Michael summation packets she'd put together.

"So," Kristen began, "two things sent me down this path: response time, and language."

Michael and Susan began sifting through the packets in front of them; Sumner kept his focus on Kristen. The material could be used to convince the higher-ups if need be, but right now, the proverbial horse's mouth was speaking, and he wanted to absorb every word.

"You remember how quickly Cassandra wrote back when we were in Peoria?" Kristen asked. "It was, what? A minute? Two, tops? That's how every single interaction between them took place. It doesn't matter what time of day Kimsey wrote to her. Noon, midnight, 3:00 AM, Cassandra's response came within two minutes."

"That just means we could be dealing with an insomniac," Sumner countered.

"True," Kristen agreed. "Or even a team of people responding for one account. I considered that, too, but I don't think it's either of those things. I think Cassandra is a computer. A super-computer. Artificial intelligence, basically."

Michael was slightly confused.

"Are you saying she's like the Terminator?" he asked.

"I hear where you're coming from, but no," Kristen responded. "We're getting into gray areas here, because the technology is so new. I think we're dealing with sentient, artificial intelligence, which is basically a self-aware entity that can make critical decisions and judgment calls in the same manner as a person, only without the humanity. I think Cassandra is a tool. She didn't self-evolve to this, she was programmed specifically to find, organize, and instruct The 100. Which means there *is* a person behind this."

"Cross Skynet off the suspect list," Susan muttered, causing Michael to chuckle.

"How did you reach this conclusion?" Sumner asked, either ignoring or not hearing Susan's joke.

"Her language," Kristen began, leafing through her own packet. "Look at the exchanges. They don't feel right."

"We go off data here, Kristen," Sumner admonished. "As a computer scientist, you of all people should appreciate that."

"If there's one thing I trust," Susan offered, "it's intuition."

Kristen shot Susan a glance of appreciation.

"I get that," Kristen continued, addressing Sumner. "I really do. But the language is too similar to be a group of people responding off one account. If you had someone answering for Cassandra at seven in the morning, and another person doing so at midnight, there'd be certain variances in the language. These don't read like that. And, as said, they're too awkward to be a person in general. Have you ever called customer service and gotten a robot pretending to be human?"

They all nodded. If orange was the new black, then "dealing with a computer pretending to be human" was the new "dealing with a call center in India that was pretending to be in Ohio."

"That's what each and every one of these messages reads like: trying too hard to sound natural. The messages don't read as 'real,' for lack of a better term. They're always too... proper. There's no slang in them, no emotion."

"What about someone that's ELS?" Michael asked. "Isn't the site originating from the Ukraine?"

"It could be," Kristen responded. "Or, more likely, whoever's behind it is masking the country of origin and just letting us think it's coming from overseas."

Sumner retained the skeptical look in his eyes, but the tone of his voice changed as he asked, "OK, say Cassandra is lifeless. How does this kind of system work?"

"Well," Kristen began, "you can buy software that will auto-respond to anything. Phone calls, online chats with a support representative, or email."

"Christ," Sumner muttered. "It's like a souped-up version of that old goddamn paperclip offering to help you write a letter, isn't it?"

"It's a genetically modified version of that paperclip on steroids, times a million," Kristen confirmed.

"Which brings us to the real questions," Sumner volleyed back. "Who has that kind of system? Is it readily available? Can just anyone buy it? If you think this is the path we're going down, what's our plan of attack?"

"To answer your second question first," Kristen said, "yes. It's readily available. But to carry on hundreds of conversations at one time, you'd need something good. Quality software. We're going to need to run buys on commercial-grade systems and see if anything odd stands out."

"Define odd," Susan interjected.

Michael leaned forward, indicating a desire to speak.

"Phone-related fraud is what I've been working in my time here," he began. "You look for who does, and who doesn't need this kind of software. If an insurance company buys an auto answer, it's because they're putting a call center out of business. What we're looking for is a business *without* a high call, or, in this case, email volume. We're looking for someone who, for a reason we can't figure out by glancing at their industry specs, wanted to own something like this."

"Why do you say a business?" Sumner asked, pointedly.

"Because," Michael responded, "I'm going to go out on a limb and guess the buyer didn't purchase anything as an individual, and I'm going to double down on that blackjack table with a bet he didn't use his real name or a legitimate company."

"If he did, though," Susan said, wishfully. "That'd be pure Beach Boys."

Michael's face scrunched in confusion.

"Wouldn't it be nice," Kristen explained, catching the reference.

Susan gave Kristen a quick thumbs up as Sumner continued.

"How prevalent would a system like this be?" he asked.

"Well, they don't sell like hotcakes," Kristen answered. "More like cigarettes. Decent numbers, but the number of buyers is smaller."

"Interesting analogy," Susan interjected.

"I do the best I can off the top of my head," Kristen said, moving her focus back to her packet. "Point is, yeah, they sell, but we should be able to cross off a ton of non-starters right at the top. Like Godwin said, insurance companies, credit card companies... ignore those for now. We're looking for one that stands out as odd."

"Which brings us back to Susan asking for a definition of odd," Sumner stated.

"Say a landscaping company," Michael interjected. "If we get a list of sales from the last year, and it has three insurance companies, one bank, and a landscaper, we're gonna question the landscaper."

Sumner nodded at Michael as Kristen pulled a sheet of paper from her folder.

"I've got a shortlist of the top companies that sell this kind of technology," she said, focusing on Susan and Michael. "You can start here, and then move into the smaller sellers."

"I bet he'd stick to big," Susan said while pulling the same sheet from her own folder. "Bigger company means more buyers, and therefore more anonymity."

"The future," Sumner said, looking over his own list. "Back in the day, you used to call customer support and get an actual person."

"Yeah," Michael laughed. "But that's before America took being dumb into overdrive."

Sumner, Kristen, and Susan all gave him a questioning look.

"Go ahead and call a couple businesses," Michael explained. "It'll give you great insight into where America stands IQ-wise. If you call DirecTV during football season, you'll hear 'Looking for tonight's game? Try channel 212, the NFL Network' during the hold music. So many people were calling customer support and asking for help instead of just looking for the game, that DirecTV decided to try and slow the flow of stupid to their reps."

"He's not wrong," Kristen agreed. "I called Verizon once and heard, 'Is your phone not powering up? Have you tried charging it?' I Googled that, and it actually made the news; people were clogging support techs with the most basic of problems, and Verizon wanted to head that off at the pass."

"Point is," Michael said, grateful Kristen had taken his back, "this falls right in line with what I said about Cassandra. The name is just a front. Cassandra is the computer, and the person behind that computer has an ego. Like the Cassandra of lore, he feels he has all the answers, and that he's being ignored."

Sumner mulled things over a bit before adding, "I don't disagree with anything you've said, but let's not discount the idea Cassandra still might be an actual person. A woman even."

"Returning to the software," Kristen interjected, "these systems are out there. We have to break down how many there are, and find out who's buying them."

"OK," Sumner continued. "I'm guessing there's no stock program that tells people to kill other people. Did our guy create it? Would writing a program like this take special skills? How many people could write a program like you describe, and is that someone we should be searching for? We have databases full of people we know like to infect computer systems with malware."

"It'd be difficult, but nothing tens of thousands of programmers couldn't do," Kristen responded. "If we start searching for the person who developed Cassandra, it could eat up a ton of resources and yield few results."

"Plus," Susan added, "since we've already had a hit in the Ukraine, this could be an international chase, and those things are ten times the pain in the ass than finding and arresting someone locally."

"Question," Sumner said, matter-of-factly. "Would this program be able to ID you and write to you directly?"

Kristen was confident in her reply, "One like this? No. We're dealing with something completely different. We know the webcam was turned on, and we found the malware used to control the computer remotely. Cassandra might have been programmed to figure out the identity of any person who sat at an infected computer, but the more likely scenario is that—"

"Cassandra's owner was watching us," Susan finished, the realization hitting her.

"Right," Kristen confirmed. "Knowing Kimsey failed at his task, and knowing we'd show up, whoever's behind this probably just sat and waited. And now there are probably files on anyone who walked by the camera."

"Files?" Michael asked.

"She's looking for a weak spot," Sumner explained. "Anything that can be used against one of our team in order to exploit them. People with tragedy in their past could be sympathetic to the cause, while anyone short on cash might take a bribe. Then that person could send Cassandra updates on what we're doing, or delete files off our computers... All it takes is one person to botch an investigation."

Sumner rubbed his eyes in frustration; he felt a migraine coming on.

"Which means," he continued. "I have to figure out who was in Kimsey's house and run a background check on all of them."

"Didn't we get those when we applied?" Michael asked.

"Yes," Sumner responded. "And that was it. One and done. You think we constantly monitor what all our employees are up to? This isn't the KGB. If anything has happened since the time they were hired and now, there's no guarantee we'll know about it. If someone's mom is in the hospital and they can't pay the bills, that's a shining beacon to anyone trying to bribe one of our ranks."

Sumner looked around the room.

"Anything any of you want to tell me now, just to get it out of the way?" he asked. "Any skeletons in your respective closets?"

There was a slight, somewhat awkward pause, then Susan chimed in.

"I once ordered a small french fry," she offered, mostly joking, "and they gave me a large, and I didn't point it out. I kept the upgrade and didn't pay for it."

Sumner nodded and laughed.

"You are forever the nun, Agent Chamberlain," he said. "Well, I've got my assignment, and you have yours."

A look of joy spread over Kristen's face for a moment, and then she quickly caught herself and tried to cover it with a look of neutral professionalism.

"It's OK to be happy, Richardson," Sumner told her. "You did good, and I'm buying your pitch." He turned to Susan and Michael. "Since we don't have anything more substantive to chase down, you two can stop fielding phone calls from crazies and start running down these companies. And you," he continued, turning back to Kristen. "Is there any way you can figure out *exactly* what kind of system we're looking for through Kimsey's computer?"

"That, unfortunately," Kristen lamented, "is highly unlikely."

Sumner nodded his disappointment.

"And thus, the fun part of investigative work begins," Susan said tiredly. "Paperwork and phone calls. I'm gonna get a cottage cheese ass."

"Have you tried a standing desk?" Kristen asked. "I love mine."

"I have an exercise ball I sit on at home," Michael said helpfully.

"You could look into one of those kneeling chairs, where your body weight leans forward against your knees and holds you in place," Kristen suggested.

"I like those," Michael said, possibly more excitedly than someone should be about a piece of furniture. "I had one in college. It really kept my lower back pain at bay."

It was all too much for Sumner, who cut in with, "This is the discussion we're having now?"

"It's a real condition," Susan explained.

"Fine," Sumner concluded. "Call me when there's a telethon, 5K, or gala for it. Until then, it's phone calls and paperwork."

"And cottage cheese ass," Susan added. "Sir."

Sumner rolled his eyes as he stood to leave, but Susan swore she caught a hint of smile on his face.

Chapter 24

Viral

Unsurprisingly, weareonehundred.com was one of the most popular websites on the internet.

People kept it open on another tab while working, and according to the analytics Josh had, diehards were refreshing the page every few minutes. They were all wondering: when is the next red question mark going to become an X? What would their story be? Who'd they take out?

Then everyone argued over the merits of it all. Were The 100 justified in their actions? Were they unsympathetic murderers? Everyone had an opinion. It was like a combination of Game of Thrones and reality TV.

Josh shook his head in amusement as he looked at the numbers; if only he could run ads on the site, he'd be rich!

Oh, wait. He was already rich.

Plus, anyone with common sense used an adblocker these days. Still, knowing the public interest was so high made Josh happy. This is exactly what he wanted: people in power shaking in their boots because the common man was engaged. Since the law wasn't protecting the fish from the sharks, the fish were standing up for themselves.

Do sharks even eat fish? Josh wondered. *Maybe just seals?*

He brushed the thought aside and focused on the task at hand. After the debacle with Kimsey's computer, Josh had doubled down his oversight of the remaining members of The 100. He was pleased to find many still wanted to go through with their task, and could tell when someone was waffling. A half-dozen cut off communication outright, meaning it was highly unlikely they would make the news.

So be it. He'd expected there'd be a few flakes.

Josh was curious, though. The FBI hadn't released a statement regarding his control of Kimsey's computer. Letting the public know about the malware might have pissed off those who remained in queue. It's one thing to wonder if you're being manipulated; it's another to actively know it. If you know you're being manipulated, you're more likely to opt out of whatever you've been told to do. Letting The 100 know Josh had control of their computers might have saved lives. Was that an oversight, or were they holding on to that information on purpose?

Whichever way it fell, it worked in Josh's favor, so he didn't dwell on it.

Now, when a member completed their task, Josh logged in and checked their computer. Three followed instructions and had sent their computer to electronic heaven. One had left his up and running; Josh wiped it remotely. He beat himself up a little for not handling things like that from the start, but life is only understood in the rearview. Live and learn, as they say.

Plus, he justified, it's not like he didn't have a ton on his plate already when dreaming this all up. It made sense he'd had a blind spot or two during setup.

Josh pushed back from his computer and stood up. He didn't enjoy being confined to the warehouse, but his discipline meant he could withstand it. The closest he came to the outside world was by running the course between here and the garage. Even though he had the route memorized, he still marked it with fluorescent paint.

Just to be safe, he thought.

In addition to his exit drill practice, Josh spent his spare time wondering. He daydreamed, and wondered: what was the FBI up to now? What had Agent Richardson gotten from Kimsey's computer, and what steps were they taking to track him down?

Josh leaned over and clicked his mouse; the monitors shifted. Instead of showing webcams from The 100—which was usually an empty room, unless the member was actually using their computer, that is—the exterior of his warehouse appeared. Cameras covered every angle of the surrounding neighborhood.

Ain't no one sneaking up on me, Josh mused.

Chapter 25

Breakthrough

Michael uncovered the first clue, even if he didn't realize it at the time.

It happened on the second day of paperwork, phone calls, and cottage cheese ass. Running down every company that had purchased auto-response software over the past few years was as tedious as they'd expected, and the ten-plus hours dedicated to eyeballing lists was already mind-numbing.

Susan and Michael split Kristen's list in two, and from there created a chart on a whiteboard. Companies were broken down into three categories: those that turned things over willingly, those who needed a nudge, and those that balked immediately and would require a court order to give a glimpse behind Oz's curtain.

"Not that we have anything to hide," their point of contact would explain. "But customer privacy is of utmost concern."

Even in the innocuous world of office supplies, some companies didn't trust the FBI to snoop around their client list.

Susan and Michael set up shop in a small conference room, turning it into their joint office. Doing so allowed them to toss ideas back-and-forth, and coordinate 'who's calling what company' more easily than sending constant emails to one another.

Several hours in on day two, Michael came across an investment bank on Wall Street.

It almost didn't make Michael's radar, but unlike, say, Goldman Sachs, he'd never heard of GGA Investments. It sounded small, like a boutique firm. A place not fielding phone calls, emails, or general inquiries from the masses.

Michael didn't think he really had a lead, exactly, but he took the time to Google the company and couldn't find anything. No webpage, no address, no phone number. According to the internet, GGA Investments didn't exist. They weren't listed on the NYSE, NASDAQ, or the Cboe BZX Exchange. Michael searched insurers and couldn't find a bond on GGA.

The only hit Michael got was a listing on a website, Custom Construction, out of New York City. GGA Investments was in their *Satisfied Clients & Testimonials* section. No testimonial existed, but Custom Construction listed GGA as a company they'd done exceptional work for. On a whim, Michael called them.

It took several holds and a transfer, but after several minutes he was told that a foreman currently out on a worksite probably did the GGA build. Did Michael want his cell number?

Michael did.

Again, not because his intuition had kicked in, but he was... curious. It was odd, and that's what they were looking for: something out of the ordinary.

Michael called the foreman, Kurt Stemig.

"Yeah," Kurt said, a cigarette-throaty tone to his voice. "I remember that build. They wanted to turn an abandoned warehouse into an entertainment center. Laser tag, I think. Built out the entire building and then nothing. Never opened. Don't know what happened to it, but I thought it was a bad idea all along. Wrong neighborhood. Our checks cleared, though, so we kept working. Ain't our place to tell anyone how to spend their money."

"Do you remember your point of contact with GGA," Michael asked.

"No..." Kurt responded thoughtfully, as if trying to bring a memory to the forefront of his mind. "Tell you the truth, they were the perfect client. Some of 'em nitpick every step of the way. They have an idea of what they want, and they want to tell you exactly how to do it, blueprints be damned. These GGA guys were all trust. They sat back and let us work."

"Who designed it? Was there an architect that gave you the design?"

"Hate to tell you, but that was all in-house, too. Client said 'gimmie this,' and we did the rest."

Kurt paused a moment.

"I think..." Kurt was hesitant. "If I remember correctly, this guy would show up at night, after we'd all left. If there were notes, they'd be there when we showed up the next day. But mostly we just got attaboys. Good job and such. No real bad stuff or 'change this' bullshit."

"Who received the initial call? Who might know the point of contact?"

"I don't think anyone did. They reached out to us for a quote, I think via email, and then a couple days later we had a check in our mailbox. I think that's the only reason I remember it. Ask me about a client from a month ago, I probably couldn't tell you who they were. But this one was different, so, yeah. I remember 'em."

Kurt's voice was the audible representation of a shrug.

"Who could tell me what bank that check came from?" Michael continued.

"I bet Janet can look it up." Kurt responded helpfully. "She's our secretary. Answers all the calls. You probably talked to her before getting to me."

"I think I did, thanks."

"I know you probably can't, but since you said you're FBI and all, can you tell me what you're looking for?"

"Unfortunately, no."

"Well shit. I was hoping it had to do with all that hullabaloo on the news."

"Nah," Michael said casually. "This is boring stuff. People using the internet to move money around in ways that cheats Uncle Sam of his fair cut."

"Which makes us working men pay more," Kurt said, disgust in his voice.

"That would be the case."

"Well, they didn't screw us. We got paid."

"Good on that," Michael said, trying to connect with Kurt in case he had to call him again later. "Thanks for your help. I'll be in touch if I think of anything else."

"OK," Kurt said, hanging up. It wasn't curt, it wasn't rude, it was just business. Talk was done; phone gets hung up.

Michael looked at the notes he had taken.

Was this really anything? It didn't have a feel to it, and Susan said she always trusted intuition.

Well, even if his gut wasn't telling him to follow the lead, it wasn't telling him to move on. There wasn't anything better to research, and it's not like he'd eventually call a place and they'd say, "Well shucks, you caught me. I'm behind it all."

"You look lost in thought," Susan said, bringing Michael out of his head.

"I am," Michael confirmed.

"Anything interesting?"

"I'm not sure."

Michael brought Susan up to speed with his discovery, even going so far as to downplay it as "probably nothing."

"Don't say 'probably,'" Susan cautioned. "You can say 'maybe,' but don't negate anything. If you ignore information, you'll ignore clues."

Michael nodded; that made sense. If he got into the habit of second-guessing himself, he'd become hesitant, and therefore inefficient.

"If you can figure out how the money moved between the investment firm and the construction company, do it." Susan continued. "Always follow the money. Even if it doesn't relate to what we're doing, it's still good experience for a future case."

With that, Susan went back to her list of companies, crossing off some and making notes by others.

Michael decided to call—he checked his notes—Janet. Couldn't hurt to find out how GGA paid their bills.

Janet was kind, but skeptical.

"Giving you an employee's company cell number is one thing," she cautioned. "Asking for a client's financial records is another. It's not that I'm doubting you, really, but in all honesty, *anyone* can just call and say they're an FBI agent. What proof do I have you are who you say you are?"

With that, Janet got the owner of Custom Construction, Justin Schroder, on the line. He agreed to do a video conference call.

"Just so I can get a look at who I'm talking to," Justin explained.

Only after Michael showed his badge, and frustratedly offered to walk a phone to the entrance of the building to show the FBI logo, did Justin agree that the call probably wasn't a ruse. And if Michael *was* faking, he was "doing a damn fine job of it."

After solidifying all credentials, Justin explained that all contact was done via email, and the email address used by GGA Investments was company owned.

"No Gmail for them," Justin said. "It was Kevin, underscore, Michael, at GGA investments dot com. GGA investments was all one word, too."

The checks came from an independent bank in Manhattan, Grassroots Financials.

Michael thanked Justin for his time and efforts, and before saying "goodbye" had already started Googling Grassroots Financials. Michael couldn't figure out if he was surprised nothing came up, or that it made perfect sense.

"This means we have a bank that doesn't exist," Susan said, digesting the information, "paying bills for an investment firm that doesn't exist."

"Pretty much," Michael confirmed.

"Which means that unless they both happened to go out of business, which does happen, they were fronts."

"Now we're speculating," Michael cautioned.

"Not really. If they'd been real and gone out of business, you'd have had hits for them online. Maybe a small news story about them going under or being bought out. The fact there's nothing, is something. Maybe not for our case, but something. Given that it's New York City, best bet is that it's mafia-related."

Michael was surprised. "Really?"

"We're no longer in the days of *The Godfather* or Jimmy Hoffa," Susan explained. "But yeah, they still do big business. We just don't hear about it, because MS-13 has a better publicist."

"So I should follow up on this?" Michael asked.

"Follow all leads," Susan said, an upbeat tone in her voice. "The lead you ignore could be Robert Frost's road."

"And that makes all the difference," Michael concluded. "Well, we don't have any addresses or phone numbers... but Kevin Michael at GGA investments existed at one time... Maybe Kristen can use her computing powers to run a trace on that? Archived websites, maybe."

"Maybe," Susan agreed. "And there's the warehouse itself. That's a lead."

"It is?"

"You have a dummy company financing a build for another dummy company. Whoever wanted that warehouse built out didn't want their name on it. Could be nothing, or hell, it could be someone going through a divorce trying to hide their assets. But it's sketchy, and sketchy is worth examining."

"What's next? Do I call our counterparts there and ask them to give a lookie-loo?"

"Sometimes yes, sometimes no," Susan began. "Handing off projects is how things get fumbled. It's easier and more cost-efficient to ask someone in New York to knock on that door, but taking action yourself means you know it's getting done. And it eliminates leaks."

"You just want to get out of the office again, don't you?" Michael laughed.

Susan half-shrugged, a smile on her face.

"There's a little 'column A, column B' there," she admitted.

"Do we just go ask if we can fly to New York and knock on a random door?" Michael asked.

"Not yet," Susan cautioned. "I have an idea."

"OK…"

Michael trailed off, expecting Susan to explain herself, but she had already picked up the phone. Not her cell phone, Michael noted with interest, the office phone. This was an internal call.

"Hey," Susan said when the line was answered. "It's Susan. Who's our contact at New York Gas and Electric?"

Susan grinned and winked at Michael. Her gesture said, *I'm on this*.

Whatever the answer was, it pleased Susan, because she scribbled a name and a number with her free hand, said, "Thanks. Appreciate it muchly," and hung up the phone.

"What's the address of the warehouse?" Susan asked, one hand already dialing the number she'd written down.

Michael slid a piece of paper her way as Susan put the phone back to her ear. Michael could hear the other end ringing, but not the other person's voice when they eventually answered.

"Hi John," Susan said politely. "Susan Chamberlain, Kansas City branch of the FBI. I understand you're our point of contact there."

Michael made note of her tone; most people in that situation would have inflected the final word, indicating a question: I understand you're our point of contact there? Susan had said it politely, but firmly. She was going in with authority. It was subtle, but people picked up on subtle unconsciously. Subtle is what defines most human interactions, in fact.

John must have confirmed the assertion, because seconds later Susan was reciting her badge number and a confirmation code for clearance. After everything was confirmed as kosher, Susan read the address, and started her pitch.

"I'm looking for energy usage," she stated. "Is the power on, and if so, how much are the using every month, and who's paying the bill?"

There was a pause as said information was looked up. Michael used the opportunity to mouth the question, "Is this legal?" to which Susan whispered back, "Public records."

After a few more exchanges, Susan thanked her New York Gas and Electric contact, John, and hung up the phone.

"You might shit your pants," she told Michael.

Michael looked at her expectantly, waiting for more.

"Let's see what we can sell the boss on," Susan told him, pushing her chair back from the table.

Michael stood and stretched. He had no clue what just happened, but he was damned curious.

Plus, even if they got shot down, getting off the phone and away from the desk for ten minutes made the walk over to Sumner's office worth it.

Chapter 26

Another of The 100

The bad news was that everyone was clean.

Cassandra hadn't found any dirt on agents Richardson, Godwin, or Chamberlain. And Sumner? He was a goddamn Boy Scout. There was a reason he rose through the ranks and made head of a division, and the reason was that the guy was solid.

Richardson had a cat, which made Josh laugh as he dreamed up ways of using that against her. A kitty kidnapping, maybe?

Slow down the investigation, or you'll never see Mittens again!

Even if it was remotely feasible, it wasn't Josh's style. Hurting people who deserved it, yes. Innocent people and animals? Nope. Oh well. He hadn't counted on turning an agent to the dark side, but there was always that crossed-fingers hope something would land in your favor.

Only a couple days remained before the party. After that, Josh could stop monitoring everything. After the party, it would all become que será, será.

Josh was happy whenever a member completed their task, like Adam Bishop did when he shot Marcus Amble.

Marcus ran an LGBTQ conversion therapy practice. The place had clocked three suicides in one year alone by telling teens they should be ashamed of who they are.

One of the suicides was Adam's best friend.

Together they'd struggled with intolerant parents, mocking classmates, and legislation designed to squash their rights.

Adam decided that while hateful politicians come and go, someone like Marcus Amble could hurt people forever; private enterprises don't get voted out of office. No, shooting him wasn't the most exciting or newsworthy way to rid the planet of evil, but it got the job done.

Josh was less than pleased with the several others who had gone dark. They stopped responding to Cassandra, so Josh disabled their computers, just in case. While no one explicitly said anything about alerting the authorities, it was best to be safe at this juncture.

That brought the total number of people who had followed through to fifteen, and the number that had backed out to ten.

Not a bad batting average, Josh mused. *Everyone strikes out sometimes.*

Plus, that left 75 people still in play. And he knew with absolute certainty one of them was going through with things...

Yeah.

Seventy-four possibilities.

That would keep everyone on their toes for a while.

Chapter 27

Clearance

Sumner took convincing.

"You know how some people have resting bitch face?" Susan asked Michael as they approached Sumner's door. "He has resting skeptic's face, so don't be turned off if it doesn't look like things are going our way."

Michael understood, and when they got inside Sumner's office he stood back as Susan pled their case. Things were amicable, but forceful. Susan would parry, and Sumner would riposte, and the two built on one another's arguments quite well.

They've done this dance before, Michael noted.

"Look," Susan said pointedly. "You know as well as I do that every agency thinks the leads they're working are the most important leads, *ever*. If we call asking for help, our request gets put on the bottom of the pile, after whatever they want to do first, including lunch."

"You say that like you're forgetting the paradox," Sumner countered. "You think this lead is the most important, ever."

"I do, because right now it's our only lead."

Sumner leaned back in his chair and looked out his window.

"Saying your only lead is your best lead is like saying you found the stripper with the least amount of daddy issues," he stated. "It's not really helping your cause."

Sumner waited to see if either of them would respond, and when neither did, he turned back from the window and asked, "How many companies did you find?"

"Over two hundred," Susan answered. "We have sales sheets from the last three years from most of them, and we've been calling every client that even whiffs of suspicion."

Sumner arched an eyebrow. "Suspicion?"

"You know what I mean. Any business that doesn't automatically look like it needs a system like this gets marked and contacted. And right now, this non-existent bank paying bills for a non-existent investment firm is the strangest one we've seen. That might not scream 'guilty,' but it does give us something to look at."

"Maybe they're anti-social. Maybe they have billionaire clients and don't want to talk to the non-rich. Not wanting to talk to people is a thing. Its why people get frustrated when their phone rings and they wonder why the other person didn't just text. Hell, didn't just Michael lecture us on the merits of leaving recorded information for customers on hold?"

"While that's true," Susan acknowledged, "every business wants to make money. To do that, you need customers and clients."

Susan paused.

"And you need to exist," she finished.

Sumner took it all in. He knew in the end he was going to let them go, but he didn't want it to be a given. They had to earn this.

"What do you think?" Sumner asked, turning his attention to Michael. "You've got Agent Chamberlain on board, but do you think this is worth following up?"

Michael chose his words carefully.

"Do I think this is going to lead to The 100?" Michael asked rhetorically. "Honestly? No."

Sumner shot a glance at Susan to see if she flinched. He was impressed when her poker face didn't betray whatever she might have thought of that response.

"But I couldn't find anything on either of these companies online," Michael continued. "No trace of them anywhere. Even if they don't help us to the finish line of our case, they're dirty. If we accidentally stumbled across another crime while working on this one, would that be the worst thing to happen?"

Sumner didn't answer; he resumed the process of countering their beliefs with his own internally. When he finally came up with a good rejoinder, he spoke.

"You said you didn't find any history of them online," Sumner began. "Did you check with the IRS?"

Michael's face betrayed his surprise. He hadn't thought of that. Fortunately, Susan was forever one step ahead.

"No," she explained. "We can, but I don't think we'll find anything. You only need to register your business with the government if you want a trademark..."

Susan trailed off as she pulled out her phone and started tapping away, pulling up a website.

"In fact," she continued, now reading off her phone, "according to the U.S. business administration, in some cases, you don't need to register your business at all. If you don't, you miss out on personal liability protection, legal benefits, and tax benefits. If you're not legitimate, those things don't matter to you. Most businesses don't need to register with the federal government to become a legal entity, and small businesses sometimes register with the federal government for trademark protection or tax-exempt status."

Susan looked up from her phone again, making direct eye contact with Sumner.

"If the only reason to register a business is to get tax breaks or to make sure you're protected if you get sued," she stated, "then it's highly unlikely either of these places would have done so."

Sumner didn't smile outwardly, but he was impressed. The move wasn't checkmate, but it was still damned good.

"Yes..." he volleyed, "but you're still running on the assumption they never existed, because they're not online. Just because they don't have a Facebook page doesn't mean they're not real, and just because they didn't apply for tax breaks doesn't mean they didn't file their taxes."

"It's more than 'no Facebook page,' sir," Michael injected. "Neither of these companies was registered anywhere. They had no presence on the stock market, and no insurance company seems to have covered them. If there's one thing every company has, it's insurance."

"We talking health insurance for employees?" Sumner asked. "Or liability insurance in case they're sued?"

For the second time in five minutes, Michael's face gave his answer before his voice.

"Didn't check both, did you?" Sumner laughed. "OK, that's one thing you have to figure out before I send you anywhere. Another thing is, how do you know anyone is even in the warehouse? You're just going to knock on a random door and see who answers?"

"Thought of that one, sir," Susan responded. "I contacted New York G&E. The power is on there, and someone is using it. The meter shows enough for undetermined usage, but definitely not enough for a building that size."

"What does that mean?" Sumner asked.

"It means a warehouse would be using a ton of energy if operating in the capacity a warehouse would operate at, or would be flat if sitting dormant. Right now, there's usage, and someone is paying the bill."

Susan let the last statement hang in the air a moment, which Sumner picked up on quickly.

"I assume you didn't finish that sentence, because you have a supposed bombshell?" he asked.

"Thank you," Susan smiled. "I wanted to be dramatic. Did you like it?"

Sumner rolled his eyes, but she could tell he wasn't angry.

"GGA Investments is covering the power bill for the warehouse," Susan said. "The company that doesn't exist is still spending money on that property."

Michael was mildly stunned, but more than that, he was pleased. If Sumner was impressed, he didn't show it. Instead of offering compliments, he fired right back with questioning.

"You're telling me that the company that bought the property, is *paying the bills* on that property?" he said cynically. "That's not unexpected."

"The money is wire transfer, though," Susan explained. "No bank is fronting it this time. A company that we can't find is buying electricity. That means the location is active."

Sumner relented. He'd wanted them to push, and they did so in all the right ways.

"OK," he began, "this is what we're going to do..."

Sumner leaned in and crossed both arms across his desk.

"I'll put two seats on hold on a plane to New York. I'm not making reservations yet, but I'll start the process. And yes, that means you're flying commercial. I'm not filling out an expense report for a private to New York off a hunch. You two go double check everything you've already covered, and then check everything you missed. If when you're done you haven't shot your theory in the foot with a discovery, then you can leave first thing in the morning."

Both Susan and Michael knew to celebrate internally; high-fives, should there be any, would take place in the hallway, out of sight.

"Sir?" Michael offered, a mischievous look on his face. "Buying any last-minute airline ticket is usually ten times more expensive than buying it weeks in advance. I could run the numbers and see if you'd actually be saving money sending us coach over just scooting us over in an FBI-chartered plane."

"Get outta here," Sumner barked.

He tried to scowl, but couldn't through his laugh.

Cocky little shit, Sumner thought. *I like him.*

Chapter 28

Confirmation

Michael quickly brought Kristen up to speed; she met him and Susan in their combination office/conference room.

"Well, here's the bad news," Kristen told him. "Just because they had an email address with a domain name on it, doesn't mean that webpage actually existed."

"How so?" Susan asked.

"Routing and bouncing," Kristen explained. "All you have to do is buy the domain you want, set up an email address, and then have it forwarded to whatever account you want. You could make 'Susan Chamberlain at Susan Chamberlain dot com' and send that to your Hotmail, Gmail, or Yahoo account. Basically, 'Kevin Michael at GGA investments' didn't require the existence of 'GGA investments dot com.'"

"It still went somewhere, obviously," Susan said.

"Yes." Kristen said cautiously. "But finding it will be problematic. Right now, you're searching a pond. A company buying software has limitations, and once you define those limitations, you narrow your search and make it easier. Finding a company hosting a specific domain name is like searching the ocean. Everyone knows GoDaddy, but that's because they're huge. Beneath them are more places to buy a domain than you could shake a stick at, and unfortunately, many of them won't be as accommodating as the big companies have been."

"Anything internet involves secrecy, doesn't it?" Susan said wearily.

"Could you…" Michael began, slowly, as if he were expressing the thought as it came him. "Could you figure out if it's hosted at the same place as The 100 site? If it popped up as being in the Ukraine…"

Michael trailed off, allowing them to pick up where he was going. Both did, and Susan spoke first.

"If they're both sourced there, that would be a pretty rare coincidence," she agreed.

"I could find that out," Kristen replied. "When I discover who hosted the domain. Which, as said, is a slog. Not impossible, but a slog."

"OK," Susan said thoughtfully. "Let's put that on the back burner and start on it tomorrow. Can you help quick-confirm our current findings?"

"Meaning make sure the company never existed with the IRS or with any insurer?" Kristen asked. "Sure. That should be less time consuming. I can also see if I can find out where the money going to the power company is coming from."

"Great," Susan said. "Let's divide and conquer. The IRS is a single call, so I'll hit that. If you two scour insurance companies, we'll move through those more quickly. And I can jump on after I've exhausted every angle of Uncle Sam's collection agency. Hopefully that'll get the two of us," Susan gestured to herself and Michael, "on an airplane tomorrow, and with us out of your way, you can run that wire transfer down."

Kristen gave a nod of agreement, and they all hunkered down and began re-tracing steps in search of missed information.

Each person finished their own task in two hours. Following that, they handed off their findings to the next person to double-check the results, and after that handed the findings off again in a version of round robin.

"Sumner wants us to double check everything," Susan said with a smile. "He can't have any complaints after he sees it's all been triple-confirmed."

By seven in the evening, with the obligatory (and somewhat cliché) empty boxes of Chinese takeout strewn across the table, they believed they had everything confirmed. Kristen said goodbye with a wave as the field agents readied themselves to make their case.

"Is Sumner still in his office?" Michael asked.

"Probably," Susan responded. "But we can call to make sure."

Susan grabbed the office phone and punched in Sumner's extension; he answered on the first ring.

"We've got our results," Susan explained. "And from where I'm sitting, we're going to New York. Want us to come up, or do you want to come here?"

"Neither," Sumner responded. "Go home and get your bags. Your tickets are already waiting for you."

Susan didn't respond, exactly, but she made a sound akin to "Um," or "Uh." Sumner couldn't tell which.

"What?" he asked playfully. "You think I don't trust you? I bought the tickets as soon as you left my office. What's that old saying? Trust, but verify. Go home. Tell Michael to pack. The two of you have a 9:00 AM flight. Oh, and I called the boys in blue; NYPD has an undercover sitting on the place, watching to see who's coming and going. I'll send you the details so you can check in with them when you get there."

Sumner hung up quickly; he liked the idea of leaving her in stunned silence.

Susan looked over at Michael.

"We leave in the morning," she explained.

Michael leaned back in his chair, put his hands behind his head, and stared up at the ceiling.

"I've never been to New York," he said, anticipation in his voice.

Chapter 29

Flying High Again

On the plane, Susan and Michael had the same conversation dominating every water cooler and chat board across the country: were The 100 justified in their actions?

"I mean," Michael said, "I get where the frustration is born from. Having your wife die because the price of her medication got raised? It's gross that we live in a world that puts profits before people."

"That doesn't mean you can take the law into your own hands," Susan countered. "In 2019, the attorney general of Connecticut filed charges against a handful of drug makers involved in price fixing, including the one Evan was angry with. From Al Capone to cigarette makers, everyone eventually gets caught. You can't just have vigilante justice be the end-all, be-all to placating society, because that'd make road rage acceptable."

"But how long should people have to wait when they're hurting? Evan didn't act in the moment, he waited years, and from everything I've seen, opinion polls are on his side."

"Popular doesn't mean legal."

"Why not?"

Michael's question was genuine, not flippant.

"Popular opinion decides our politicians, right?" he continued.

"Except for the presidency every so often, sure," Susan countered. "Are you suggesting people vote on laws?"

"I think it'd be an interesting experiment. Look at seatbelts. It's illegal to drive without wearing one. I bet if you took a vote on it, most people would uphold the current law. People get that seatbelts are good. While there would be people who'd vote against it, they'd have to understand majority rules, and not complain about big government regulations, or whatever it is they complain about."

"I don't think you'd get too many people to the polls by offering that at the ballot box."

"OK, how about guns?" Michael asked. "All we hear are polls saying 'people want this' and 'people want that.' How about a definitive 'let's find out what people really think about guns' vote?"

"Because," Susan began slowly, "you know as well as I do that sometimes people can't be trusted. Would Americans have voted for desegregation? Would they have legalized marriage equality? Women's suffrage?"

"Was America ready for those events?" Michael countered. "You could say 'yes' to marriage equality, 'no' to desegregation, and 'doubtful' to suffrage. Do you think there would have been less violence surrounding civil rights had America been allowed to grow into the idea of equality for all?"

"Are you really saying Black Americans should have waited for rights to be handed to them?" Susan was more than a little surprised by the inference.

"No," Michael cautioned. "I'm asking if white people would have been less violent towards Black people had equality played out longer and not been forced upon them from above."

Susan allowed his words to bounce around her head a moment before responding.

"I'll answer your question with a question," she began. "Didn't the televised violence help sympathize the cause, and bring a certain number of white Americans off the sidelines?"

"I don't know," Michael replied carefully. "You can never tell where America stands on violence. I found that out when I visited Kent State."

"How so?"

"Today we look at the Kent State Massacre as the turning point in the Vietnam War protests. Back then, turns out that most good, God-fearing Americans dismissed it as just a couple hippies getting shot. Did you know that?"

Susan was taken aback.

"I did not," she said.

Michael laughed, causing Susan to give him a stern look.

"Are you mocking me?" she asked.

"No, no," he said, gently waving her off. "It's just that you love references, and two popped into my head, and then I couldn't decide which was more appropriate."

"Hit me with them," Susan said, relaxing.

"I was going to go with either 'History is written by the victors'—"

"Attributed to Churchill, but unverified," Susan interjected.

"Right. And since the anti-war protesters ultimately 'won,' because Nixon withdrew the troops, they could say Kent State was the turning point, making them the victors."

"And your second reference?"

"We have always been at war with Eastasia."

"Meaning people will believe whatever they're told to believe, even if it's a lie."

"Right."

"So cynical, for such a young fella," Susan joked.

A shadow crossed Michael's face.

"Yeah," he said distantly.

Michael paused, then looked at Susan earnestly.

"Does it get worse?" he asked.

Susan was thrown.

"Does *what* get worse?" she responded, confused.

"The cynicism," Michael explained. "I spend several weeks working in phone fraud, seeing people getting taken advantage of, and I get..."

Michael paused again, as if he didn't like admitting what he was about to say.

"I get angry," he concluded. "I get angry at those willing to take advantage of other people, and I get angry at the victims for being such gullible rubes."

Michael looked away, then whispered, "I get angry at the victims. I victim blame. I never used to do that, and I'm worried it's going to get worse as the crimes get worse."

Susan didn't answer straightaway; the question had taken her by complete surprise. After a moment, she put a hand on Michael's knee.

"We see the worst in people," she confirmed softly. "We see a side of life most people are insulated from, or in the least, they're detached. They can read a headline about a man killing his family and think 'Oh, how horrible,' but they're not on the scene firsthand."

Susan paused before continuing. While her first words had been gentle, she now added a firmness to her empathy, removed her hand, and looked Michael square in the eyes as she spoke.

"I look at it like this: emotions are good. Anger, sadness, sorrow... they're all good, because you're feeling something. I'd say you should get worried when you go numb; when it all becomes rote and you don't have any thoughts one way or another about the perps or their victims."

Susan then flipped back to a quieter, more compassionate tone.

"I'll tell you a secret," she said. "It gets to me, too. I've been doing this a long time and it still gets to me. You solve a case, and there's another one waiting for you. You put one perp away, and there's another murderer or rapist standing in line to take their place. You wonder if it's all worth it, or if you're making a difference, but you are. There will always be evil in the world, so there will always be a need for someone to hunt that evil down and lock it away."

While Michael was digesting that thought, a synapse fired inside Susan's mind.

"Let me ask you a question," she began.

Michael nodded; fine by him.

"Have you ever given up on anything after only a few weeks?"

"No..." Michael responded hesitantly.

"Then don't give up on this," Susan finished, matter-of-factly. "If everything gets worse, maybe it's not for you. But allow yourself an adjustment period, OK?"

Michael nodded.

"OK," he agreed.

"Good," Susan said with a light smile. "Now, if you tell anyone that sometimes the job still gets to me—"

"You'll have to kill me?" Michael interrupted, seemingly finishing her sentence.

"Oh no," Susan laughed. "That would be letting you off too easy. No, if you tell anyone, I'll photoshop a nude picture of you that will be less than flattering, create a dating profile in your name, put it on every app that's available, and any woman that contacts you will get that picture in response."

"Goddamn," Michael said, impressed. "You do not play."

"I do not play," Susan echoed.

It was at that moment the flight attendant came by and asked if they were interested in breakfast. Having had enough in the way of personal conversations, the two concluded the flight playing *"is it edible?"* with the onboard meal.

(The answer, for any concerned wonderers, was 'No.')

Chapter 30

Stir Crazy

Josh didn't like feeling powerless.

No one does, but when you're a Master of the Universe—as Tom Wolfe might have labeled Josh—feeling powerless left you with nothing.

The current buzz was that weareonehundred.com might get shut down.

Josh couldn't tell if it was legitimate or (hashtag) "fake news." Apparently a few concerned citizens didn't like the site, and thus several of their "concerned representatives" said they would back legislation to block weare-onehundred.com from American servers.

Even the hint of censorship started debates.

"Free speech!" some argued.

"The government can shut down websites if they threaten national security!" others responded.

Josh knew he was in sketchy territory.

Both the 'free speech' and 'government discretion' sides were technically right; free speech didn't include yelling "fire!" in a crowded theater. As far as policing the web goes, Josh's thoughts turned to the guy who'd posted directions on how to make a gun using a 3D printer. Because such a weapon could make it through airport security (and any other metal detector), the government had put an end to that nonsense quite nicely.

The frustration came from not being able to add his voice to the fray; Josh couldn't fight the good fight to keep the website alive. To do so would invite scrutiny.

If he reached out in support of the website, even if by Tweet or 'like' or phoning his representative, it would put him on the radar, even if in the smallest of ways. He'd already screwed up once by communicating with Kristen Richardson directly, and wasn't about to risk another peek out of the groundhog's hole. If anyone saw his shadow, it'd be 'spend the rest of your life in jail,' not just six weeks of winter.

Maybe the ACLU will take it on, Josh mused. *They're always sticking their nose into... well, everything.*

The very idea his website might disappear annoyed Josh.

ISIS still had websites up and running, and the most popular social media sites had allowed them to recruit right off their platforms for years. But if one were to use a little ultra-violence to do good, not evil? Well, gotta nip that in the bud immediately.

The hypocrisy didn't surprise Josh, but it did annoy him to no end.

He needed a backup plan, and quickly. The good news was that nothing ever really disappears from the internet. Sure, you could delete a picture, tweet, or video, but chances are someone, somewhere, saved it.

Especially if it was salacious.

Basically, the message would always be out there. The problem was how to make sure the remaining messages were received by the masses.

Cassandra was programmed to unlock a user's video within an hour of their death. That would still happen, but it would only be seen abroad. Sure, people would rip it and post it in too many places for anyone to censor, but that method of distribution would take a while to filter back to the United States, which is where it *needed* to be seen.

News outlets would still have to cover it, right?

As Josh had the thought, he frowned.

That was a maybe, at best. The media had the attention span of a gnat. Today's biggest, scariest story was yesterday's news only hours after it happened. The media represented the biggest example of the *What have you done for me lately?* attitude.

Viewers didn't drive the news; the news drove society. It told people what to be afraid of, what to purchase, who was an honorable celebrity, and who was mean.

To stay in their good graces, the machine had to be fed. If a member of The 100 didn't complete a task for several days, it'd all fade from memory.

Josh had two options: dwell on it and grow angry, or let it go.

So be it, Josh decided. *Lord grant me the strength to accept the things I cannot change and all that jazz.*

Josh took several deep breaths to center himself and let his anger dissipate. He could only do what he set out to do; everything else was out of his hands.

That said, he really believed there'd be no way to ignore what was going to happen next.

It all started tonight.

Chapter 31

New York

"You should have gone at the airport," Susan chided playfully.

Michael gave a hard stare, but didn't respond.

The two were trapped in traffic, in a taxi.

"We don't get to drive ourselves?" Michael had asked as they passed the rental counter.

"Apparently the powers that be believe there's a difference between driving yourself in New York City and lesser-traveled sections of America. Our insurance will cover one of the two, and keep us on the hook for the other."

"You mean the FBI can't drive in New York? That's absurd."

"No, residents can drive, *we* can't."

"Huzzah," Michael deadpanned. "Do we Lyft, or Uber?"

"You want to front the money for that and then have to wait for your expense report to clear to get it back?" Susan responded.

"Point taken. A taxi on the company card it is."

The duo was headed from JFK, to Industry City.

"Apparently it's quicker from Newark," Susan explained. "But it's about $200 more expensive per ticket to fly in there."

"Wouldn't want us to be on the scene more quickly when there's money to be saved," Michael said.

"We're not exactly headed to an active crime scene," Susan explained before changing gears, and asking: "How're you holding up?"

"I'm fine," Michael lied.

Susan laughed, and pulled out her phone.

"There's a coffee shop a block and a half east of our destination," she said, looking at a maps app. "We'll drop you there, and I'll check in with the NYPD unit watching the warehouse."

"Great," Michael said. "Is there an urgent care nearby? I think my bladder is going to rupture."

"I told you to go at the airport," Susan repeated, still smiling.

"Thanks, mom."

Michael felt dumb.

He hadn't been in the field all that long, and this was embarrassing. He tried to go at the airport, but when he walked into the bathroom it smelled like someone died in one of the stalls. Michael turned on his heels while gagging and left feeling sorry for the janitor on duty.

That was 65 minutes ago.

The total trip was supposed to take just under an hour, but that hadn't happened. Their driver didn't know what the holdup was, he just knew, "This is not right, this traffic. It's not right."

Whatever had every car along the Belt Parkway backed up, it was turning their attempted sprint into an exceedingly slow marathon.

They'd left Kansas City at 9:15 AM—a fifteen-minute delay wasn't all that bad, they agreed—and landed at 1:30 PM eastern. Neither had checked a bag—they just had overnights which they carried on—which meant they were on the curb by 1:50 and in a cab by 1:51.

"Do we have a game plan?" Michael asked. "Do we just knock on the door and ask, 'Hi, who are you, and why is an investment firm that doesn't exist paying your bills?'"

"I find it's best to go into these situations with a loose agenda," Susan responded. "If you're too fixed on a certain outcome, you don't get taken where the current wants to take you."

"Fair enough," Michael said, understanding.

"If there's someone there," Susan continued, "who is that person? A security guard with zero information? A squatter trying to live rent-free? After that, we have to pay attention to their response to us; how do they react to the FBI showing up at their door? Are they alarmed? Confused? Worried? What's behind that emotion? They might be afraid they're about to receive bad news. Or they can be worried because we're going to ask to come inside and they have something to hide, something as small as a joint.

They don't know why we're here, so they might be afraid of getting arrested. There are hundreds of things to watch for, and plenty of opportunities to misread a situation."

"So," Michael began, "what's your loose plan?"

"At first, we leave everything open-ended. We show up, say we have a few questions about the property. We can say we're investigating tax fraud, or we can say nothing at all. Depending on how that goes, maybe we ask for permission to enter and look around. Hell, we could get a door slammed in our face. Without a search warrant, that's always on the table."

"People love their search warrants, don't they?" Michael laughed.

"People watch entirely too much television," Susan confirmed.

Susan took a glance at her phone.

"We're only a few minutes away," she noted. "After you're dropped at the coffee place, and I'm left with the stakeout crew, do you want me to have our driver pick you up some Depends?"

Michael scratched an eye using his middle finger, but truth be told, his eye didn't itch.

Chapter 32

Decisions

Josh didn't know what time the Crown Vic parked down the street from his warehouse, but when it caught his eye he noticed two men sitting inside.

Not being one to dismiss anything, Josh started reviewing footage. He didn't like what he found.

His cameras showed that the car had shown up at 6:00 AM. Which was fine, but when it arrived, the two men had parked, gotten out, exchanged pleasantries with two men parked in a different Crown Vic across the street, and then that car had left.

Going back further, Josh watched as the first car arrived right around 6:00 PM the night before. Those two men in that hadn't left their vehicle all night.

Twelve-hour shifts. A stakeout. The police were here.

Josh paused before allowing his imagination to run away with itself. Was he positive they were watching his warehouse? The neighborhood wasn't the worst borough in the city, but it was a place people went to stay out of the sunlight. His cameras had recorded drug deals aplenty, and he was pretty sure a warehouse-turned-loft a block away was a brothel.

Josh monitored the car all day. Not obsessively—he didn't want to be paranoid—but Josh had to assume the worst. Which meant he had to assume they were there for him.

That assumption was laid to rest when a taxi pulled up alongside the Crown Vic at 3:25 PM and Susan Chamberlain got out. She walked over to the plainclothes officers, who got out of their car, and then everyone shook hands and introduced themselves. One of the officers pointed at Josh's warehouse; Susan followed his gesture and nodded.

Josh was too stunned to even feel an emotion. He wasn't angry or afraid. If anything, Josh was in a mild state of denial.

After a minute of chit-chat, Agent Chamberlain gave the officers instructions, turned, and began walking toward Josh's warehouse.

The two officers returned to their car and resumed waiting.

They aren't driving off, Josh noted. *They're backup.*

Josh took a deep breath. He had about 45 seconds before Agent Chamberlain got to his door and rang the buzzer.

How did he want to play this?

In rapid-fire sequence, Josh weighed his options: *just don't answer, answer and play dumb and try and get her to spill what she knows...*

The thought stopped Josh in his tracks.

Wait, what do they know? He wondered. *She's walking up here alone; this isn't an assault.*

No S.W.A.T. team was coming to bust down his door, he was positive of that. Ever since discovering the undercover, Josh had been watching every monitor carefully. He'd reviewed all the tapes and there wasn't anyone hiding around corners or ready to bust in through windows. His neighborhood was clean, save for the stakeout crew.

She doesn't know who's in here, Josh realized. *Something led her here, something I missed, but she doesn't know it's me. If she did, she wouldn't be walking here so casually, or alone. This is an information mission, not an arrest.*

Josh glanced at his phone.

Technically, he could leave for Chelsea Piers now. He'd planned on leaving at five, but if he wanted to skedaddle and avoid any facet of law enforcement, he could just get over there early and not risk anything.

That said, he had plenty of time to stick around and either talk to Agent Chamberlain, or just watch her and the police on the monitors and see what their next course of action was.

Josh didn't like indecision; he was a man of action. You set a course, and then you sailed it. Which is why it tore him up inside that he couldn't immediately figure out what to do here.

On the one hand, leaving was the prudent move. On the other hand, he really liked the idea of talking to the FBI. When it was all over, Agent Chamberlain would have an epiphany, "That's the guy I met at the warehouse! I talked to him and let him go!"

The thought amused him. It would be like a predator toying with its prey. Technically, she was supposed to be stalking him, but he had the upper hand in this situation, because he had knowledge.

With ten seconds left before Susan reached his door, Josh made his decision: he would visit with Agent Chamberlain and see if he could figure out how they found him. He'd been meticulous, and the idea the FBI made it to him was mind-boggling.

What had he missed?

Chapter 33

Face to Face

As she approached the warehouse, Susan examined every inch of the building she could.

The final building before the Hudson—technically called the Bay Ridge Channel here—was eight stories high and took up a quarter of the block.

She'd done some research on the flight and learned that most of the construction in Industry City took place before 1910. Susan figured Wikipedia had gotten that one correct, as many of the buildings showed their age. Not because they were dilapidated, but in the style of architecture. Nothing was modern; everything had a turn-of-the century look to it.

In its heyday, the unit had probably been a hub for trade; now, all the shipping docks were bricked up.

Only one entrance on this street, Susan noted as she neared the drab-gray metal security door. Its placement on the westernmost end of the building made it look as if it had been an afterthought during construction.

Looking back over her shoulder toward Brooklyn, she saw the officers keeping track of her, which she appreciated. There was no sign of Michael.

His bladder must have been full to the brim, she thought, chuckling to herself.

Upon arriving at the only door she could see, Susan hit the buzzer and made note of the camera monitoring her.

Glancing around casually, she pretended to look at the neighborhood. In reality, Susan was counting every security camera adorning the building.

This place has good security for a building on the crap-end of the street, she noted.

Cameras generally meant value. If you had nothing to protect, then you didn't need security. She wondered what was inside while counting down the time she wanted to wait before buzzing a second time. Just because someone didn't answer immediately didn't mean the building was empty. The place took up a decent chunk of real estate, after all, which meant it might take a couple minutes to respond.

While she waited, Susan dropped one hand into her jacket pocket. Given the presence of cameras, she suspected that after she introduced herself the first question would be to ask for her identification. She'd beat them to the punch on that one.

When her internal clock said enough time had passed, Susan buzzed again.

Mentally, she crossed her fingers in the hope someone would answer. If she and Michael flew all the way here for nothing, Sumner would be less than pleased. He wouldn't be angry, exactly, but it would mean a wasted trip.

He also wouldn't allow them more than a day or two in the hotel; he'd have them back in the office and on the phones. Worst case scenario, he'd suggest she and Michael join the police in their stakeout. Normally, the police would watch all their own and call with updates. If someone arrived, then the agents would show up and knock on the door again. If anyone left, the police would follow them and allow the agents to catch up and question the person in public.

But if he were in the right mood, Sumner might just punish them slightly by saying, "Why don't you two sit on the building, too, just to be safe."

Susan hadn't done a full-on stakeout in a while, and she didn't like the idea of doing one now. If there was one thing worse than phone calls and paperwork, it was stale coffee and gas station bathrooms. At least in the office you could stand, stretch, and walk around every so often.

With that last thought, the speaker finally buzzed. A male voice said blandly, "Hello? Can I help you, lady?"

Susan held her identification up to the camera as she introduced herself; "My name is Agent Chamberlain, I'm with the FBI. Could you come to the door and answer a few questions for me?"

"OK," came the response.

Susan put away her identification and frowned thoughtfully. "OK" was an odd response. Most people, when told they needed to talk to the FBI, were a bit confused. *About what?* was a typical reaction. *OK* was not.

Susan began counting again. Given the size of the warehouse, she wanted to determine how long it took the man inside to get from wherever he was, to the door. Not that such knowledge would help her with the layout of the building, but it never hurt to keep track of such things. If it took two minutes to answer this time, and she had to come back and re-question him later and he hadn't shown up after four minutes, then she could wonder if he was rabbiting out a side door.

Off that thought, Susan began wondering how many exits the place had. The NYPD had surveillance on the main door; what would it take to keep the place completely covered?

Since one thought begets another, she wondered what this man would have to say or do to compel her to ask for more coverage. Off-duty officers were always happy to take a gig involving light lifting. They earned over-time, and the FBI picked up the tab. While it was easy enough to budget two people watching the front door for anyone coming or going, putting a team around the building required more than a hunch.

We need evidence, but evidence of what? Susan asked herself. *This guy isn't even a suspect. He's just some random dude in a warehouse that has sketchy financials.*

Susan half-laughed to herself. She was inside her head, examining every possible angle, and that always drove her a little batty. It was like being slightly OCD, only in this case, showing attention to detail usually provided solid results.

As she counted, Susan saw Michael step out of the coffee shop a block and a half up. Since the neighborhood had little foot traffic, a single person stepping onto the sidewalk was noticeable.

I don't imagine I would have seen him had we been in Times Square, Susan mused.

Her thoughts were interrupted by the sound of a bolt sliding back on the other side of the door, followed by a light click from the knob.

Handle lock and a bolt, Susan noted. *Seventy-five seconds.*

The door opened.

The man who stood in the doorway before her was a white male, late thirties to early forties, dark brown hair worn short, probably around six two and 180 pounds, give or take. He had two or three days of growth on his face, but it looked as if by design—like he kept a scruffy face, not that he had forgotten to shave. He was dressed in running shoes, athletic pants, and a designer T-shirt, the kind people with money paid $60 for.

Susan took it all in quickly, trying to assess him before they spoke. The man carried himself with an unassuming air; casual, like the "OK" he'd given when asked to speak to a member of law enforcement.

"Agent..." the man spoke, and then paused. "Chamberlain, was it?"

"Yes," Susan affirmed.

"Do you mind if I see your credentials again?" he asked. "The monitor is good, but not that good."

Susan fished in her pocket for her FBI placard.

"Do you think you'd be able to spot a fake up close?" she asked.

The man laughed in response. "No, I guess I wouldn't."

Susan showed him the identification, but having just called him out on his inability to know whether or not it was counterfeit, he only took a passing glance at it.

"I suppose this is about the prostitution ring up the street," the man suggested.

The statement threw Susan. That's why he was relaxed. He had nothing to fear, because he didn't think this was about him.

"Actually, no," Susan countered. "I'm here to ask about this property."

"Oh?" he responded, startled, but not yet alarmed. "What about it?"

"Before that, can I get your name, please?"

"Didn't even think to offer it," he stated, holding out a hand. "I apologize. Paul," Josh lied.

"Paul..." Susan trailed off, allowing him to offer his last name. While she did so, she accepted the handshake.

"Sorry, Hewson. Paul Hewson."

"Thank you. Mr. Hewson—"

"Paul," Josh interrupted politely. "Sorry, are you supposed to be formal? I've never talked to the FBI before."

"We're supposed to be respectful," Susan explained. "But that can involve referring to you according to your preference."

"Then please," Josh said warmly. "Paul."

"Paul," Susan began. "Do you work here?"

"Sort of," Josh responded, amused, but not mockingly so. "I live and work here. This has a loft inside it."

"How long have you lived here?"

"I'd say... six, seven months?"

"And do you rent your loft, or do you own it?"

"This is definitely a rental," Josh laughed. "Even down here property is too expensive to own."

Though he was answering casually, Josh's mind was working overtime. *Financials?* He thought. *That's how they traced me? OK, think... she's going to ask who I pay rent to. How should I answer?*

"Do you know who owns the building?" Susan asked.

"No," Josh responded. "I don't even know who owns my loft. The agency found it when the owner needed to work abroad for a year. Europe, I think?"

Shit, Susan thought. *A sublet. We're going to go back to Sumner with nothing, and he's going to laugh at us for chasing ghosts.*

"What agency did you go through?" Susan followed up.

"Plum Guide," Josh responded. "They're like a version of Airbnb, I guess. Only for long-term stays."

"How many units are inside?"

"Just the one. It's nice. No one above me stomping around, and no one next to me blasting music at 3:00 AM."

As Josh spoke, he noticed Agent Michael Godwin up the block, making his way to them. An idea crossed his mind. How far did he want to take this? If he left things as they stood, there'd be a couple more minutes of discussion, then they'd leave, do five minutes of research and discover everything he'd said was a lie. Which wouldn't matter, because he'd already be gone, down the sewers and out through the garage.

Where's the fun in that? Josh wondered.

Nothing they did could stop him, so why not push some boundaries?

Because that's probably why they're here, now. He chided himself. *You tossed out Agent Richardson's name, and now the FBI is knocking on your door. Think that's a coincidence?*

As quickly as he had that thought, Josh countered it with, *yeah, but once this door closes, I'm gone.*

"Sorry?" Josh asked. He'd been lost in his head and missed Agent Chamberlain's question.

"What do you do for a living?" Susan repeated. "You said you live and work here."

"App developer," Josh lied proudly. "I've made three games, one of which is doing OK by app standards."

"Define OK."

"I make enough money to rent this place," Josh laughed. "But not own it."

"When something breaks, who do you call?" Susan probed. "Is there an on-site maintenance man, or a specific local contact, like a plumber?"

Susan was hoping for more leads into the financials of the place. *Anyone* that got money from this property was someone she wanted to talk to.

"I just call the rental agency," Josh responded. "They take care of everything. I've never had an issue, but they said that if anything happens, even if it's at two in the morning, a service will be on hand to help me."

"And, just to reiterate, you don't know the owner of the loft, or building? Not even a name?"

"Nope. Nothing."

"Has any mail arrived not addressed to you? Something that could have been for the actual owner?"

"Nope. If there's even mail service here, I wouldn't know about it. I rent a box a couple blocks away and have everything sent there."

"Was the loft furnished when you rented it?"

"Nope. I was told I'd have to provide my own furniture, because the owner was a bit of a germaphobe and didn't want a stranger touching anything. I think his stuff is in storage."

"Do you know where?"

"Nope. But the agency might."

"Plum Guide," Susan confirmed.

"That's the one."

"Well, I think that's about everything I have for you, then," Susan said as Godwin came up behind her. She acknowledged him with a look that said, *waste of time*, then reached into her wallet, took out a card, and extended it to Josh.

"If anything comes to mind regarding your loft—a name, or something you didn't think of in the moment—please give me a call."

"Absolutely will," Josh said, taking the card and looking it over.

"Thank you for your time, and have a nice day Mr. Hewson," Susan finished.

"Not a problem, Agent Chamberlain."

Josh paused, shifted his attention ever-so-slightly to Michael, and then said with a casual nod, "Agent Godwin."

With that, he closed the door.

Chapter 34

Chase

The move had been so subtle, so natural, that neither Michael nor Susan had noticed it for three seconds.

They'd turned back toward the NYPD and realized at the same time—

"Holy shit," Michael said.

"He knew your name," Susan concluded. "I didn't introduce you, and he knew your name."

"That's Cassandra!"

Michael didn't like the fact that he'd shouted, but he was stunned, excited, and had blurted out before he could catch himself.

Susan was a bit more measured in her response. She was just as surprised, but immediately went into action, signaling for the stakeout officers to join them. She exaggerated her wave, because she wanted the officers to drive over, not get out of their vehicle and saunter.

It worked, because within seconds the car had started, a flashing cherry was slapped on the roof, and it was screeching to a halt next to them.

By that time, Susan had turned her attention back to the door.

When it closed, she rightly assumed it had locked automatically. But she hadn't heard the bolt slide into place, which meant they were only dealing with the doorknob lock.

"Do you have a Blackhawk or an Enforcer?" Susan shouted at the officers leaping out of their car.

Without responding, one of them went immediately to the trunk, popped it open, and grabbed the handheld battering ram from within.

Both were aside Michael and Susan moments later.

"Our suspect is inside," Susan explained hurriedly, but clearly. "We're going to bust in. Call for backup. Get several squad cars into the neighborhood and set up a perimeter for a white male, six-foot-two, one hundred eighty pounds, brown hair, light beard. Put out an APB on Paul Hewson. Find a record of him, find a picture, and get it out there."

"Clothes?" one of the officers asked.

"Don't bother," Susan responded. "He's probably changing them now and heading for a side exit. Just give the physical description. Also, assume he's armed and dangerous. If you have vests, put them on."

With that, the undercover not holding the battering ram rushed back to the car to call everything in.

"Go grab our throws," she ordered Michael, who broke out in a jog toward the undercover vehicle.

"Ready?" Susan asked, turning to the remaining officer.

He nodded as she reached out to take hold of half of the battering ram.

"On three," Susan ordered.

They centered the ram with the doorknob, swayed it back-and-forth to a count of three, and then hit the knob full force. It half-collapsed within the door.

"Again," Susan said commandingly.

The duo repeated their action, and on the second hit the doorknob clattered to the ground and the door opened slightly.

They dropped the ram as Michael returned with her FBI-emblazoned jacket; he was already wearing his. The second officer returned with a walkie-talkie in one hand.

"Here," he said, holding it out to Susan.

"Thanks," Susan acknowledged, taking it and attaching it to her belt. "Agent Godwin and I are going in. I need the two of you to circle the building and watch for him coming out of another exit."

The two officers immediately separated and darted along the building, heading for their respective corners in search of other ways in and out of the warehouse.

"No one shoots without a positive ID and warning first," she shouted after them.

She looked at Michael as she retrieved her firearm, readied it, and nodded.

"You good?" she asked.

"I'm good," Michael responded firmly, gun now in hand.

"In on three," Susan proclaimed, and then counted.

As she hit "three," Michael kicked open the door in front of them...

...and was greeted by another closed door.

Susan and Michael had begun charging, and immediately pulled up. Each had a variation of "What the fuck?" race through their mind, with Michael verbalizing his reaction one second after thinking it.

Chapter 35

Below the City

Josh was giggling.

Keep it under control, you idiot, he thought. But he couldn't. He couldn't contain his amusement. Josh wished he could have seen their faces once they realized what he'd said. Part of him wanted to stop and check the security footage, but that would be pushing things too far. He'd allowed himself this little poke, and that was going to be it.

Josh zigged and zagged as he giggled and jogged. A left here, a right there... every so often he'd pause long enough to close or open a door, but that was it.

He'd run the route a hundred times in preparation. Every time he completed the path he'd wonder, *Am I even going to get to use this?*

The fact Josh was now playing a variation of hide and seek, albeit with pretty extreme consequences for losing, thrilled him. Even if the deck was stacked in his favor.

It took Josh approximately 45 seconds to get to the center, to his office and living quarters. By the time he made it, he heard the distant thud of the battering ram knocking down the front door. A quick glance at the security monitors confirmed it; the FBI was coming inside, and the police were running around the building.

Guard those exits, boys, Josh smiled. *I've got a different way out.*

Josh grabbed his laptop; no need to leave behind extra evidence.

Other than the laptop, the location was clean. Yes, there were clothes, and they could find his DNA all over the place, but big whoop. He wouldn't be trying to hide his identity after tonight, he just wanted to protect what remained of The 100.

Access to the sewers came via a tube that looked like a submarine hatch. Josh unscrewed and lifted open its lid while taking one last glance around the room. Two boxes containing several dozen folders were all that remained. He wanted the authorities to find those; they were left behind on purpose.

Josh tossed his computer down the tube and watched it smash onto the concrete below.

Damaged, but not destroyed, Josh realized while eyeballing it. *Probably still works, which means they can get information off it if they find it.*

With that, Josh climbed into the tube. He closed and locked the lid before descending, then climbed down. Arriving at the bottom, Josh kicked his laptop into the sewer water rolling by lazily.

And that's that, he concluded.

Josh started walking briskly. Things were slippery down here, and while he could probably manage a jog, there was no need to risk anything. How stupid would he feel if he turned an ankle, or fell into the floating cesspool next to him?

Pretty stupid, Josh determined.

When he came to the first fork, Josh smiled. He was done giggling, but his plan still amused him enough for the involuntary reaction to spread across his face.

Always follow orange, Josh thought, glancing at the wall before him.

He knew the path like the back of his hand, but he'd still put two large arrows up at every junction. One was in green, pointing the wrong way, and one was in orange, pointing the correct way. If anyone made it through the maze and into the sewers after him, they'd be stymied again. It wasn't much of a misdirect, but because people are creatures of habit and 'green means go,' it would probably throw off a few less-than-thoughtful people.

Plus, even if it didn't fool anyone, the ruse would peel people off at every turn. Say an entire S.W.A.T. team was in pursuit; every time they got to a set of arrows, they'd have to send a couple people one way, and a couple people the other way. It was standard operating procedure: pair off and give chase.

Which meant that should someone, somehow make it all the way to the garage, it'd be two on one at best, not a team versus lonely old Josh.

At a decent clip, he could make a half-mile in a couple minutes. Down here, trial walks had him doing it in seven.

Once he got to the garage, Josh would take in his surroundings. He couldn't imagine they'd have enough manpower to cover the entire neighborhood, but nothing could be taken for granted.

Josh marveled at how alive he felt, how real everything was.

All week he'd imagined walking this path leisurely, with nothing to fear. The sheer fact agents Chamberlain and Godwin had knocked on his door blew his mind and charged his body with an adrenaline that felt like electricity was coursing through his veins.

The financials, Josh thought. *What did I miss there? They made it to the warehouse, but not to me...*

Josh went over everything he could during the walk, but couldn't piece together his mistakes. In the end, whatever it was, he was just happy he'd used fake names everywhere.

If he hadn't, then the FBI wouldn't have knocked on his door, they would have come through it with guns drawn.

With that, Josh did what he believed he did best: took a deep breath, let everything go, and focused on the moment.

And at the moment, he had to make it to the garage.

Chapter 36

Separation

Both Susan and Michael recovered from their surprise quickly.

Busting down a door and discovering another door was nothing either of them had expected, but almost as fast as they'd seen it Michael had picked up the battering ram.

Susan reached out, jostled the handle, and then upon discovering it locked, grabbed her half of the doorbuster.

"Had to check," she explained.

The second door only took one hit to collapse; turns out it was more for show than an actual deterrent. Kicking the door open and stepping inside, Susan and Michael found themselves in a long hallway that ran side-to-side, with a wall directly in front of them. About thirty yards in either direction, the hallway turned inward, into the warehouse proper.

"We have to split up," Susan determined.

"Have you ever even seen a horror movie?" Michael asked, reaching into his pocket. "That's how shit goes south."

"The people in horror movies never have guns."

Susan's phone rang; she pulled it out and was surprised to see Michael's number on her caller ID.

"Answer," Michael explained. "Put the phone upside down in your chest pocket, so the speaker and microphone are facing up."

Susan understood immediately. Since they didn't have radios, this was the best way to keep one another informed of their respective locations. She tapped answer, put the phone on speaker, then dropped it in her pocket.

"Quick thinking," she complimented.

"You going east, or west?" Michael asked.

"I'm already on your left," Susan countered. "You head west."

Michael nodded as he started moving in an up tempo, deliberate and focused manner down his side of the hallway.

"Let the NYPD know we've split up," Michael said over his shoulder. "Black man with a gun on premises, and that Black man is wearing an FBI blazer."

Susan nodded as she headed down her end. Before rounding the corner, she paused to check in with the officers outside; they radioed back that they'd seen no movement, and that a second squad was pulling up.

"Keep them in their car," Susan ordered. "Have them drive in a grid pattern around the neighborhood. If anyone even close to the description is dashing through an alley or even walking too quickly on the street, detain them."

Susan didn't want too many people inside, and it wasn't just Michael she was worried about. You put too many tense people in one location, each of them armed. One of them turns a corner, sees movement, panics... Anyone could get shot in this kind of situation.

"Can we get air support?" Susan asked, depressing the button on the NYPD radio.

"It's on the way," came the response.

"Good. As more units show up, have them expand the perimeter."

Susan returned the walkie-talkie to her belt and raised her weapon. Turning corners in a building was always a crap shoot; a blind hallway was a great place to catch a bullet.

"You hear all that?" she asked.

Michael's voice came out of her pocket; "I did. It's just us?"

"It's just us," Susan confirmed. "Too many chefs in the kitchen causes stress and makes a mess."

"I heard that. Going silent."

Susan understood.

In an empty building, the two of them talking to one another would give their position away to anyone listening.

Off that thought, Susan took a moment to glance around.

No security cameras inside, she noted.

Susan did a tactical turn around the corner, but the hallway in front of her was empty. It ran for about 25 yards, and then split three ways.

"Shit," Susan muttered.

"Dead end?" Michael asked quietly. It wasn't really a whisper, but he wasn't using a normal speaking voice now; stealth in all areas was his mindset.

"No, too many options."

"Ah... I hit a dead end. I'm retracing my steps and trying another way."

On his side of the warehouse, Michael was lost. In the short time since they'd separated, Michael had come to two forks, made a decision at each, gone through a door, come to a hallway that had two doors at the end, made a decision, and found an empty room behind the one that was unlocked.

He had toyed with the idea of kicking in the other door, but that generally only worked in the movies. Michael thought about getting the handheld battering ram, which is when he discovered he didn't know exactly which way led back to the entrance.

That's when it hit him.

"Chamberlain," he whispered.

"Go," she responded.

"We're in a maze," he stated.

Susan quickly checked her surroundings, and then paused, confident she was clear.

"Say again?" she asked, taking time to focus on Michael's words.

"The construction crew foreman said they built an entertainment center. He said it was laser tag, but it's a maze. That's why the dude dropped my name. He led us in here because he's toying with us."

Susan dropped a couple swear words internally before responding.

"He's escaping," she determined. "He's toying with us, yes, but there aren't any cameras in here, so he's not watching us. Fucking with us isn't how he gets off, it's just an added bonus. He's got an exit plan, and we need to figure out what that is."

"The roof," Michael said without hesitation. "He knows NYPD is outside on the ground, and this warehouse has a skyway attached to the building to the east."

"We have a helicopter inbound. He'll have to move quick."

"What's your call? Do we continue pursuit, or pull back and hit this from another angle?"

Susan answered without hesitation: "Continue pursuit. We have to trust NYPD to do their job. If we rush out there and micro-manage, they won't like it. This is their city, and they know it better than we do."

"Copy," Michael stated.

With that, Michael had second thoughts about the locked door he'd considered kicking in. The front door took two hits from the battering ram, but that second door, that fell like an asthmatic tenth grader in the ring against Mike Tyson.

Since this was a maze, maybe the doors were more props than actual reinforced material.

Michael made his way back to the door—he couldn't find his way out, but he was only twenty yards from where he'd realized he was lost—and jiggled the handle again.

Feels light, Michael determined. *OK, one kick. If it doesn't go down, I'm not gonna hurt myself bashing away at it.*

Michael lined himself up, squared his shoulders, and raised his right leg. *Don't kick the doorknob,* he thought.

With that, Michael kicked forward with his foot perpendicular to the floor, ensuring that his heel would strike first. He didn't want to break a toe.

Were Michael staring in a comedic movie, what happened next would have been considered funny. His foot went through the prop door, and because of his momentum, his leg followed all the way up to his thigh.

Michael swore, hopping on his left leg in an attempt to maintain balance, and extracted his leg from the reinforced cardboard.

"What was that?" came through his phone.

"Tried kicking in a door and discovered it wasn't a door," Michael replied.

Michael put his hand through the hole he'd created and unlocked the door from within. As he opened it, he explained his discovery to Susan.

"This place is like a movie set," he said, looking things over. "Nothing is real; this door I just kicked in is made out of cardboard. If you come across a locked room you want to get into, just apply force, and voila."

"Copy. Just making sure you're OK."

"Trust me," Michael laughed. "I'm embarrassed, but I'm fine."

"Don't be embarrassed," Susan explained, a light tone to her voice. "No one saw you. Just make sure you tell me all about it later, so I can share the story back at the office."

While speaking, Susan had made her way to her three-way choice. She hadn't made enough lefts and rights to get lost, so she decided on the straight-and-narrow center hallway. As she moved, her eyes darted. Not nervously—every look was focused. Though she believed the man she'd talked to was making his escape, that was just an assumption. He could be lying in wait, and truth be told, he could have left booby traps strewn throughout the place.

The hallway Susan was in ran for 25 yards, then split left and right. When she arrived at the split, Susan saw that one path was lined with closed doors, and the other split again in two directions. Neither option was inviting, and Susan had to weigh her options: what did she feel like doing, kicking open a bunch of doors, or getting lost in the madhouse?

Though the latter didn't seem all that much fun, the idea of movement appealed to her. Stopping at every door felt like a tactic to slow a pursuit; she'd take the other option and continue forward.

Just keep swimming, just keep swimming... crossed her mind, which then caused her to roll her eyes. *Jesus, even when I'm alone I reference pop culture. Maybe I should see a psychologist about that. Psychologist? Psychiatrist? OK, what's the difference, and Goddammit why is my mind wondering that now?*

Susan took a moment to focus, and then resumed scanning the hallway.

At the same time, Michael was pulling his phone out and tapping the flashlight icon.

The room he'd stepped into was, aside from whatever light made it in through the doorway, pitch black. The space looked empty, but Michael decided that in this place, looks could be deceiving.

Michael moved his phone in a slow arc across the room; his gun was up, and tracing the light with its muzzle. His finger was down the barrel of the gun; he didn't want to be startled and accidentally pull the trigger.

When the light showed nothing, Michael inched forward. He had no clue how big the room was, but his light hadn't reached a back wall.

It took about five steps, his light tracing back and forth in front of him the whole time, for Michael to reach a wall.

Empty, he thought.

As he turned to go, something caught the corner of his eye. One section of the room seemed a little darker, if that was possible, than the section Michael was in.

Goes back farther over there, Michael realized.

Again he tip-toed forward, slowly, silently, gun up.

After several feet, he saw a stairwell built into the side wall. The stairs led up, presumably to the second floor.

Well that's interesting.

The silence was unnerving. So much so that Michael took comfort in the sound of a helicopter overhead. Even though he was inside, and the helicopter was above the building, it made Michael feel not so alone as he arrived at the inviting stairs.

Perfect place for an ambush, Michael thought as he looked up the stairwell.

FBI issued tactical flashlights whose beams carried 1,000 meters, easy. The light on his phone only lit up the few immediate feet surrounding him, meaning Michael wished he'd brought his gear bag from the car. It didn't contain much, but the necessities were always there.

Michael placed his foot on the first stair, paused, and then lifted all his weight off the back foot. After balancing a moment, he bounced once, and then again a second time. There were fake doors made out of cardboard; what was to stop there from being fake stairs?

But if there is a fake stair, Michael realized. *It wouldn't be the first one. A dummy stair would be in the middle, or top, in order to maximize someone's fall.*

That in mind, Michael tested each stair for weight before actually stepping up onto it. The going was slow, and the higher he climbed the more the darkness enveloped him.

Michael had no idea what he would find, but after fifteen steps he could make out the top. After ten more, he realized he had come to a dead end; the stairwell ran directly into a wall.

Shit. Michael thought. *That was a waste of time.*

Frustrated, he had just turned to leave when he had a change of heart.

This entire place is an illusion.

Michael turned back to the wall and stared at it.

This entire place is an illusion, and everything is designed to confuse.

Michael approached the wall and began looking it over inch by inch.

His mind flashed back to Evan Francart's house, and Susan's words about searching a location; "It's meticulous, which means monotonous, which means it can be boring. You have to keep your senses heightened..."

Michael gave the wall a little shove, and it showed a little give.

Drywall wouldn't do that so easily, Michael thought.

Running his fingers down the edge, where the stairwell walls met the wall in front of him, he felt a gap.

Shoddy construction, or something done on purpose?

When he reached the bottom of the wall, Michael noticed an even larger gap than on the side. The gap was so wide, in fact, the wall was floating about a quarter inch above the floor.

This isn't a wall, Michael determined. *It's a door.*

Michael placed his hands on the wall before him and tried moving it side-to-side, to see if it was a slider. There was a little give, but not much.

Locked. But by bolt, or latch?

Michael wanted to find out, and applied more pressure dead on. This wasn't cardboard, but it wasn't solid plaster. What was the best way to get through it? If the wall had been at the bottom of a stairwell, he could have braced himself and given a decent kick, or maybe even a little run-and-jump into the wall to see if it'd give. But trying to force his way through while fighting gravity, well, that made things more interesting.

And by interesting, I mean difficult, Michael mused.

Michael decided to use body weight. He'd press against the wall as hard as possible and pray something gave. Turning to his side and holding one shoulder against the wall, Michael braced his feet and gave a powerful shove. On his test run, the wall had moved an inch. This time it moved six inches.

He eased off and squatted down to the base of the wall again, where the gap was. Shining his phone's flashlight under the crack, it looked like the floor ran way back.

OK, Michael decided. *If I go through this, I'm not dropping two stories.*

Michael turned to the side again, braced himself, then rammed the wall as hard as he could.

It cracked, but didn't break, but that was enough. The crack gave Michael a handhold, and he began tearing at the wall until he'd created a hole wide enough to look through.

This is the most batshit insane place I've ever seen, Michael thought.

Through the wall was another set of stairs, only this one went down, back to the first floor.

Well, in for a penny, in for a pound...

Michael tore at the wall until he could climb through, causing Susan to ask, "What are you doing over there?"

"Secret staircase," he responded. "Found it by punching through a door disguised as a wall."

"Sounds neat," Susan quipped. "For the record, I think I'm officially lost."

Michael laughed.

"I am, too," he told her. "Just because I'm finding interesting things doesn't mean I have a clue where I am."

"Going silent."

"I'd say the same," Michael said jokingly. "But since I just tore out a wall, it's safe to say that my position has been compromised."

Susan smiled, but didn't laugh. She was too busy trying to get her bearings. After so many lefts, rights, and hallways that split, she was officially disoriented.

According to her NYPD backup, two squads were driving the neighborhood, and two others were setting up roadblocks one block over. The two officers she'd met upon arrival had each found a side exit, and were sitting put as per orders. Susan could hear the helicopter overhead, and each and every bit of information that arrived gave her crossed-fingers hope. The more people they had outside, the better their chances of grabbing their perp.

Susan made her way around a corner, paused, and wondered if she'd just done a loop. Everything was too similar, everywhere she looked was déjà vu. Susan was considering turning around and attempting to make her way back to the entrance when Michael's voice sounded from her phone. He was alarmed.

"Radio the NYPD," Michael said in a rush. "I called it wrong. Our guy isn't on the roof, he's in the subway."

Chapter 37

Escape

Josh made quick work of his sewer walk.

From the moment his feet hit the slimy ground to the time they were up the ladder putting him inside the garage was six minutes.

Beat my record, he thought, a mix of impressed and amused.

Six minutes wasn't long, but he could already hear a police helicopter in the distance, most likely hovering over his warehouse.

By now, Josh assumed, *they've got squad cars on the streets and officers in the alleys. Better move fast.*

Josh stripped down to his underwear, throwing his clothes and now-filthy shoes into a garbage can in the corner.

Retrieving his keys from a nail, Josh popped the trunk and grabbed the bag of clothes contained within. Looking himself over, he determined that most of the sewer filth had gotten on his shoes and pants cuffs. Overall, his hair, arms, and face were clean.

Which was good—he didn't want to arrive at the cruise smelling like the feces of a million New Yorkers.

Josh changed into the captain's uniform he'd purchased, leaving off the jacket. He'd throw that on when he arrived at the Chelsea Piers.

A last-minute purchase was the cherry on top of his quick-disguise sundae: a blond wig.

He hadn't spent much on it; it wasn't high quality like you'd find on a real housewife of Beverly Hills. But, it was enough for a quick glance. Upon close inspection, yeah, it was obviously a wig. If the police had the description of a man with brown hair, and a blond guy drove by? Well, they wouldn't give him a second thought.

It's always the little things, Josh realized during his planning phase. *Something small, like altering your appearance ever so slightly could be the difference between getting caught, and getting away.*

To that end, Josh opened the passenger door and reached into the glove box. A wallet was inside, and it contained his actual driver's license. As it stood, Josh Hodges could get pulled over and not even raise an eyebrow.

Not that he wanted to test that theory.

Josh didn't want to talk to another member of law enforcement, local or federal.

Unlike after outing himself to Agent Richardson, he had no regrets. This was a calculated move; could he fire a parting shot across their bow and get away with it? Josh believed he could, so he dropped Agent Godwin's name.

Josh stepped over to a window and looked around; the concrete jungle surrounding his garage was desolate. He didn't see any squad cars on the street, nor any flatfoots patrolling the immediate area.

Well, Josh decided, *it's now or nothing.*

The Honda Accord was old, but reliable, and started on the first turn of the key. Josh smiled, his head and heart full of nostalgia. Starting his getaway car in test runs had always pleased him; today, cars all fired up at the push of a button. Josh didn't mind that, but there was something... not exactly romantic, but more pleasing, in the least, to turning a key. Turning a key *felt* like starting a car; pushing a button was too benign an action.

The garage door opened in front of him, and Josh inched out casually. He was taking in his surroundings, but didn't want to give the impression of hesitancy.

I don't know, fly casual, crossed his mind, and he laughed.

All looked well, so Josh drove across the lot, made his way out of the industrial section of the neighborhood, and onto city streets.

Coming to one corner, he did the customary left, right, left. Before pulling out into traffic, a flash of red light caught his eye in the rearview: the police had set up a checkpoint a block and a half behind him.

They didn't just come in after me, Josh thought. *They marked off a perimeter.*

Josh exhaled a slow sigh of relief. Giving away his identity had nearly cost him everything.

Realizing that sitting and staring at the police would probably draw unwanted attention, Josh eased into traffic. His radar was now up; were they going to pull over random cars exiting the neighborhood?

It took a few blocks, but eventually his nerves steadied, and a calmness returned.

Once he hit the Gowanus Expressway, Josh knew he was safe.

Chapter 38

Realizations

Michael had followed the stairway down into what he quickly surmised was their suspect's home base.

There was a refrigerator, bed, what looked to be a bathroom off to one side, and a wall of security monitors to Michael's left.

Shining his phone around, Michael found a light switch on the wall, flicked it, and was happy to discover it worked.

With the light, however, came understanding. In the corner of the room was a hatch, like you'd find on a naval ship or submarine. As soon as he saw it, Michael knew their man hadn't gone up, he'd gone down.

He told Susan, Susan told the NYPD, and that was about all they could do. One good tug revealed the hatch was locked from the other side, and getting such a sturdy hunk of steel open wasn't going to be easy. In the least, it was nothing Michael could do alone. They'd need an acetylene torch; something that could cut through steel.

Michael considered asking Susan to call in the FDNY.

They have to cut through steel all the time to save people who'd been in car accidents, right?

As he had the thought, he dismissed it. The guy they were chasing was gone. A ghost.

Michael felt defeated. His first big case, and he blew it. Michael thought a moment and realized he had two options: play the 'what could I have done differently?' game and beat himself up, or see what he could salvage by finding a new lead.

Beating himself up wasn't going to change anything, so he began looking around for anything "Cassandra" might have missed.

The first thing that caught Michael's eye was, of course, the boxes.

Those aren't sitting there by accident; he wants us to see what's inside them.

Keeping Susan's words of wisdom in the back of his mind, Michael examined the boxes thoroughly before opening one. He didn't really believe they were booby-trapped, but it was always better to be safe than sorry.

After Michael opened the boxes, he immediately wished he'd searched elsewhere. In fact, he almost threw up.

Inside were files, and while the files started out normal—pictures of men, names, information breakdowns—soon after came the horror. Pictures of children. Pictures of children in awful situations.

"Agent Chamberlain," Michael said, his voice hollow.

"Go," Susan responded.

"I found his next targets…"

Michael trailed off, setting the folder he had been thumbing through back on the box it came from.

"Are you OK?" Susan asked. "Are you hurt?"

"No, to both," Michael replied. "I'm not hurt, but I'm not OK."

Michael paused, then determined he didn't know what else to do but to be forthright with Susan.

"Child porn," he said flatly. "I found child porn."

Susan winced.

"Jesus," she whispered. "I didn't see that coming."

"It's not for our guy," Michael informed her. "He's got files on pedophiles. These are his next targets."

Susan exhaled a sigh of relief, and then caught herself. She was happy their criminal wasn't *more* of a criminal?

"I've got to make my way to you," Susan determined. "Can you describe where you are?"

"Yes," Michael answered. "But that won't help you."

In the end, they played a rousing, albeit frustrating, round of Marco Polo. Michael made his way back to the entrance of the living quarters, where he'd initially busted in the door, and after ten minutes of call and response, Susan was close enough to find him.

During that timeframe, her radio came to life; the NYPD was contacting her.

"You want the bad news?" the officer asked, "or the bad news?"

Susan felt her shoulders slouch involuntarily. This was defeat. To have come all this way, to have come so close... face-to-goddamn-face with him, and now defeat.

"Go for it," she responded.

"Your guy? He's not in the subways. Those lines are a couple blocks from here. Your guy is in the sewers, and with this kind of head start, he's gone."

"Copy that," Susan said, her voice neutral. "And the bad news?"

"You got a phone on you?"

"Yes."

"Google Paul Hewson."

Susan didn't like games, but she did as requested.

When the response popped up, Susan nearly smashed her phone in anger. According to Google, there was only one "Paul Hewson," and that man was better known by another name.

"Fucking Bono," Susan muttered, still controlling the urge to chuck her phone at a wall.

Of course the guy at the door had given a wrong name. And not just *any* wrong name; not 'Brian Jones' or 'John Doe,' no. He wanted to embarrass her, to make her look foolish. All it did was make her angry.

When she got to Michael, he showed her the hideout and gestured to the boxes, but truth be told he didn't want to go rummaging through them a second time.

"We blew it," Susan said resignedly. "Let's wrap things up and go workout."

Michael was confused. "You want to hit the gym? Now?"

"No," Susan explained. "Not the gym. The bar. It's liver day."

Chapter 39

Josh Hodges

When Josh's question mark faded and became a clickable photo, it revealed a video unlike the others.

Every video to date had been one person, telling their story to the camera with a bland background behind them. Some were angry, some were wistful, but all betrayed the sadness each had been living with.

Josh, by comparison, never appeared on screen. He spoke from behind the camera, narrating as opposed to staring in his confessional. Where the others explained their actions, Josh was going to show his. Plus, his face would be all over the news anyway. The media had a way of finding photos of a person.

Josh's video faded in from black to reveal the Atlantic Ocean. Vast, gray, and cold, water stretched the horizon; wherever the video was taken, it was in the middle of nowhere. The sky was overcast and the surface choppy, but not dangerously so.

"I once read that having a child meant having your heart exist outside your body," Josh began. "When my daughter was born, it hit home how accurate that assessment was."

Josh paused.

"I don't think I knew what love was before I became a father," he eventually continued. "I mean, I loved my wife, yes, but becoming a father was like love on steroids. I never knew I had it in me to feel so powerfully about anything."

On the screen, small, two or three-foot waves crested and fell, bumping into one another like drunk Oompa Loompas.

"I once read tales of men coming back from war, men who had lost arms and legs. They said that decades later, they would wake up in the middle of the night, scratching at phantom limbs, itching at flesh long since absent that their mind couldn't accept as truly gone."

Josh slowly panned left and right, showing the vastness of the ocean's expanse. No land, birds, or boats were anywhere to be seen. Just the waves dancing their rhythmic dance.

"Imagine, then, what it's like to lose your child."

Josh took a moment to collect his thoughts.

"Imagine what it's like to be missing a part of your soul, a piece of your heart..."

Josh had practiced his words; he didn't want emotion getting in the way of what he had to say, and took several deep breaths to steady himself. He'd practiced, but this part killed him.

"My daughter Beth was diagnosed with lymphoma when she was two."

Josh had said the words matter-of-factly, but tears were forming in his eyes. He took two more deep breaths, and repeated himself.

"Beth was diagnosed with lymphoma when she was two. We were told that she had a very good chance of survival. That was the quote, 'a very good chance.' Turns out, Beth had a compromised immune system..."

The words drifted off so Josh could compose himself.

On screen, the waves continued to create mini-whitecaps and then recede back into the expanse of water from whence they came.

"She didn't make it to her third birthday," he concluded.

Even though the tears had started flowing, Josh was holding it together. He was over the hump now, and his voice had remained steady.

"I'm sure there will be those who say, 'Why didn't you give your money to cancer research?' I have. It's all gone. I don't need money anymore, so I gave it away anonymously to research foundations, medical grants, anywhere and everywhere I thought it might make a difference."

Josh sighed.

"But I don't know that it will. For as long as I've been alive, the cure to just about every disease has been 'right around the corner.' At some point you begin to wonder if they're just raising money to raise money. So many pharmaceutical agencies create pills that mitigate diseases, because if you keep a disease at bay without curing it, you can continue to profit off it."

Now Josh's voice began to harden, if only slightly.

"I don't like being cynical, and I don't like being bitter. I gave my money away and I cross my fingers that something good comes of it."

Josh gave a hollow laugh.

"And, I gave it away because I know there are lawyers out there who will completely miss the point I've tried to make with all this. I got rid of my money so that no one could sue my estate and get paid because I influenced someone to hurt their loved one. Sorry, leeches. If one of my hundred took out someone you love, maybe take a good, hard look at whatever that person was doing, and ask yourself why you defend them."

Josh paused in reflection. When he continued, his voice was softer, as if he were in confession.

"There is barely a moment that goes by I don't think about Beth. That I don't miss her. And the worst part? If I do have a moment of peace, if I have a moment of happy, or a moment of forgetting... then when it all comes flooding back, I feel guilty. I feel guilty for the one second I didn't mourn. I feel that if I were to be happy, it would be a betrayal."

The yacht swayed gently with the waves. Josh believed the motion would be nice to fall asleep to.

"My wife and I drifted apart," he continued. "We had to. I don't blame her for anything, and I don't think she blames me, it's just that it became impossible to be with someone who was a constant reminder of what you'd lost. The delivery had been hard on her... when our daughter was born, we were told that my wife couldn't survive another pregnancy. Which was fine, we had our Beth, and that was more than enough. That was everything. Beth was our everything..."

Josh took a moment to change gears. The confession was over; it was time for the explanation.

"So," he continued. "You're probably asking what we're doing out here today."

As he spoke, Josh stood up and turned, the camera still facing outward.

He had been on the bow of his yacht, and as he walked down the side—port, starboard he couldn't remember which was which—he continued narrating.

"When I set sail, I left behind two boxes of files. Those files contain the names and addresses of over two hundred pedophiles. They also contain evidence. Evidence no one should have to see. Children having their lives ruined to appease the sick thoughts contained within diseased minds. The FBI has possession of those files, and God willing have already started making arrests. Ten men won't be home, though. They're out here, with me."

Josh reached the yacht's stern, and began a slow zoom into the distance. After a moment, little orange blobs were seen bobbing in the waves. As the camera focused, those blobs became men. Their faces were full of panic, and their mouths were wide; they were obviously shouting, but were too far away to be heard.

"Those men fell asleep last night on this boat. They woke up this morning in the ocean."

The men were flailing; some were trying to swim toward the yacht, but they weren't making any headway. The wind, though light, was enough to blow them around. Two-foot waves aren't suitable for surfing, but they do tend to make swimming difficult.

"They're wearing life jackets, because I didn't want them to go straight to the bottom," Josh explained. "That would be too quick. No, I want them to think about what they've done. I want them to think about what they've done for however long those things keep them afloat."

Josh's voice was now emotionless. Neutral. It contained neither anger, nor sorrow. Emotions were saved for the deserving, and the drowning men had earned no empathy.

"As I pulled away, I read their crimes to them, and truth be told, they said all the right things. They were sorry, they promised to never do it again, they needed help, they'd *get* help... It was all self-serving remorse that only comes with being caught. When they're getting away with their crimes, they keep committing them. They never get the help they say they need when having the sick thoughts, they act on their impulses. And every single one of these men acted on their impulses. They fed their compulsions. This is their punishment."

Josh became reflective, and answered a question he figured those watching might be asking.

"My daughter died of cancer, yes. But I can't punish cancer. These men harmed children. They damaged children in ways that might never be repaired. I can't punish cancer, but I can punish them. I was powerless to help my baby. All I could do was sit by her hospital bed, useless. The children these men hurt were powerless. Now, these men know what it's like to be on the losing end of a horrible situation they cannot control."

Josh began a slow pull back to normal; the men became blobs, then were lost from sight altogether.

"We're not in any shipping lanes, so chances are they won't be found accidentally. I guess if you want to begin a search and rescue for them, you can... but how many taxpayers want their money used to pay for that? If you do come looking, good luck. By the time this video goes live, they'll have been out here for two days."

Josh became wistful for a moment.

"In a way, I'm giving them what they never gave their victims: a fighting chance. I mean, it's a slim chance, but it's something. It's more than they gave, and more than they deserve, but what the hell? I'm generous like that."

Josh's tone shifted again. Neutrality came easy to this section, because it was mere explanation. He figured there'd be someone who had ideas on how to find him, the boat, or those men. Josh wanted to nip that in the bud so they didn't waste any time.

"For the record, I turned off the transponder on this yacht the day we left port, so you won't find me through any emergency channels. As soon as my video loads, I'll set it to post in a couple days, turn off the onboard internet, and smash my phone."

Josh smiled, though he knew no one could see it.

In a way, he was proud of himself. Not for his actions, but for holding it together throughout his speech. Though he'd cried, that emotion hadn't spilled over into his voice.

Not yet, at least.

Not until his last sentence, when his voice finally cracked as he choked up.

"I'm going to take some sleeping pills now," Josh said through tears. "I'm going to drink a warmed glass of milk, duct tape a plastic bag over my head, and see if my daughter is somewhere out there waiting for me."

And with that, Josh's video stopped.

Epilogue

It took six months, but Kristen Richardson eventually found Cassandra.

Kimsey said he met Cassandra in a support group, so Kristen joined as many as she could and posted notices inquiring about exchanges with the now-famous computer. She also made it a point to chat with group moderators, most of whom didn't even remember Cassandra.

"She never contributed," they'd say. That and, "I forgot she was even in here."

As it turned out, Cassandra never really interacted with anyone publicly. She monitored the groups—or, more likely, Josh monitored the groups—and when a likely candidate showed up, they received a private message. That kept everything in the shadows, which is where secrets live.

While a majority of tips from these groups led nowhere, every so often someone who had interacted with Cassandra would send a useful bit of information Kristen's way. She would request access to the person's computer, run traces on Cassandra's messages, and thank the civilian who'd come forward.

Just as Kristen believed, Cassandra used an ever-changing multitude of dummy IP addresses to hide her location. Thankfully, such tricks only work for so long. Everything has to have an origin, and over time Kristen was able to unearth patterns, similarities, and ultimately Cassandra's true location.

Unsurprisingly, she wasn't in the Ukraine; Cassandra was in Flatbush, minutes from Industry City. Josh had wanted her close, but not under the same roof as he was. He was cautious, even if he'd neglected to cover his tracks when purchasing Cassandra's software.

Cassandra sat in an empty studio apartment where the air conditioning ran 24/7 to keep her cool. She just sat there, carrying on conversations with anyone Josh targeted.

After shutting her down and getting her to the FBI offices, Kristen and her team attempted to hack into Cassandra, but she was too high-end for even government codebreakers. Cassandra had a 26-character password, which meant the likelihood of cracking it within Kristen's lifetime was zero.

(Josh didn't have a problem remembering the password. It was simply his daughter's first initial, uppercase 'B,' followed by her birthday forward, backward, backward, and forward again, and then a lowercase 'h' at the end. He made it absurdly long because according to a codebreaker website, "Nine-character passwords take five days to break, ten-character words take four months, an eleven-character password would take ten years, and if you make your password twelve characters long it will take a supercomputer 200 years to crack." Josh wondered if 26 characters was overkill, then decided it wasn't, thus frustrating Kristen Richardson once she saw what she was up against.)

The bad news was that they'd never discover who the remaining 100 were. Their identities were sealed within Cassandra's hard drive, locked away forever. The good news, then, was that no more videos could go viral. Since Cassandra was programmed to update The 100 website whenever a member wiped their computer—the signal they were about to act—and Cassandra was out of commission, that meant no more new content for civilians to gossip over.

With their source of attention cut off, no one could get their message out. Members realized that if they were going to die for a cause, they'd do so anonymously. Sure, they could leave a note stating they were part of The 100, or even film a new video. But once people have had a taste of something big, getting them excited over amateur hour isn't an easy sell.

Since people love fame, and fame was no longer happening, dramatic exits from life slowed to a trickle, then halted altogether. After Josh posted his goodbye video, a few stragglers had been re-inspired and had put forth their violent foot, but the numbers were not great.

The public at large wasn't inspired to take things into their own hands, and in fact quickly moved on to the next sensationalistic story to hit the airwaves. If Josh had hoped for a revolution, he would have been disappointed.

The ADHD minds of the American public kept clicking on their computers, forever in search of the newest, bestest, and most exciting (and popular) trend.

In all, 27 people, Josh included, completed their tasks. That left 73 remaining in the ether. Susan, Michael, and occasionally Sumner would speculate as to how many would eventually complete their task, but the numbers were always low.

"One, maybe two more," Sumner believed, and no one was willing to go much higher than that.

Once the newness wore off, once the magic was gone, even the most passionate adherents lost interest.

Michael, despite his initial beliefs otherwise, had proven himself in the field. He was thus removed from phone fraud duty and given more 'energetic' assignments. Sumner acknowledged his hand in, if not catching Josh Hodges, putting him out of business early.

Susan was once again offered a promotion out of the field and into a cozy office, managing a team of agents. She once again declined.

"Maybe when my mind don't move and my knees don't bend I'll stop doing legwork," she explained to a forgiving Sumner. "But it's still more fun going places than staring out a window."

Sumner understood. He knew Susan would make a great leader, but only when she was ready. Thankfully, she was a hell of a field agent, so losing her in the office meant retaining her on important cases.

Since they had found Josh's hideout, and the files of pedophiles Josh left behind, Susan and Michael headed the team of investigators tasked with making the arrests. Confirming the evidence took several weeks; coordinating the arrests took several days atop that. Once all ducks were in a row, 217 human traffickers across the United States were removed from society.

Forty-seven children were rescued from various locations.

At the six-week mark, The 100 all but forgotten by the public at large, a body washed ashore in Senegal. The body was swollen beyond recognition, was missing its eyes and most of its fingers, and bites aplenty had been taken out of it by various aquatic creatures, but DNA eventually confirmed its identity as one of the pedophiles from the yacht.

No other body from that final video was found.

Josh's yacht is still drifting out there somewhere.

Acknowledgements

To my Mrs., the one and only Lydia Fine, thank you.

You gave this book the first and third edit, took the pictures, and designed both the front and back covers. You're good like that, even if you don't realize it.

Also, thanks to Kristine Bjork, who now goes by the God-awful moniker "Roggentien," a name I refuse to acknowledge. Apologies to your husband, Reece, but in my defense spellcheck says "Roggentien" isn't a real word anyway. So there.

Quick thanks to Nick and Shannon Arnold, two more fine folks who gave this the once over and found mistakes both big and little for me to fix.

If this book contains an error, it's my fault. Because I am a stubborn mule, sometimes I just like the way something looks, or "sounds" in my head. Grammar-check often tells me, "Hey! NO! Bad writer! Get that comma outta there!" Thing is, I like adding a pause sometimes, rules of grammar be damned. My editors both saw and corrected technical errors aplenty, and then I went ahead and kept it the way I liked it.

To my small humans, Hillary and Truman. While you didn't contribute to this book, except to distract me from completing it, I still love you so much with my one heart.

About the Author

Nathan has been writing since he could scribble using crayons. As a comedian, he has released six albums that can be streamed on Pandora, Spotify, or anywhere else you stream your audio-based entertainment. Should you be interested in parting with your hard-earned cash, these albums can be purchased anywhere and everywhere (e.g., Amazon, Apple Music, Google Play, etc.).

Nathan has told jokes all over the world, Iraq and Afghanistan included, for American troops stationed far from home.

Nathan currently lives in Iowa (on purpose) with his wife, kids, and cat named Turtle.

(You can thank the daughter-unit for that.)

He is an avid fan of Billy and the Boingers, and enjoys a fine pair of pants.

Nathan has written more nonsense than you can shake a stick at, including:

- *I Was a White Knight… Once*
- *It's OK to Talk to Animals (and Other Letters from Dad)*
- *Hey Buddy (Dubious Advice from Dad)*

Please visit nathantimmel.com for anything and everything Nathan-related. Look for his podcast, "Idiots on Parade," wherever you find your favorite podcasts, and his vodcast, "Artificially Intelligent," on YouTube.

If you can, go see Nathan perform live. Failing that, dial up his YouTube channel. You'll giggle and have a good time.

Promise.

Author's Note

Hi!

I wanted to take a moment to say, "Thanks for reading."

So... thanks for reading.

All any unknown author has going for them is word of mouth. If you enjoyed this tale, please, tell your friends, family, fellow parishioners, your cellmate, various passersby on the street, and the police officer currently giving you a ticket for reading this on the Kindle app on your phone when you were supposed to be focused on driving.

(If you're reading a paperback copy while driving, kudos to you, old school!)

Share your happy thoughts on social media, and if you could leave a nice review somewhere, that would be wonderful.

If you hated my word salad of a book, buy copies for all your enemies. Maybe they'll hate it, too.

Hugs,

nathan

Made in the USA
Middletown, DE
22 April 2022

64624776R00144